Susan K Phillips

On the Seaboard

And other Poems

Susan K Phillips

On the Seaboard
And other Poems

ISBN/EAN: 9783337206635

Printed in Europe, USA, Canada, Australia, Japan

Cover: Foto ©Andreas Hilbeck / pixelio.de

More available books at **www.hansebooks.com**

POEMS.

ON THE SEABOARD

AND OTHER POEMS

BY

SUSAN K. PHILLIPS

LONDON

MACMILLAN AND CO.

1878

OXFORD:
BY E. PICKARD HALL, M.A., AND J. H. STACY,
PRINTERS TO THE UNIVERSITY.

Many of these Poems are reprinted, by permission, from Macmillan's Magazine, All the Year Round, Tinsley's Magazine, Cassell's Magazine, Belgravia, and The World.

DEDICATED

TO

HARRIETTE WORSLEY,

BY

HER FRIEND,

SUSAN K. PHILLIPS.

CONTENTS.

POEMS.

ON THE SEABOARD.

WHAT do you know about it?—you who dwell
In the calm safety of the inland hush,
Seeing bright corn-waves ripple on the.fell,
And sparkling becks by floating lilies rush.
Why, if the great winds sweep across the moor,
And shake the branches of your spreading trees,
Have I not heard you, smiling, say secure,
'Hark, how the forest mocks the sound of seas!'

The sound of seas! Draw closer round the hearth,
Hope that your oaks face bravely to the storm,
Let the wild music blend with household mirth,
As fair false fancies 'mid your dreamings form.
The sound of seas! What does it say to *us*,
When the surf 'calls' along the hollow strand,
With its deep thunder, low and ominous,
While the white foam flakes, warning, stud the sand?

It tells how the fierce blast is landward blowing,
How ships are drifting to the cruel reef;
It tells how crested waves are landward flowing,
Back sweeping hope of rescue or relief;
It bids skilled watchers gather on the pier,
And daring crews to loose the life-boat ready,
To see the rocket lines are taut and clear,
To feel the rowlocks strong, the rudder steady.

Old men that gather on the harbour side
Point to the drum, and mark the falling glass,
Gaze at the threatening storm-pack spreading wide,
And scan the tossing sail that strives to pass,
Whisper old ghastly tales of gallant ships
Lost with all hands, out on the stormy sea,
And missing barques round which in sad eclipse
Close years of sorrow, prayer, and mystery.

For you there is no cadence in the wind,
Caught from the sailors' last despairing cry,
Your careless untaught glances cannot find
Promise or presage in the changing sky;
For you, when wakened from your quiet sleep
As sudden gusts dash on the window pane,
No thoughts, like ours, of danger on the deep,
Forbid your weary eyes to close again.

We live our lives, who on the seaboard dwell,
Lives face to face with peril, death and heaven;
The strong sad sea in its eternal swell
Something of strong sad fellowship has given;
Stern as its tempest, solemn as its roar,
Keen, true, and frank as sunlight on its breast,
Its signet stamps their souls, who on the shore
Dare, love, and labour; die, and sleep in rest.

HOW THE SMACK CAME IN.

'SHE ought to be in, she ought to be in,
Here's another moon begun;
She sail'd last Friday was a week,
And it is but a four days' run.

'I've left our Jane at home,
She'll nor sleep nor bite, poor lass;

Just toss her wedding duds about,
And stare at the falling glass.

'The banns were out last week, you see;
And to day—alack, alack,
Young George has other gear to mind,
Out there, out there in the smack!

'I bade her dry her tears,
Or share them with another,
And go down yonder court, and try
To comfort Willie's mother.

'The poor old widow'd soul,
Laid helpless in her bed;
She prays for the touch of her one son's hand,
The sound of his cheery tread.

'She ought to be in, her timbers were stout;
She would ride through the roughest gale,
Well found and mann'd—but the hours drag on;
It was but a four days' sail.'

Gravely the gray-haired sailor spoke,
Out on the great Pier head;
Sudden a bronz'd old fishwife burst
From the anxious group, and said,

'Jenny will find her lovers anew;
And Anne has one foot in the grave;
We 've lived together twenty year,
I and my poor old Dave.

'I 've a runlet of whisky fresh for him,
And 'bacca agen he comes back;
He said he 'd bide this winter ashore,
After the trip in the smack.

'We have neither chick nor child of us,
Our John were drown'd last year;
There is nothing on earth but Dave for me.
Why there's nought in the wind to fear.

'He's been out in many a coarser sea.
I'll set the fire alight;
We said "Our Father" before he went;
The smack will be in to-night.'

And just as down in the westward
The light rose, pale and thin,
With her bulwarks stove, and her foresail gone,
The smack came staggering in.

With one worn face at her rudder,
And another beside her mast;
But George, and Willie, and stanch old Dave?
Why, ask the waves and the blast;

Ask the sea that broke aboard her,
Just as she swung her round;
Ask the squall that swept above her,
With death in its ominous sound.

'The master saw,' the sailor said,
'A face past the gunwale go;'
And Jack heard 'Jane!' ring shrill through the roar;
And that is all we know.

'I can't tell. Parson says grief is wrong,
And pining is wilful sin;
But I'd like to hear how those two died,
Before the smack came in.'

Well, this morning the flags droop half-mast high,
In beautiful Whitby Bay;

That's all we shall know till the roll is read
On the last great muster-day.

THE BLACK NAB.

Sᴡᴇᴇᴛ June sunshine in the heavens, sweet June
    sunshine on the seas,
Where the blue waves broke in silver, tossing kisses
    to the breeze;
Crisping, curving on the shingle, laughed and leapt
    the wavelets near;
High above the clovered meadows, larks were sing-
    ing shrill and clear;
Nature, in her lavish beauty, royal-handed flinging
    forth,
Wealth of warmth, and light, and colour, on the
    seaboard of the North.

Foam defined the glorious sea-line, bay and point
    in distance spread,
Kettle Ness, and rocky Runswick, on to mighty
    Huntcliff Head;
Round the cliffs at sunny Saltwick chafed the
    breakers' ceaseless war,
Slowly, softly, rose and wavered the brown sea-
    weeds on the Scar,
And the Black Nab 'mid the glitter frowned defiance
    stern and dumb:
Surely in a world so lovely, naught of cloud to-day
    can come.

Gliding 'mid the tumbled boulders, past the tangled
    slippery stones,
Springing over wave-worn channels, where the tide
    imprisoned moans,

Always gazing, gazing seawards, even as she presses
    on,
A slight girl the Scar is crossing, till the Nab's
    huge crest is won;
And fearless on the Point of peril, all her tossed
    hair floating free,
Shades her eyes with frail white fingers, gazing,
    gazing o'er the sea.

'Nay, she's safe enough,' an old man answered to
    our cry of fear,
'Well she knows the path she's taken, shade or
    shine she's ever here,
Poor fond lass, still watching, watching, for a sail
    that never more
Will bear her sweetheart's home-bound coble to
    the cottage on the shore.
Poor Jem, he took the long lines outward, just a
    year ago it was:
Here, I say, the wind's agen him, he'll not come
    to-day, my lass!'

Turning as the sailor's hollo, borne upon the wind,
    she heard,
Down the dizzy path towards us, fluttering like a
    wounded bird,
Sinking by us on the shingle, lifting piteous wistful
    eyes,
Their sad question dimming for us half the glow
    of seas and skies,
As in strange pathetic accents the pale lips ap-
    pealing said,
'Not to-day? and oh! to-morrow is the morn we
    are to wed.'

Child, the bright blue treacherous ocean, fathom
    deep above him roars,
That true heart is waiting for you, where no wild
    waves lash the shores,
And the God who called him from you, in mercy
    to the wildered brain
Sent the hope that lulls to 'waiting' broken life's
    dull yearning pain.
But to us the golden memory of June's glory on
    the Bay
Blends for ever with the echo of her plaintive
    'Not to-day?'

THE SECRET OF THE SEA.

Who knows the mighty secret,
The secret of the sea?
I love its beauty passing well,
I love the thunder of its swell,
I love the glory of its play,
The glitter of its feathery spray,
But its secret is hid from me.

Who knows the mighty secret,
What gives the sea its power?
Its laugh will chime with the gayest mood;
It gives the friend to solitude;
It frets with the fretted heart or head,
It mourns the past, it wails the dead,
It lulls the dreamy hour.

Who has the mighty secret?
Never a mortal knows.
By the shells alone is the riddle read,
As they lie deep down in their coral bed,

In the depths of the sea-weed forest brown,
Where the August sunshine quivers down,
And the great tide comes and goes.

They know the mighty secret;
They are cast upon the sand;
We gather them up from the creamy foam,
We bear them away to our inland home,
As relics of happy sea-side days,
We bear them to dwell where the soft breeze plays
Over the flowery land.

They know the mighty secret;
They murmur it all day long.
With a passionate wail, with a yearning cry,
For the shadowy reef where the surf beats high,
Where the great waves roll for ever and aye,
And their roar swells up to the hanging sky,
And the wind blows wild and strong.

They know the mighty secret;
We hold them to our ear,
We hear the mystical sound again,
We hear the voice of the restless main,
We know the long monotonous roar,
As the billows break on the rugged shore,
But that is all we hear.

We cannot read the secret.
We cannot find the key.
Ah! sully not by earthly guess
Its grandeur and its loveliness;
Take the infinite gladness of the main,
And fling the poor shell back again,
Back to its parent sea.

I'LL DIE AT HOME.

Oh aye, it is very likely, it's mostlins what I have
 heard;
She comes of an honest stock, you see; the egg
 bodes best of the bird;
And we were girls together, we've laked through
 many a day,
Though now she's mistress up yonder, and I'se
 upon parish pay.

And I'se no call to shame for it; I'se but taking
 back my own,
I'se never owed cess, or rent, or rate, it's known
 through all the town;
It's not much I want—a sup of tea, a bite of bread
 to eat,
But sooner than go to' t' House for them, honey,
 I'd die i' t' street.

What, she 'keeps all straight and tidy,' Mrs. Jones
 we mun call her now:
It was Sal, and Polly, long ago, in the cots upon
 the brow.
O she's a canny body, was always hearty and wick,
Never let a job stand still for her, nor dirt have
 time to stick.

And I'se a cobweb i' t' corner. I seed thee tak'
 heed of it,
And thou'd fain ha' dusted the settle, when I bade
 thee come and sit;
I seed thee, bairn, and I'd ha' liked to up and tell
 thee then,
Thou'd, mebby, be no better off at thy threescore
 and ten.

It's 'Home, be it ne'er so homely,' as my old man
    used to sing,
When, after supper at father's farm, he sate by me
    in the ring;
And here he brought me when we were wed, and
    here the childer were born,
And here he bade God bless me, and went, one
    dreary Christmas morn.

I sate all night by yon pillow, where he lay dead
    and cold;
The little 'uns climbed about me, as the passing-bell
    was tolled;
Well, it's all past and half forgot, and my time has
    soon to come,
But they needn't crack of the House to me,—I tell
    thee I'll die at Home.

That's his stick set by the clock, dost see, and his
    cap upon the pin,
And yon's the corner our bonnie bairns were fond
    of hidelin' in;
Why, when the ashes are dying, I sit, and listen,
    and look,
Till I see it all afore me, as plain as a printed
    book.

And I can steek my door, and clean, or pray, or
    cry my fill,
Or set it wide, and rake the logs, and call a neigh-
    bour at will,
And go where I like, and have who I like, and
    watch them go and come;
Bed and board may be good up there, but, for me,
    I'll die at Home.

I 'se had little but labour all my life, bread has been
  hard to get,
But I 'se done as my old man bid me—kept clear
  of begging or debt;
I want but a hole of my own, in this world of the
  rich and blest;
Well, it all raffles my worsted, but for sure the Lord
  knows best.

It 's His will. I've striven to do it; to be honest,
  and pure, and brave.
His Word says naught of the Workhouse, and naught
  of a Parish grave.
I 'se put by what 'll bury me, i' t' teapot up on t'
  shelf,
And what I can't get I 'll do without, and make my
  moan to myself.

Mrs. Jones may come and see me. I 'll give her a
  cup of tea,
We 'll talk of times when we little thought of differ
  'twixt her and me;
She 's nobbut keeper of a 'gaol, as may be to the
  liking of some,
But, faring hard, or sleeping cold, I'll die, as I've
  lived, at Home.

'HE'LL BE A MISSED MAN.'

Aye, 'twas a homely epitaph:
  'A missed man'—that was all.
The stern lips quivered as they spoke,
The rough voice just for a moment broke,
And the brown hand brushed across his eyes,
  As if he felt the hot tears rise:
    He would not let them fall.

And I, who had wept him sorely;
  I, who had words at will,
Felt there was more in the simple phrase
Said in the accent of early days,
Than eloquent praise of pulpit and press,
Or the lines of pious tenderness
  Read on the marble still.

A missed man in the village street,
  Where still I can picture him,
With the sunshine upon his good gray head,
His stalwart form and his swinging tread,
His keen quick noting of all he saw,
His shrewd firm words of peace and law,
  And the smile no care could dim.

A missed man by the cottage hearth,
  Where the bairns stood at his knee,
And the good wife told her eager tale,
And sought the aid that would never fail,
Gentle counsel and mild reproof,
And the blessing on the honest roof,
  And the kindly jest and free.

A missed man by the dying bed,
  Where he held the stiffening hand,
Patient watched through the fevered hour,
Soothed and guided with words of power;
Friend, physician, and priest in one,
Help to the mourner when all was done,
  With the heart that could 'understand.'

A missed man in the country side,
  Where every labourer knew
His cheery call, as he passed them by,
With the happy light in his clear brown eye,

And the greeting given to each and all,
From cot, or farmstead, or lordly hall
  Alike frank, kind, and true.

A missed man in the grey old church,
  Where his majestic voice
To every litany, collect, and prayer,
Gave the soul their framers had planted there;
While he taught in language, simple and clear,
Our hope in heaven, our duty here,
  Bade man in God rejoice.

Missed in all social gatherings,
  Bright host and welcome friend.
Missed by young and old, and grave and gay;
Missed in his life-paths, day by day;
Missed as men miss their truest and best;
Loved and honoured, and mourned and blest,
  A missed man till the end.

IN HOLDERNESS.

THE wind blew over the barley, the wind blew over
    the wheat,
Where the scarlet poppy toss'd her head, with the
    bindweed at her feet;
The wind blew over the great blue sea, in the golden
    August weather,
Till the tossing corn and the tossing waves show'd
    shadow and gleam together.

The wind blew over the barley, the wind blew over
    the oats,
The lark sprang up in the sunny sky, and shook his
    ringing notes;

Over the wealth of the smiling land, the sweep of
    the glittering sea,
'Which is the fairest?' he sang, as he soared o'er
    the beautiful rivalry.

And with a fuller voice than the wind, a deeper
    tone than the bird,
Came the answer from the solemn sea, that Nature,
    pausing, heard,—
'The corn will be garner'd, the lark will be hush'd,
    at the frown of the wintry weather,
The sun will fly from the snow-piled sky, but I go
    on for ever!'

WHY?

From the butterfly crushed on the daisied lea,
    In its brief life's brightest hour;
From the blighted bud on the fair green tree,
    That never had time to flower;
From the sea-bird, shot on the merry waves,
    As it basked 'neath the summer sky;
From all earth's countless, needless graves,
    Swells up the piteous 'Why?'

From the child in the hideous London court,
    'Mid sin, and want, and gloom;
From the cripple, the cruel rabble's sport,
    From the workhouse' dreary 'home';
From the strong man, with his darling gone,
    From the woman's agony,
As Death strikes down her All, in One,
    Wails Nature's helpless 'Why?'

Worst pang in sorrow's bitter blow,
 Worst pain in trial's time,
The goad that drives the restless woe
 From misery into crime.
Pale fiend, that will not rest or part,
 Dull ache that will not die;
Mocking in every mourner's heart
 With 'Thou art broken, why?'

Nay, try no earthly argument,
 All learning does but fail;
The keenest shaft, most deftly sent,
 Blunts 'gainst that cold black mail.
One answer from God's Word we take,
 One Comforter and Guide;
For He has promised 'when we wake'
 We 'shall be satisfied.'

THE SQUALL.

The nighest shave of death I've had?
Well, wait till my pipe's alight,
Throw a log of the drift-wood on the blaze,
And I'll spin you a yarn to-night.

Danger! you'll meet it upon the deep;
Nor shun it upon the land.
I take it, the sea and the shore alike,
Are held in God's mighty Hand.

Many's the tue and the tussle,
The sea and I have had,
Since I sailed away to the whalery,
When I was a bit of a lad.

But not on the Greenland waters,
Among the floes and the pack;
And not on the great Atlantic,
With the gales upon our track;

And not where breakers whiten the reefs,
On the coast of Elsinore,
Have I won through such a perilous time,
As last week, a mile from shore.

There was me, and Bill, and Mather,
All good sea-faring men;
I can handle a rope as well as most,
Though I'm past three score and ten.

The wind was whispering like a bairn,
In the merry April weather,
The great blue sea and the great blue sky
Seemed met like friends together.

We'd got a fair lot of fish aboard:
I turned to say to Mat,
We might steer to shore, when he gripped my arm,
And swore, 'Look thou at that!'

Over the calm sea, black and keen,
Blotting the glow of it all,
Fast, and fierce, and cruel, and strong,
It came, it came, the squall!

The crested waves to its summons sprang,
Like tigers, around the boat;
Down swept the drift, wild yelled the blast,
Were we still alive, and afloat?

Gone the spot that marked the rock-buoy;
Gone the far faint line of home ;
There was nothing but hissing water and wind,
The very air was foam.

Mather baled and baled, I strove with the sheet,
She laboured—fit to fill,
None on us spoke, save just to shout
To the helmsman, ' Mind her, Bill.'

I 'm none soft-hearted, but I thought,
How the bairns, at play on the sand,
Were watching to see the boat come in,
And help with the fish to land.

I thought of the hearths clean swept for us,
And the poor old wife, and all,
While the waves poured over the gunwale,
And we tossed and drove in the squall.

And I thought a prayer to Him who trod
 On the waters, and said ' Be still !'
Mebby a Hand we could not see
Held the rudder, along with Bill.

For we weathered it, we rounded the Nab,
And cleared our eyes from the sea,
And just shook hands, and hauled down sail,
And took to the oars, we three.

They say the ways of a woman
Can puzzle the wisest yet ;
I wot she can never be harder to guide
Than the old North Sea in a fret.

I think I shall drown when my day is done ;
And I'd liefer rest in the deep,

Than moulder up in the churchgarth there,
Where the earthworms burrow and creep.

I 've served the sea these sixty year,
When it calls, as it will, I know,
I 'll be none so loath to hear its voice,
And say good-bye, and go.

I shall better sleep where the billows
Sing to the seaman's soul,
Than where restless footsteps tramp and pass,
And weary church bells toll.

But, till I hear and answer
The great sea's solemn call,
I shall never so near touch hands with Death
As on that spring day in the squall.

THE VILLAGE FLOWER SHOW.

There are the oaks; they burgeon broadly yet;
   And the horse-chestnuts, with their mighty fans;
Are those tall trees the birches that you set,
   When chase and park showed brave in boyish plans?
What! pert red cottages in formal row,
   Where thatch and lattice wore their woodbine screen;
Aye, we knew nought of progress long ago,
   But this 'great age' has spoiled our village green.

So, the white gate still guards the show. But what!
   A band that clashes, flag and uniform;
Poor Tommy and his fiddle, both forgot,
   Lie mouldering. crushed 'neath Time's persistent
      storm.
Who is that pretty child? her eyes and smile
   Carry one back; I know, it 's Patty East;

Just so she looked that April morning, while
  We watched George 'courting' her, at Marton Feast.

That must be Patty's child; and see, out there,
  A gray-haired cripple tries to lift his hat;
Speak to him; nay, years show us marvels rare,
  But yon frail wreck can't be our 'handsome Mat'?
Look at the roses, Harry Parker's glory
  They always were, and Harry Parker's dead;
These are his grandson's; ever the same story,
  Has all the past, except its shadows, fled?

We walk as strangers here, those whisperers
  Recall the name and fame their parents taught;
Just a faint light of memory glints and stirs,
  Amid the stagnant waste the years have wrought.
Come, let us leave it all; I 'll tell you where
  We two shall find a silent welcome still;
Where the lush ivy waves in sombre air,
  And the gray church lies underneath the hill.

Aye, aye, I know you, friend; so Mary brings
  Honey and poultry as her mother did;
Though the tall elm its heavy shelter flings,
  Where 'Molly' lies beneath her coffin-lid.
Come with us; 'mid the headstones, one by one,
  We'll find the names we loved in bygone days;
And smile and sigh, recalling gay deeds done,
  When others heeded both our blame and praise.

Our shows were better, were they? May be so;
  Our fruits were finer, brighter bloomed our flowers?
And Tommy's fiddle, thirty years ago,
  Gave fleeter pinions to these loitering hours?
I am not sure, old Friend; our bairns sometimes
  Talk in decorous whispers of the past;

Till mocking laughter 'mid their memories chimes,
  Admiring how such antique 'ways' could last.

Come with us; the low seat beneath the yew
  Still stands where we were wont of yore to sit;
We'll praise the old, and criticise the new,
  With the strange bitter yearning born of it.
They look so happy out there in the meadow,
  We seem a little cold and lone, in sooth;
Well, surely o'er the dial creeps the shadow,
  Eternity renews the glow of youth.

THE BURIED CHIME.

UNDER the cliffs at Whitby, when the great tides
    landward flow,
Under the cliffs at Whitby, when the great winds
    landward blow,

When the long billows heavily roll o'er the harbour
    bar,
And the blue waves flash to silver 'mid the seaweeds
    on the Scar,

When the low thunder of the surf calls down the
    hollow shore,
And 'mid the caves at Kettleness, the baffled breakers
    roar;

Under the cliffs at Whitby, whoso will stand alone,
Where in the shadow of the Nab the eddies swirl
    and moan,

When to the pulses of the deep, the flood tide rising
    swells,
Will hear amid its monotone, the clash of hidden
    bells.

Up from the heart of ocean the mellow music peals,
Where the sunlight makes his golden path, and the
    sea-mew flits and wheels.

For many a chequered century, untired by flying
    time,
The bells, no human fingers touch, have rung their
    hidden chime,

Since the gallant ship that brought them, for the
    abbey on the height,
Struck and foundered in the offing, with her sacred
    goal in sight.

And the man who dares on Hallowe'en on the black
    Nab to watch,
Till the rose-light on St. Hilda's shrine the midnight
    moonbeams catch,

And calls his sweetheart by her name, as o'er the
    sleeping seas
The echo of the buried bells comes floating on the
    breeze,

Ere another moon on Hallowe'en her eerie rays has
    shed,
Will hear his wedding peal ring out from the church
    tower on the head.

SONG.

I LOVE her with every pulse of my heart,
    What would you more, what would you more?
With her cold sweet smile she draws apart,
    What would you more, what would you more?

Fair, still, she stands, like a passionless saint
That Behrens might fashion or Herbert paint,
It is naught to her if men madden or faint,
   And oh, what would you more?

I told her it all last night by the river,
   What would you more, what would you more?
How I 'd loved her for years, and would love her for
      ever,
   What would you more, what would you more?
She nor trembled nor blushed to hear my pleading,
She yielded no sign to my interceding,
In her gentle courtesy hearing, not heeding,
   And oh, what would you more?

I know that my beautiful dream is naught,
   What would you more, what would you more?
With its hope, and fancy, and centered thought,
   What would you more, what would you more?
Yet I know too, while life in my bosom stirs,
Mute and patient among her worshippers,
I shall waste my heart for one smile of hers,
   And oh, what would you more?

DRIFTING APART.

Drifting apart,
Hand from hand and heart from heart;
Striving with a patient will
To keep the sweet old fashion still;
Striving with a passionate pain
To join the breaking links again,
To act the impulse of the heart,
Drifting apart.

Drifting apart,
 With a strange, hid, bitter smart,
Speaking old familiar words,
Striking old familiar chords,
Feeling all the impulse dead,
Hearing all the music fled,
Reading in the secret heart,
Drifting apart.

Whose the blame?
Each so fain had felt the same;
Each would yet renew the spell,
Proved so dearly, loved so well;
Each had watched those failing ties
With clinging hands and pleading eyes,
Each the crown of faith would claim.
Whose the blame?

Let it be:
Sun nor shade will ever see,
Blooming as it wont of yore,
The fair flower whose life is o'er;
Let it wither, toss the grass
O'er its petals as you pass,
Hush the idle plaint and plea:
Let it be.

Drifting apart.
Let us with untroubled heart
Bid the sober future come,
Bid the happy past be dumb:
What avails to seek the cause,
Feeling owns no settled laws;
Hide the scar, forget the smart.
Drifting apart.

THEIR PRESENCE.

LIKE falling leaves, like drooping flowers, they pass,
The loves, the joys, the hopes of golden youth;
As shadows cast upon a looking-glass,
That mock the touch that fain would prove them
    truth;
A cold suspicious glance is all we give,
As fresh-fledged fancies woo us on our way,
Till, wrapping every darkening hour we live,
Creeps dull despondency, chill, blank, and gray.

The friends we garnered in our heart of hearts,
Grow tired of us and our failing strength;
The comrades of the drama's first gay parts,
Find fitter actors ere it wins its length.
The children that we reared our stay to be
Clasp newer loves and stronger hands than ours;
Time dims the eyes that were so keen and free,
Time dulls the senses, saps the boasted powers.

The books we loved pall on the wearied mind,
The arts we practised jar, or halt, or fade,
Silent and sad the standard is resigned
As the fresh-knighted champions seize the blade.
Young lips laugh lightly, and young voices soothe,
Young eyes dissemble half the scorn they feel,
But oh, we once won battles in our youth,
We scarce with patience due can sheathe the steel.

Where wave the grasses round the marble cross
Lie those who trusted, honoured, prized, and loved;
And memory, drooping 'neath the weight of loss,
Feebly recalls the glory life has proved;

Only when musing by the fire alone,
In the gray evenings of the lonely home,
With gentle touch, and low endearing tone,
And steps we know, our Dead around us come.

There is an empire where you cannot reach,
O young and joyous darlings of the Spring;
There is a happiness no lore can teach,
A rest no terrors haunt, no doubtings sting;
Across the dreary valley-paths of life,
One full pure cloudless lustre yet is shed,
When we can enter from its fret and strife
The stedfast presence of the noble Dead.

BENEATH THE WILLOW.

THE roses flashed their crimson bloom over the
    mossy pillow
Where the violet couched in her own perfume, and
    the thrush sang clear on the willow;
Sang loud and sweet its joyous song,
Sang of love and hope the bright day long,
In the flush of the golden summer weather,
While two stood hearing it, two together.

There was not a violet bud to see, there was not a
    leaf on the willow,
Where the thrush lay dead by the bare rose-tree,
    lay dead on a snowy pillow,
Where the blackbird wailed its dreary song,
Wailed of sorrow and change the dark day long,
In the chill of the black December weather,
While one wept to think how they stood together.

The sleeping buds will wake again, to gem the soft
    green pillow
Where the rose-leaves shed their fragrant rain, when
    the west wind blows through the willow,
Another thrush, sweet, clear, and strong,
Carol of June the bright day long,
But never again in the sunny weather
Will those two listen its lay together.

GRANDFATHER'S STORY.

Give me the helm, child. Why, the steel is dimmed,
And on the breast-plate, gauntlet, cuisse, and all;
Our gallants now are grown so dainty-limbed,
They let the armour rust upon the wall.
See, how the dust upon the feather lies;
Out on the carpet knights! Nay, never pout,
Go, bid them do their devoir for thine eyes,
The old mail sickens for one rousing bout.

There, put thy little finger in the cleft,
Through which the life-blood poured like summer
    rain,
When, 'mid the best of Astley's riders left,
I lay and groaned on Edgehill's fatal plain;
Aye, if old Gilbert there, at break of morn,
Had not come back to seek me 'mid the dead,
No saucy wench had in these halls been born,
To try my casque upon her golden head.

Those covenanting knaves struck hard and deep.
See, here a sword right through the plating shore;
That dint a lance-head made on Naseby steep,
When our wild charge their bravest backward bore.

But this jagged hole! fiercest and fellest stroke,
Of all I gave, or took, in days of old,
I had it when our line at Marston broke;
Sit here, child, thou shalt hear the story told.

When the gay sun on black Long Marston rose,
Thy mother was a bride of seventeen.
Aye, just thy years, like hers thy soft cheek glows,
But thy blue eyes are scarce so blue, I ween!
And as we mustered in the castle court,
She came to me as she was wont to come,
And whispered, masking fear in wistful sport,
'My father, bring my Harry safely home.'

Poor Harry, frank and joyous out he rode,
Waving the flag she wrought him in the van,
And as ranks closed, and war's fierce fever glowed,
He bore him like a gallant gentleman;
And Ouse ran redly through each willowed bank,
Ere the dark day was done, and all was lost,
And with the sun the hopes of Stuart sank,
And, snow-like, melted all the northern host.

Fast to the sheltering walls of loyal York
Fled proud Newcastle, all his projects o'er;
And keen Prince Rupert, whose hot morning's work
Had wrecked the royal bark in sight of shore.
What did it boot to linger there to die,
'Neath traitor lance, or rebel axe and cord?
Better to wait beneath a happier sky,
Till God saw His anointed line restored.

Yet ere I turned old Warrior for the flight
(It irks me yet, girl, though 'tis past so long),
I heard our Harry's shout ring through the fight,
I saw his crest struck backward 'mid the throng,

I saw the bright head down amid the spears,
I saw the Roundhead's arm was up to strike,
And dashing in, amid our comrades' cheers,
I flung myself between him and the pike.

Our brave lads rallied round us.   Masterless
Full many a steed of Fairfax ran, I trow,
We tore our bloody way amid the press,
And I had Harry on my saddle bow.
And not till many a league of heather lay
Behind our thundering hoofs, I reeled and fell,
But as I sank, I heard old Gilbert say,
'See, see, the boy breathes yet,' and all was well.

Poor Harry! Aye, he died at red Dunbar,
And, like a blighted flower, she followed fast;
And thou, safe in thy convent walls afar,
Wert left to cheer thy grandsire's hearth at last.
But thy sweet mother, ever on that day,
At gloaming, creeping to my side would come,
And bid me tell her of the desperate fray,
When her old father brought her Harry home.

THE FISHERMAN'S FUNERAL.

Up on the breezy headland the fisherman's grave
      they made,
Where over the daisies and clover bells the birchen
      branches swayed;
Above us the lark was singing in the cloudless skies
      of June,
And under the cliffs the billows were chanting their
      ceaseless tune:

For the creamy line was curving along the hollow
    shore,
Where the dear old tides were flowing that he would
    ride no more.

The dirge of the wave, the note of the bird, and
    the priest's low tone were blent
In the breeze that blew from the moorland, all laden
    with country scent ;
But never a thought of the new-mown hay tossing
    on sunny plains,
Or of lilies deep in the wild wood, or roses gem-
    ming the lanes,
Woke in the hearts of the stern bronzed men who
    gathered around the grave,
Where lay the mate who had fought with them the
    battle of wind and wave.

How boldly he steered the coble across the foaming
    bar,
When the sky was black to the eastward and the
    breakers white on the Scar !
How his keen eye caught the squall ahead, how his
    strong hand furled the sail,
As we drove o'er the angry waters before the raging
    gale !
How cheery he kept all the long dark night; and
    never a parson spoke
Good words like those he said to us, when at last
    the morning broke !

So thought the dead man's comrades, as silent and
    sad they stood,
While the prayer was prayed, the blessing said, and
    the dull earth struck the wood ;

And the widow's sob, and the orphan's wail, jarred
  through the joyous air;
How could the light wind o'er the sea, blow on so
  fresh and fair?
How could the gay waves laugh and leap, landward
  o'er sand and stone,
While he, who knew and loved them all, lay lapped
  in clay alone ?

But for long, when to the beetling heights the snow-
  tipped billows roll,
When the cod, and skate, and dogfish dart around
  the herring shoal ;
When gear is sorted, and sails are set, and the
  merry breezes blow,
And away to the deep sea-harvest the stalwart
  reapers go,
A kindly sigh, and a hearty word, they will give to
  him who lies
Where the clover springs, and the heather blooms,
  beneath the northern skies.

?

Did that garden glow so brightly?
Did that brook in silver foam?
Did the deer bound by so lightly
In the wooded glades at home?
Did the oak tree where we idled,
Burgeon o'er such sweep of grass ?
Did the dark gray mare you bridled
O'er such gap so bravely pass?

Dear, you turn in pretty passion,
At the doubt I dare to hint,

Yet, Time keeps the sober fashion,
Learnt in life and preached in print;
Young eyes have their own fond glamour,
Memory deepens every line,
Love and Fancy, in sweet clamour,
Join to make the Past divine.

If we read the dear old stories,
If we tread the dear old ways,
If we wake the joys and glories
Of the dear old vanished days;
Dwarfed, and dull, and weak, and failing,
Do they show to older eyes,
And we ask in vain bewailing
What has changed the earth and skies?

Better leave them in their sleeping,
Bygone days, half lulled to dreams,
Tender thoughts true vigil keeping,
Memory shedding moonlight gleams;
Gold's no purer for the testing,
Question never steadied trust,
Where our early joys are resting,
Fading flowers make gracious dust.

Life is full of task and duty,
Age steals steady on our track;
Leave the Past in all its beauty,
Never gaze regretful back;
Pity to disturb the vision
By Reason's calm unpitying glare,
Not hers the light on fields Elysian,
Which our childhood found so fair.

THE TENTH BEATITUDE.

A pale pure pearl that is chosen to grace
    A young queen's royal crown;
And another, as meet for a diadem,
That fades—a fair neglected gem
    In its shell 'neath the sea weeds brown.

A blossom plucked from a beauty's wreath,
    A lover's pledge to be;
And another, as rich in its scent and grace,
Wasting them both on a moor's blank face,
    Where the winds sweep lone and free.

As varying, on from source to goal,
    Runs many a human life:
One cold and empty, one full and blest;
This, lapped in the sunshine of happy rest,
    That, spent in the world's hot strife.

And, musing how each different fate
    By one common spring is moved,
We think a Beatitude, half divine,
Might complete the roll of the sacred nine,
    For 'Blessed are the Beloved.'

THE HELEN.

'So you're back again among us;
I 'se glad you 've gien us a call;
Step in, and welcome, and take a seat,
The pot 's on the boil, an' all.

'Oh, I 'se well and purely, thank you.
I is but dowly a bit,
I gets thinking of the old man, you see,
When I has the time to sit.

'He 's master of the Helen;
She 's sailed for the North, you know,
I feel as a knife went through my heart,
When the wind gets up to blow.

'But there 's not a braver bark afloat,
Nor better manned and found ;
George says to me, as he walked her deck,
They 'd not match her, England round.

'Our Mary? come thou hither, I say.
She 's shamefaced there, fond lass.
She 's promised to young Charlie Clare,
As bides above the Pass.

'Her father made him mate this spring.
I heard him tell her int' court,
The banns should be up the very day
The Helen rode in port.

'The neighbours? Oh, aye, they mind on you;
Old Bess? Well, her man was lost,
In the fearful gale when the Royal Rose
Struck on the Norway coast.

'Her little un 's grown a bonny lad;
Our George has ta'en him afloat,
He said, how 'he 'd be a sailor too,'
When first he framed in the boat.

'And Bess was fain her one son's start
Should be with my good old man,

He 'll give the fatherless kindly heed,
And the pick of the berth and the can.

' And Annie ? her with the golden hair ?
Aye, she thought too much on her curls ;
But she steadied when she married Bill,
It 's often the way with girls.

' Poor lass, he sailed in the Helen,
Three days or the bairn had come,
She 'll talk to the morsel half the day
How " Daddy will soon be home."

' Who else is in the Helen ?
Why Ned, from the cot by the beck ;
You made a picture of him and his lads,
Heaping the nets on the deck.

' And John, who steered the life-boat
Right through the surf on the shore,
When the blue lights burnt from the Niobe,
On the reef where the breakers roar.

' His blind old father ? he 's yonder,
He 'll say as he sits on t' pier,
" I can't see the Helen heave in sight,
But I 'll know my brave boy's cheer."

' And Harry Hudson, do you mind ?
His father were drowned at sea,
And the mother faded like a bud
When a blight has struck the tree.

' And Harry, who 'd hardlins twenty year,
Kept the bit of a home together,
And worked for it, and the eight poor bairns,
Summer and winter weather.

'George has ta'en him out in the Helen,
Where was a good wage to be had,
He wrought a'most too hard ashore,
For nobbut such a lad.

'Aye, owners may talk of her cargo,
But we mun give our prayers,
For a richer and dearer freight than that,
The hands that the Helen bears.

'Was the drum up as you passed it?
I reckon I'm fond to speer;
She's far enough from the angry winds,
That lash our sea-board here.

'But oh, we women who sit at home,
With our men so far away,
It is only we who know how the waves
Can thunder in Whitby Bay.'

*   *   *   *   *   *

Oh, long, long may the ingle side
Its blaze of welcome keep;
And long, long may the pale wife strain
Sad eyes o'er the tossing deep;

The wedding gauds the maiden prized
May yellow where they rest;
The bright babe spring to the sunburnt boy,
By a father's lips unblest;

The widow may pine her gray life through
For the help of her son's right hand;
The kindly fisherman's nets may rot
In the boats, far up on the sand;

The blind old man may see his son.
Where the light of Heaven shines clear,
And know his voice in the angels' song,
But not upon Whitby Pier.

For the Helen never showed her flag
In the Roads beyond the Scar,
And never echoed the joyous cheers
As she swept o'er the harbour bar;

A smack picked up a broken boat,
Adrift at sea, on the flow,
With her timbers stove, and her rudder gone,
And 'The Helen' upon her prow.

And that is all we shall ever hear,
As the desolate months go by,
Of the ship that sailed with her gallant crew
'Neath the calm October sky.

MY CHILD LOVE.

How we played among the meadows,
My child-love and I;
Chasing summer gleams and shadows,
My child-love and I.
Wandering in the bowery lanes,
Making rose-tipped daisy-chains;
Storing fairy treasure trove,
Tender chestnuts from the grove,
Juicy berries, sweet and red,
Violets in their leafy bed,
Peeping 'neath the old oak tree,
All for my child-love and me.

How we sped the hours together,
My child-love and I,
In the blue unclouded weather,
My child-love and I.
Two gold heads—ah, one is gray,
One is pillowed cold in clay;
Two bright faces—one is grave,
One hid where pale the willows wave.
Two laughs—I wot my smiles are few;
Do angels sport as mortals do,
Or as we did in days gone by,
We, my sweet child-love and I?

What infant mysteries we had,
My child-love and I;
What little things could make us glad,
My child-love and I.
What fair castles did we build,
Every room so gaily filled
With sun and flowers ever new;
I so brave, and she so true.
Endless pleasures, boundless wealth,
Ceaseless joy, and cloudless health,
Nought should change, and nought could die,
So ruled my child-love and I.

We were parted in our youth,
My child-love and I;
In our fearless baby-truth,
My child-love and I.
She in virgin freshness died,
I stood weeping at her side,
Turning to the world again,
Gathering many a deepening stain.

Other loves their empire held,
Newer dreams such empire quelled,
Till far as trackless sea from sea
Seemed my fair child-love from me.

Yet 'twas an idyl that we had,
My child-love and I;
Ere death dimmed all its glory glad,
My child-love and I.
Though deeper sorrows, deeper pleasures,
Fill for me life's foaming measures,
Yet, fairest mid my hopes and schemes,
Purest of my wandering dreams
Is, how when all is past and done,
Forfeit paid and pardon won,
In some calm sphere there yet may be
A home for my child-love and me.

BAFFLED.

I WILL plant a tree for myself, she said,
With clusters of crimson bloom,
Whose beauty shall dazzle the waking sight,
Whose scent shall fill all the dreamy night
With the breath of its sweet perfume.
But the blight fell down with the morning dew,
And the rose tree died ere its first bud blew.

I will twine a wreath for myself, she said,
Of myrtle and laurel and bay,
Whose glory shall halo my living head,
And over the grave where they lay me dead,
Speak of me and my fame alway.
But the canker was deep and the thorn was keen,
And the bright leaves withered her clasp between.

I will carve a dream for myself, she said,
Its loveliness fixed for ever,
A thing of beauty and joy and life,
We will pass serene through the world's hot strife,
I and my work together.
But Death's strong hand struck sudden and cold,
The chisel dropped from her fainting hold.

They tossed them aside in a useless heap,
Dead root, and blossom, and half-wrought stone,
Where the river of time flowed swift and deep,
And they left not a trace thereon.

LET IT BE.

Let be the river!   What does it avail
  To struggle with the current's destined course?
The strongest effort does but faint and fail,
  Skill yields, out-tired, to resistless force.
The highest rock is overleapt by spray,
The silent waters fret each bar away.

Vainly the bulwark fashioned deep and wide,
  New bed contrived, new turn by cunning wrought;
Steady, resistless, onward flows the tide,
  Each gathering wave with gathering purpose fraught,
Till, full and free, rejoicing in its strength,
It sweeps to ocean's mighty arms at length.

Let be the river!   Let the loved alone
  To meet the fate, and shape the circumstance.
We dream the future, fancying all our own,
  What does but wait the call of time and chance;
Foredoomed, the path before the pilgrim lies,
The sunset lurking in the morning skies.

Let be the river! Hail its rippling smile,
  Listen its song, and shiver to its sigh;
Let its chafed beauty weary hours beguile,
  Watch how it darkens to the darkening sky;
We cannot cloud or brighten, speed or check,
Nor alter on its way the tiniest beck.

Let be the river then! Where lilies float, ·
  And blue forget-me-nots beside it shimmer,
Take gladness in its suns' reflected mote,
  And soothing from its moonlights' dreamy glimmer;
Happy if still your faltering footsteps tend
Beside its varying currents to the end!

THE FISHERMAN'S SUMMONS.

THE sea is calling, calling.
Wife, is there a log to spare?
Fling it down on the hearth and call them in,
The boys and girls with their merry din;
I am loth to leave you all just yet,
In the light and the noise I might forget
The voice in the evening air.

The sea is calling, calling,
Along the hollow shore.
I know each nook in the rocky strand,
And the crimson weeds on the golden sand,
And the worn old cliff where the sea-pinks cling,
And the winding caves where the echoes ring.
I shall wake them never more.

How it keeps calling, calling;
It is never a night to sail.
I saw the 'sea-dog' over the height,
As I strained through the haze my failing sight,

And the cottage creaks and rocks, wellnigh
As the old 'Fox' did in the days gone by,
In the moan of the rising gale.

Yet it is calling, calling.
It is hard on a soul, I say,
To go fluttering out in the cold and the dark,
Like the bird they tell us of, from the ark;
While the foam flies thick on the bitter blast,
And the angry waves roll fierce and fast,
Where the black buoy marks the bay.

Do you hear it calling, calling?
And yet, I am none so old.
At the herring fishery, but last year,
No boat beat mine for tackle and gear,
And I steered the coble past the reef,
When the broad sail shook like a withered leaf,
And the rudder chafed my hold.

Will it never stop calling, calling?
Can't you sing a song by the hearth.
A heartsome stave of a merry glass,
Or a gallant fight, or a bonnie lass,
Don't you care for your grand-dad just so much?
Come near then, give me a hand to touch,
Still warm with the warmth of the earth.

You hear it calling, calling?
Ask her? why she sits and cries!
She always did when the sea was up,
She would fret, and never take bit or sup
When I and the lads were out at night,
And she saw the breakers cresting white
Beneath the low black skies.

But then in its calling, calling,
No summons to soul was sent.
Now—well, fetch the parson, find the book,
It is up on the shelf there if you look:
The sea has been friend, and fire, and bread;
Put me, where it will tell of me, lying dead,
How It called, and I rose and went.

THE FOURFOLD ASPECT.

THE lovers stood in the deep recess
Of the old ancestral hall,
Where the storied panes their gold and red
Flung o'er the grace of her bended head,
As he whispered, 'Nothing on earth is bliss
Like a silent hour, such as this,
With the soft hush over all!'

The children played on the flowery lawn,
Darting from glade to walk.
'And see,' they said, as they glanced above,
To the two, in their happy trance of love,
'How Maud and Charlie waste the day,
Though night is coming to stop our play,
They do not even talk.'

With weary eyes and sable robes
The lonely lady passed;
A sudden cloud her pale face crossed,
The anguish of one who has loved and lost;
Then from laughing babes and dreaming pair,
She turned away with the gentle prayer,
'My God, may their sunshine last!'

The old men glanced from the lighted hearth,
Where they sate over cards and wine,
To the two unconscious of aught the while,
Save Love and each other—then shrug and smile,
As one, draining his glass, said, 'As they choose,
But yon blaze is better than chill night dews,
Your trick, and the deal is mine.'

The twilight deepened into night,
The stars through the dusk air shone;
Age and infancy calmly slept
O'er a dark-eyed portrait the mourner wept,
And the lover still murmured, 'Not yet, not yet!
Ah, why should such hour in parting set?'
And so the old world rolls on.

'GIVE ME A CHANCE.'

FACT.

'GIVE me a chance, Jack!' Fierce and fast thun-
    dered the flowing tide,
The breaking billows flashed in foam, where the
    coble lay on her side.
But three bare feet from the rising wave, the mast
    of the sunken boat
Stood firm 'mid the terrible surge and swirl — it
    might keep one man afloat.

Just one, and home lay close and safe, not a shot's
    length from the Scar;
Just one, and already the life-boat strove, 'mid the
    rollers on the Bar;

Just one; and Will, clinging desperately, as men
    cling for life and death,
Felt his mate clutch round him as he strove, in the
    boiling surf beneath.

It quivered and bent, the poor frail mast; his whole
    brain reeled in the roar.
Were those his bairns out there on the pier? Did
    the wife shriek then from the shore?
' Jack, give me a chance!' death's agony from his
    lips the sentence wrung.
' I will; God bless thee, mate; good-bye;' and he
    smiled up as he clung.

Then, quietly loosed his iron hold, with never a
    moan or cry,
Down 'mid the tangled seaweeds, the brave man
    sank to die;
Stalwart, and strong, in manhood's prime, dear love
    and life he gave,
The simple hero, who all unsung lies 'neath the
    northern wave.

Just dying — no thought of glory, no dream of an
    honoured name,
To ring through the coming ages, from the fiery
    lips of fame;
No flutter of flag, or dazzle of steel, or thrilling of
    trumpet blare,
Only cold gray sky, and cold gray sea, drowning
    and death were there.

Untaught, untrained, save to courage here, and trust
    in the good to come,
Only to give his friend ' the chance,' the fisherman
    faced his doom;

Such men our Yorkshire seaboard rears, such men
    make England's glory,
Touching to light sublime the tale that tells our
    Island Story.

' HARD LINES.'

Have you raised a fragile rose-bud
From tangling weed and dew,
And fenced it aright, from glare and blight,
And trained it as it grew;
Was it not hard to see it,
When its beauty was all you had,
Glow and expand for the stranger's hand,
Who won it his life to glad?

Have you nursed a bright-eyed fledgeling,
While the days were dark and long,
Till its plumes shone rare in the sunny air,
And you thrilled to its joyous song;
Was it not hard when its echo
Brought an answer to the lay?
The dream was sweet, and the lot was meet,
But—the gay mates flew away!

But oh, we left in the shadow
This solace at least may gain,
The victor may keep of the corn he will reap
From the seeds we sowed in pain;
But we had the first sweet waking
To light, and life, and love,
And memory's store told o'er and o'er
May the wealth of the lonely prove.

CHOP HEAD LOANING.

ALL day long at Boro'bridge the battle swayed and
    roared,
Where Lancaster and Hereford unsheathed the rebel
    sword.

The Ure came glittering plainward, all bright with
    moorland dews,
But she ran red with gallant blood or ere she met
    the Ouse.

For on the gray bridge arches, and by the willowed
    banks,
Was Hereford's last desperate stand against the
    royal ranks.

And when upon the Welshman's spear poured the
    lifeblood of de Bohun,
His followers melted from the fray as the tides
    beneath the moon.

From violated sanctuary Earl Lancaster they tore,
The best and bravest of the north to prison doom
    they bore.

Fast galloped John de Mowbray from the field of
    Boro'bridge,
Fast to where Upsall's massive walls nestle by
    Boltby ridge;

There stanch hearts to the Mowbray would render
    homage due,
There bold hearts to the Mowbray give refuge close
    and true.

But close upon his traces stern Barclay's riders
    came,
Eager for traitor Mowbray's head, Despencer's gold
    to claim.

All in the darkening Loaning was the brief unequal
    fight,
And helpless in fierce foeman's hands stood Mow-
    bray's noble knight.

The jury of the battle day, all form as mercy lacks,
A fallen ash-tree bole the block, a soldier's sword
    the axe;

Among the ferns the headless trunk in rough dis-
    honour flung,
The gilded armour on an oak, in mockery they
    hung,

To rust in summer showers, in winter storms to
    sway;
No more to flash the tourney's star, to lead the
    tossing fray.

It was five hundred years ago; calm flows the bright
    brown Ure,
Upon her banks the little town stands quiet and
    secure.

Who on the bridge at Boro'bridge thinks of that
    day in March
When the brave blood of Hereford, stained all the
    dark gray arch?

The ancient church where Lancaster fled in his last
    despair,
How few they be who yet can point, and say " it
    once was there!"

Gone shrine, and oak, and Milan mail; de Mow-
    bray's haughty race
Have vanished from the land where yet their name
    marks Vale and Chace.

Yet still tradition treasures the tales of long ago;
And still when from Black Hambledon the fierce
    north-easters blow,

The fearful peasant passing by 'Chop Head Loan-
    ing,' hears
The sough of boughs, and clash of steel, fall on his
    shrinking ears,

As on the unseen branches the knightly harness
    rings
Defiance to the veil that time, o'er name and glory
    flings.

AT THE BAR.

'Who speaks for this man?' From the great white
    Throne,
Veiled in its roseate clouds the Voice came forth;
Before it stood a parted soul alone,
And rolling east, and west, and south, and north,
The mighty accents summoned quick and dead:
'Who speaks for this man, ere his doom is said?'

Shivering he listened, for his earthly life
Had passed in dull unnoted calm away;
He brought no glory to its daily strife,
No wreath of fame, or genius' fiery ray;
Weak, lone, ungifted, quiet, and obscure,
Born in the shadow, dying 'mid the poor.

Lo, from the solemn concourse hushed and dim,
The widow's prayer, the orphan's blessing rose;
The struggler told of trouble shared by him,
The lonely of cheered hours and softened woes;
And like a chorus spoke the crushed and sad,
' He gave us all he could, and what he had.'

And little words of loving kindness said,
And tender thoughts, and help in time of need,
Sprang up, like leaves by soft spring showers fed,
In some waste corner, sown by chance-flung seed;
In grateful wonder heard the modest soul,
Such trifles gathered to so blest a whole.

O ye, by circumstance' strong fetters bound,
The store so little, and the hand so frail,
Do but the best ye can for all around,
Let sympathy be true, nor courage fail;
Winning from the dense ranks of poor and weak,
Some Witness at your trial hour to speak.

WORK.

Strong gales keep the clouds from raining;
Work lulls the sad heart's complaining;
Through the fret and the toil runs the weary ache;
Yet Duty grows dear for her own grave sake,
And muscles are stronger for straining.

Each life has some prize for gaining,
Each wound has a balm for its paining;
So we seek for it long in faith' and in prayer,
For the finger of God is everywhere,
While the days are dawning and waning.

Though the mildew its leaves are staining,
The rose has some scent remaining:
Through the darkest hour still trust in the light;
What the hand has to do, let it do with its might;
Strong gales keep the clouds from raining.

WAS IT I?

In the morning the light breezes shiver,
  The soft cloudlets flit o'er the sky;
Who ran in her mirth by the river?
  Was it I? Was it I?
Whose voice rang out, as clear and gay
As the joyous breath of the wakening day;
Who cheered the dog to the flashing leap,
Where the pebbles shone and the banks were steep;
Who lay on the daisies to watch the lark
Lose its twinkling wings in the great blue arc;
Who laughed at the brown hares darting by?
Was it I? Was it I?

In the sunset the lithe willows quiver,
  The rose-tint is flooding the sky;
Who loitered of old by the river?
  Was it I? Was it I?
Who watched the blue forget-me-nots gleam,
And the water-lilies float on the stream;
Who blushed as a strong arm drew them near,
And a low voice whispered close and dear,
How fair the waxen flowers would show,
'Mid the golden braids in the ball-room's glow?
Oh! the happy silence, hushed and shy.
Was it I? Was it I?

The black ice-bands crackle and shiver,
  As the pale wintry sun lights the sky;
Who stands by the cold sullen river?
  Is it I? Is it I?
With hair that is touched by the fallen snow,
And a step that was eager, long ago;
Ah me! since then its faltering tread
Has followed the train of belovèd dead,
And has learnt the watcher's cautious ways,
And must needs go softly all its days.
And memory owns, with a patient sigh,
It was I! It is I!

OLD LETTERS.

Ay, better burn them. What does it avail
To treasure the dumb words so dear to us?
Like dead leaves tossed before the autumn ga'e
Will be each written page we cherish thus,
When Time's great wind has swept them all away,
The smiles, loves, tears, and hatreds of to-day.

Living, we hoard our letters, holding them
Sacred and safe, as almost sentient things;
So strong the yearning tide of grief to stem,
So true, when doubt creeps in, or treason stings;
Parting may smile, such golden bridge between;
Change cannot come, where such stamped faith has
      been.

Dying, we leave them to our children's care,
Our well-prized solace, records of the time
When life lay spread before us, rich and fair,
And love and hope spoke prophecies sublime;

Lore slowly gathered through laborious hours,
Wit's playful flashes, sweet poetic flowers.

All these to us, to us—and for awhile,
Our loved will guard the casket where they lie,
Glancing them over with a tearful smile,
Touching their yellowing foldings tenderly;
A little while—but Life and Time are strong,
Our dearest cannot keep such vigils long.

And by-and-by, the cold bright eyes of youth,
Lighting on such old flotsam of the past,
The shattered spars of trust, and hope, and truth,
On the blank shore of Time's great ocean cast,
Will read and judge, with naught of soft behoving,
Dissecting, sneering, anything but loving.

So, let us burn them all, the tottering words
The guided baby fingers wrote us first,
The school-boy scribble—lines the man affords
To the old eyes that watched, old hands that nurst,
The girl's sweet nonsense, confidence of friend,
And these, our own, ours only, till the end.

Heap them together, one last fervent kiss,
Then, let them turn, ere we do, into dust,
Ashes to ashes. Well and wise it is,
To meet the end that comes, as come it must;
And leave no relics to grow gray and rotten,
Waiting the certain doom of the forgotten.

THROWING STONES.

Nay, the lake lies quietly,
Do not fling the stone;
You cannot stop, you cannot guide;
Pause once ere it is thrown.

It will fright the bird, just resting
On the quivering willows there;
It will scare the May-flies, dancing
Where the sunlights gleam so fair;
It will crush the water-lilies,
That float upon their track;
Do not throw the stone so rashly,
You cannot call it back.

What? it will but for a moment
Break the surface of the stream,
And make a million facets
Of that steady noonday gleam;
Just a splash in the warm silence,
Just an instant's stir, no more,
Ere the thrush renews its melody
Upon the wooded shore;
And the midges whirl their endless waltz,
Where on its broad green throne
The waxen water-lily lies,
Forgetful of the stone.

Nay, much more in its flashing fall
That pebble flung will do,
Than cleave its own swift burial-place
Beneath the waters blue.
Bethink you how the tiny ring
Its sudden dart will make,
Will spread in widening circles,
Across the placid lake;
On, on in broadening power
Till it touch on either hand,
The mosses and the fern leaves,
That fence the flowery land.

Pause, ere you hurl the missile.
Pause, ere you say the word.
Long ere the lake recovers,
The calm that you have stirred;
Long ere the foolish echo,
Of a light phrase idly spoken,
May cease to thrill and vibrate,
Through the chords its jar has broken;
While in smile of youth and nature
Calm hearts and lakelets lie,
Fling not the stone, oh trifler,
But pass in silence by.

C'EST LA GUERRE,

1870.

GAUNT blackened walls where lately smiled the home;
The chill winds whistle for the household mirth;
Pale hungry babes the ravaged orchard roam,
Or crouch in silence by the empty hearth;
The old man moans beside the dying child,
The widow's wailing thrills the heavy air;
The wounded peasant 'mid the ruin wild
Says in despairing calmness 'C'est la guerre.'

Stolid submission, sullen smouldering wrath,
Broods o'er the land that once was fair Lorraine;
The desolation of the conquerors' path,
Marks broad and black each long Alsatian plain.
Shun every wooded knoll, and bosky hedge,
Keen men, with levelled rifle lurking there,
Deem stealthy murder patriotic pledge,
And brave the stern avenger—'C'est la guerre.'

Eager to dye their laurels doubly red,
The Teuton circle narrows day by day,
Where Paris rears her fair defiant head,
And famine hovers o'er her helpless prey.
O'er beautiful indomitable France
Settles the heavy cloud of last despair,
While Prussia, spite triumphant sword and lance,
Wails from her orphaned thousands, ' C'est la guerre.'

War's fatal seed is never sown in vain,
Her bitter harvest—hate, revenge, and scorn,
Long after peace resumes her golden reign,
Europe will reap by children yet unborn.
And now, while yet each desperate wrestler strives,
From homes laid waste and smiling uplands bare,
And countless graves, and broken hearts and lives,
Swells the accusing chorus, ' C'est la guerre.'

THE LETTER ON THE BATTLE-FIELD.

'We found in the dead hand of a captain in the Chasseurs d'Afrique, a letter in text hand, signed "Ta petite fille qui t'aime. MARGUERITE."'—*Times' Special Correspondent*, 1870.

AYE, take it from the stiffened hand,
    The pretty childish letter,
And smooth it out on the clay cold bed,
Where you lay the soldier-father's head,
To wait, till the last account is read
    Of ' War, Love's mighty debtor.'

See, the blood-stain red on the baby words,
    ' Ta petite fille qui t'aime,'
They had lain on the heart that, full and large,
Throbbed for the Chasseurs' fiery charge.
Ah, Marguerite! such a feeble targe
    'Gainst the keen Bavarian aim!

One moment bold in his champion's place,
  For the sunny land of his birth,
'For Home, for Honour, for France, for France,'
As MacMahon's trumpets rang 'advance.'
Then, Landwehr bullet, or Uhlan lance,
  And the blood-drenched soil of Woerth.

Where is that desolate home of thine,
  Poor little Marguerite?
By the storied Loire, or the swift Garonne?
Or where the Moselle's blurred waters run?
Or where Paris waits for the Prussian gun,
  Where the Seine and the sunshine meet?

How is it in that sad home of thine,
  Where 'maman's' heart will break,
Where no loving words, no playful ways
That the dear dead Father used to praise,
The widow's swollen lids can raise,
  For the glance his step would wake?

Alas! pale, pretty Marguerite,
  In grief thou art not alone;
Thousands of homes are darkened like thine,
Thousands of widows and orphans pine,
While from Berlin to Paris, for Seine or Rhine,
  The deadly game whirls on.

And thy Father's spirit, Marguerite,
  As it rose from the gory sod,
Did it carry its wail of sorrow and pain,
With the cloud of witnesses round him slain
For greed of glory, or power, or gain,
  To the throne of the Saviour God?

THE WIDOW OF DUNKERQUE.

FACT, 1870.

ALL! must France have them all?
Jules and Alphonse are gone;
I have only Henri left to share
The lonely widow's humble fare,
And kneel at night for the evening prayer.
Can they not leave me one?

We lived contented here,
'Neath summer and winter skies;
My boys worked early and late for me,
Toiling in market, and field, and sea,
And every Sunday they knelt, all three,
By the cross where their father lies.

Cannot kings live in peace?
Alphonse was brave from his birth,
His father's spirit was in his glance,
There was not a stronger arm in France;
Men say, spite the terrible Uhlan lance,
He died *with* his foe at Woerth.

I cannot tell who's to blame,
Now the weary siege is o'er;
But I know I shiver and shrink in pain
When I hear them clamour of great Bazaine;
The walls of Metz may be won again,
But they shelter my Jules no more!

Our Empress has her boy;
Mine lie in a bloody grave,

Killed—fighting for something, I cannot tell;
In Dunkerque we love our country well,
But the trumpet to me is a funeral knell,
And Henri is all I have.

Well, if he must go, he must.
My time cannot now be far.
Will these kaisers and kings have as calm a rest
When, conquered or conquerers, which is best?
Men dig them their graves in the earth's fair breas,
All scarred and defaced by War?

THE HOUR-GLASS.

SPARKLING, dancing downwards,
Merrily drop the sands.
While the golden hours so gaily pass,
Amid rose, and lily, and soft green grass;
Wherefore so eager to turn the glass,
Oh dimpled baby-hands?

Glittering, flashing downwards,
In the glow of the April sun.
Ah, sweet white fingers, and shy blue eyes,
And cheeks as rosy as western skies;
'Tis pity in Youth's first Paradise,
That the sands so swiftly run!

Stealing for ever downwards,
Gray tinging their virgin gold.
Pulses still quiver, and hearts still beat,
But the road grows hard for the tired feet;
Surely the sky had more warmth and heat,
And the sands showed brighter of old!

Dropping drearily downwards,
The evening is wellnigh o'er.
The brightest and best the river have crossed,
The bolt is shot, and the venture lost;
The barque on the last long wave is tossed,
The glass needs to turn no more.

BILL IS WASHED ASHORE.

SILENCE in the cottage.
Only the widow's moan
Breaks out sometimes from the curtained bed,
Where she buries mutely her desolate head.
Or the babe the neighbours won't take away,
'For its wail might wake her to cry,' they say,
Murmurs and stirs in its rosy sleep;
All else in a solemn stillness keep
And the woman is let alone.

Let alone in her trouble,
In the wisdom by sorrow taught;
We learn the ways of grief, who live
Where the mariners on the seaboard strive,
Each with his life in his hand to hold,
In the war with tempest, hunger, and cold;
Strong and stedfast they needs must be
Who win their bread from the Great North Sea,
Stern task in quiet wrought.

Silence in the cottage.
Only the mighty sound
Of the long waves crashing upon the strand,
And thundering far down the hollow sand,

And the moan and shriek of the angry blast
Shaking the lattices, sweeping past;
And sometimes the sound of heavy feet,
As the fishermen stride down the narrow street,
On their dangerous labour bound.

Hark! 'tis a strange weird cry
Piercing the deepening roar;
Up to the hut must the echo come,
For the woman starts from her mourning dumb,
Great tearless eyes on the threshold strain,
Pale lips are parting in throbbing pain,
Kind hands to aid her, kind friends to watch,
But she is the first the words to catch
That 'Bill has washed ashore.'

A voice of praise in the cottage,
A torrent of saving tears;
She has him again, cold, bruised, torn, dead,
With seaweed twined round his comely head,
His strong arm helpless, his gay voice hushed,
But she has him; to lie in his kindred dust,
To kiss, to touch, ere they put him away,
Where his bairns may plant o'er ·his honoured clay
Bright daisies for coming years.

Think of the depths of sorrow,
When a woman thanks God for this;
Just to have·her Dead in a hallowed grave,
Not left to toss with the tossing wave,
Not hidden in caves where the fishes play,
And the lithe brown sea-flowers wreathe and sway,
But laid to his rest with blessing and prayer,
To wait, till she creep beside him there.
Such life on our seaboard is.

LIFE.

Down from the moor, all flushed with purple dyes,
    Dances the bright beck 'neath the morning ray;
Now tossing lily-leaves to laughing skies,
    Now bathing mimic rocks in fairy spray;
Broadening its banks, and deepening its tune,
Till the great stream reflects the blaze of noon.

Stronger and graver, onward rolls the river,
    Heather and woodland far behind it left;
Where city lights upon its waters quiver,
    The mighty tide of shade and peace bereft.
Till burthens borne, and bridge and barrier past,
To ocean's solemn arms it sweeps at last.

So, to the golden hours of happy youth,
    To fret, and toil, and heat of middle life;
The evening time, through patience, prayer, and truth,
    Brings soft serenity to lull the strife;
Calm flows the river, as it nears the sea,
Hushed grows the life that nears Eternity.

FOR GOD AND THE RELIGION.

'For God and the Religion,' the simple rallying cry
That rang through Europe far and wide, in the angry
    days gone by,
Made humble shepherds soldiers stern, on the plains
    of Languedoc,
Taught peasants armed with scythe and spade to
    meet the spearman's shock,

Gave to weak women hero hearts in Poitou glen
    and dell,
And braved fell famine week by week on the ramparts
    of Rochelle ;
That spite dark Torquemada and his hecatombs of
    slain,
Spite Te Deums sung by Tiber side for murder on
    the Seine,
Brought to the quiet Huguenot the courage and the
    faith
That led him through a stedfast life to meet a
    noble death.

And for God and the Religion we had martyrs too
    at home,
When England raised her fearless head against the
    might of Rome,
Though Spain's imperial power dared 'Opinion' to
    advance,
And 'neath the golden lilies ranged the chivalry of
    France,
Though kingly threat was spoken, and Papal ban
    was hurled,
The steady English Protest spoke, alone, against a
    world ;
Till after years of doubt and dread, of axe, and flame,
    and sword,
The daughter of the Tudor took her stand upon The
    Word,
And by the crushed Armada were the glorious tidings
    known,
How for God and the Religion, old England held
    her own.

And for God and the Religion we have champions
    as of old,
Though Doubt creeps slow and subtle, though
    cherished creeds grow cold;
Though like the ebb tide as it turns upon the sunny
    shore,
The brave bright Truth that won so much, would
    fain look back once more;
As if in ancient rite and rule, to find the Peace that
    dies,
Before the sneer of modern lore, the glare of modern
    skies;
Deep in the heart of England the pulse is beating
    still,
That taught her hand to strike so hard, that taught
    her head to will;
And she has children stout and staunch to fence her
    in the fray,
If for God and the Religion she must stand once
    more at bay.

HARD SAYINGS.

Out from the tangled web of words they start,
By their own lurid light of sorrow lit,
The three sad phrases, by the human heart
Chosen the worst of human needs to fit;
Despite grave reason's dictum, 'will,' and 'fate,'
Despite pale resignation's brow serene,
Who does not shrink before the dread 'too late,'
The drear 'was once,' the wild 'what might have
    been.'

But to recall the hasty words we said,
But to give back the smile from which we turned,
For one forgiving whisper from the dead,
Speaking the patient love our folly spurned;
O passionate cry above each tended grave!
O frantic dashing 'gainst the iron gate!
Vain bitterest tears, vain all we pray and rave;
Dull comes the echo back, 'Too late, too late.'

That bitter smile 'was once' a happy laugh,
That blighting curse 'was once' a golden hope,
That broken reed 'was once' a trusted staff,
Fit to all heights to climb, all foes to cope;
The lonely mourner by the silent hearth,
The baffled warrior in the failing strife,
Turn all the sadder from their paths on earth,
Thinking how glorious 'once was' love and life.

But keenest in the poison of its sting,
Most pitiful in its appealing cry,
'What might have been' its mocking dreams can
　　bring,
To wring the hopeless heart, the yearning eye;
In other worlds what 'once was' yet may be,
'Too late' may lose its ache in calm serene,
But oh! can any Future let us see,
The glories pictured in Love's 'might have been!'

THE TWO THREADS.

A BABE, who crept from the downy nest
Fond hands had loved to deck,

Glowing and sweet from its rosy rest,
To cling, caressing and caressed,
To its gentle mother's neck ;
Another, who shrank in its squalid lair,
In the noisy crowded court,
Dreading to waken to curse and blow
The woman, whose life of sin and woe
Won from sleep a respite short.
From the darkness and the light,
Weave the black thread, weave the white.

A girl, in her graceful guarded home,
Mid sunshine, and birds, and flowers,
Whose fair face brightened as she heard
Her gallant lover's wooing word,
In the fragrant gloaming hours.
Another, tossed out, a nameless waif,
On the awful sea of life,
Mid poverty, ignorance, and wrong,
Young pulses beating full and strong
For the fierce unaided strife.
From the darkness and the light, ·
Weave the black thread, weave the white.

A wife, beside her household hearth,
In her happy matron pride,
Raising her infant in her arms,
Showing its thousand baby charms
To the father at her side.
Another, who stood on the river's banks,
Hearing her weakling's cries ;
Thinking, 'a plunge would end for both,
Cruelty, hunger, and broken troth,
Harsh earth, and iron skies.'

From the darkness and the light,
Weave the black thread, weave the white.

Her children's children at her knee,
With friends and kindred round,
An aged woman with silver hair,
Passing from life mid the love and prayer,
That her gracious evening crowned.
Another, crouched by the stinted warmth
Of the workhouse homeless hearth;
Her bitter fare unkindly given,
Knowing as little of joys, in Heaven
As of gladness on the earth.
From the darkness and the light,
Weave the black thread, weave the white.

A soul that sprang from the rose-strewn turf,
With its carven cross adorned.
Another, that left its pauper's grave,
Where rank and coarse the grasses wave,
O'er rest, unnamed, unmourned.
And two, who sought their Redeemer's feet,
By His saving blood to plead;
May He in His mercy guide us all,
For sunbeams and shadows strangely fall,
The riddle is hard to read.
From the darkness and the light,
Weave the black thread, weave the white.

THE PATIENCE OF THE POOR.

AYE, cherish them dearly, honour them well,
Our England's gallant sons,

Nursed 'mid the gleam of her bayonet points,
'Mid the roar of her thundering guns.
Honour them nobly, cherish them dear,
Write their names on the roll of glory,
Teach our children's eyes to flash and fill
O'er each high heroic story.
Honour their gay serenity,
Honour their stainless faith,
Their brave obedience to duty's code,
Frank life, and fearless death.
Give their day our eager homage,
Give their night our proud regret;
But there 's another noble host
Their land should scarce forget.

Oh, silent unrecorded lives,
In poverty stern and hard;
Oh, brave unfaltering struggle
For the workhouse' grim reward;
Oh, beautiful untutored faith
In love and help in heaven;
Oh, thankfulness for niggard boons,
Lightly or coldly given;
Oh, simple grand humility,
'Neath the ills as birth-right found;
Oh, charity that never fails,
To their fellows, suffering round;
Stedfast, and strong, and quiet,
To meet and to endure,
Sublime in its unconscious might,
The patience of the poor.

All cold unlovely strife for bread,
From the cradle to the grave,

No bright chivalric hope for fame,
No prizes for the brave.
Just labour, from the dreary morn,
Till the day drags past at length,
Then heavy slumber to renew
For endless tasks, the strength.
From month to month, from year to year,
Unceasing weary working,
For the failing hand, for the tired head,
Hunger or alms-life lurking.
All labour, labour,—fire and food,
And shelter to secure,
Borne in the calm God-given faith
And patience of the poor.

And we, we spare an idle hour,
A coin we do not need,
We pause, some lesson to enforce,
Some moral code to read.
We stoop from the rolling chariot,
To the pilgrim by the way,
To the wearied and the footsore,
Warning or rule to say.
Then talk of 'the base ingratitude,'
Of a rough or jarring word,
Of the lavish use of a careless gift,
Of a 'sullen' heart unstirred.
Ah, brothers, learn our gilded ills,
As calmly to endure,
Learn in our wrongs to emulate,
The patience of the poor.

SUN AND SHADOW.

Day's affluent glory on the glittering seas,
　　Day's fullest splendour in the beauteous skies.
Warm from the moorland blew the scented breeze,
　　The moorland glowing rich in purple dyes.
Light skiffs went darting o'er the dimpled waves,
　　The coble spread its broad brown wings for flight,
And gray and grand amid its grassy graves,
　　The noble abbey towered on the height.

Old men sate basking in an idlesse bland,
　　Gay girls and boys stood round in laughing groups,
Bright bairns built fragile castles on the sand,
　　Or watched the juggler toss his gilded hoops.
A sumptuous languor lapped earth, sea, and sky,
　　Won from the golden Autumn's brooding charm,
And through it all a man passed quietly,
　　Bearing an infant's coffin on his arm.

The heartless sunshine shone as frank and glad
　　On the poor velvet pile and silver nails,
As on the happy children brightly clad,
　　Or dancing sea, or flitting fairy sails;
Ah, did it penetrate the darkened house,
　　Where the pale mother, by her gathered flower,
Smoothed the soft curls, and kissed the waxen brows,
　　And sobbed her farewell through the anguished
　　　　hour?

Yet which of all who saw amid them pass
　　That symbol of the fleeting life we live,
Thought of the strange weird warning that it was?
　　Ah, time is all too brief such pause to give.

That narrow home waits for us all, to-day—
　To-morrow—or while years' long measure keep.
Seize then the sunny hour—yet turn to pray
　For those who in the heavy shadow weep.

THE SEVEN-NIGHTS' WATCH.

NORTH-COUNTRY SUPERSTITION.

Nay, don't turn the key, not yet, not yet, five nights
　　haven't past and gone
Since we laid the green sods straight and meet, to
　　wait for the cold gray stone;
See, his pipe still lies on the mantel where the old
　　arm-chair is set,
The knife is left in the half-carved stick—don't turn
　　the door-key yet!

How it rains! it must be dree an' all where the wet
　　wind sweeps the brow,
And it's dry and warm by the hearth-stone; don't
　　steek the lintel now!
Fling a fire-log on the ingle; he used to love the
　　light,
That shone 'haste thee' through the darkness, when
　　he was abroad at night.

Thieves? nay, they scarce come up our way, and
　　there's none so much to steal,
Just the bread-loaf in the cupboard, and the hank
　　on the spinning-wheel;
And I'd rather lose the all I have, aye, the burial-fee
　　on the shelf,
Than think of him barred out from home, out in the
　　cold by himself.

Whisht! was not yon a footstep in the path out
    there by the byre?
Whisht! I know how boards can creak. I say, pile
    sticks on the fire.
The wind sighs over the upland, just like a parting
    soul;
Get to bed with you all—I 'll stay, and keep my
    watch by the gathering coal.

For all he grew so wild and strange, my one son
    loved his mother.
Mayhap he 'd come to me when scarce he 'd show
    himself to another.
When the drink was out he was always kind, and
    e'en when he had a drop
He was mild to me. Don't turn the key! For
    seven nights here I stop.

I bore him, kept him, and loved him; whatever else
    might come,
He knew, while his mother held the door, was
    always his welcome home.
You may stare and laugh, an' it please you; but, oh,
    a glint of him
Were just a sparkle of heaven to the eyes that are
    waxing dim !

And I know, should he meet his father, up there in
    the rest and joy,
He'll say, ' A couple of nights are left, thou'st need
    to cheer her, my boy.'
So leave the key, and fetch the logs; till the
    mourner's week is done,
I tell thee I'll watch; lest I miss in sleep a last
    smile from my son.

THE HOUSEKEEPER'S STORY.

Aye, yon's Sir Guy: he fell at Bosworth fight,
All for the Boar of Gloucester and his crown:
Lord bless you, Sir! I know them all aright,
My good old master made me take them down;
'Young folk forget,' he said, 'and it were well,
Some voice of all his house had done should tell.'

She was a maid of honour to Queen Bess;
My fair young lady wears those very pearls.
Men vow that she outvies her ancestress,
When they are twined among her golden curls;
God keep her blue eyes bright! That widowed bride
Wept herself blind: her lord with Norfolk died.

Yon is Sir Bevis; he who kept the Pass
When bloodhound Cromwell dogged the Stuarts' way;
And there his son, well shown with dice and glass,
Who lost our lands, from Ure to Neville's Stray;
Sir Richard won them back—that dark-browed man,
Who fought with Marlboro' and who knelt to Anne.

Aye, there's a touch of kindred in them all,
Flashing from falcon glance and haughty lip;
In every portrait round our bannered hall
You catch the nature link of workmanship:
He has it least, my master wont to swear,
Lord James, with his cold sneer and sullen air.

No soldier he. He won his barony
By the keen bloodless weapons of the law,
And when his son, in youth's frank chivalry,
Dared to a lowly maiden's side to draw,
A pure sweet child, low born but true and good
(See, there she hangs, limned in her russet hood)

The Baron, on his deathbed, framed a will,
Barring both land and lordship from his boy,
So, knowing all, he chose to hold her still,
Who was his wife, who made his young heart's joy;
But if they'd part for ever, if she went,
Dropping his name, to life-long banishment,

Using some cunning quibble, such as yet
Parts right and law for women, to divide
The bond, the busy world would soon forget
The bond rash love for hasty minors tied,
Leaving him free to wed, as seemed his race,
Then all was his. Look at his fair weak face ;

Look at the quiet pride in her brown eyes,
And you will guess the rest. He let her go:
She withered soon beneath the stranger skies;
He, crushed and helpless, in remorseful woe
Died, with her ring clasped in his nerveless hand,
Whispering the name that Law and Gold had banned.

Yet my young lord, his grandson,—for he wed
A richly dowered dame, who bore a son
(See, there they hang; the diamonds on her head
The baby clutches, bold Sir Bevis won
At play with Villiers)—my young lord, I say,
Stands by his word, and knows, and takes his way.

That's the one blot our loyal line must own.
Our chaplain talks of faith, and wilful will.
I say 'twas too much learning, made the stone
Flung by the dead man's hand, so strong to kill.
Well, let it rest. This way, Sir, I have store
Of portraits yet in yon long corridor.

MEMORY.

Up on the headland gleamed the purple heather,
The breakers crashed, the white foam flew below,
The breezes swept from flowery vales, to blow
Where wave and tide rolled up the bay together,
Leaping and laughing in the golden weather ;
Great Nature, rousing in the genial glow,
Called, in the joyous voice her children know,
Wake ! life and I should love and hope for ever,
Forgetting care and cross and all things past,
While Earth will spread our bridal banquet thus,
And at our feet her lavish glories cast,
While her fair face unveils its charms for us.
One heard, and turning saw behind it all,
Grave Memory with sad eyes and funeral pall..

CHRISTMAS.

How shall we keep our Christmas, you and I?
'Tis many a Yule-tide since we two together
Heard childish laughters blending merrily,
When the chill sunlight gleamed through wintry
        weather,
When drifts lay deep around the old red house,
And arch and roof were gay with holly boughs.

And many a Yule since (dear, do you forget?)
You chose a spray all brightly berried over,
And as its leaves amid my curls you set,
Spoke in the first soft whisper of the lover,
And as the haze from girlish fondness swept,
 The woman's heart from trance unconscious leapt.

Then just another Christmas, hand in hand,
Troth-plighted, we two heard the midnight chime,
And knew your path lay in a far-off land,
And smiled, in youth's gay fearlessness, at time;
Easy to wait, with love and life so strong.
Easy to wait! but oh, the years are long!

How shall I keep my Christmas? here at home
I smooth my braids—there's gray amid the gold—
I wear no holly now. The children come
And clamour for the merry sports of old;
I join the dancers, lead the carol strains:
They scarce can echo in Australian plains.

How do you keep your Christmas? Strange suns shine,
    shine,
Strange flowers blossom, brighter than our hollies;
Perhaps you bend to rosier lips than mine,
And make them smile at antique English follies!
Letters come rarer, words grow cold and few;
Broad leagues of sea and land 'twixt me and you.

Dear, do I wrong you? Life is hard and short,
Fortune is coy and chill, time flies so fast;
Wiser, perhaps, the passing rays to court,
Nor hoard our all of sunshine in the past;
Women will cling to dying dreams, you see,
And memory keeps my Christmas-day with me.

· HOPE.

    The plant's first shoot was fresh and fair,
    We tended it with loving care,
    But keen the breath of April air,
    It chilled the frail new comer.

We said, 'The days roll onward fast,
The east wind's reign will soon be past,
We'll fence it from the bitter blast,
Our bud will blow in summer.'

But June had half her smile forgot,
And August suns blazed fierce and hot,
And tired of their earthly lot,
The soft leaves drooped and faded.
We said, 'When heat and glare pass by,
Beneath October's tranquil sky,
The bloom will blossom quietly,
By Autumn's calm wings shaded.'

But ah! the dead leaves heaped the plain,
And rotted 'neath the ceaseless rain,
With, like a weary soul in pain,
The winds amid it sighing.
We heard the Winter's coming tread,
The low skies darkened overhead,
'Love, Faith, and Truth are vain,' we said,
'Our treasure lies a-dying.'

And slowly with reluctant feet,
We left the snowdrift's winding-sheet,
Where lay the promise, pure and sweet,
To youth's gay morning given.
Then, angel-like, Hope whispered low,
'Life lingers 'neath yon saving snow,
On through the seasons patient go,
God keeps your flower in Heaven.'

APRIL 16th, 1746.

In the gleamy northern gloaming of that fatal April
day,
Heaped with dead, and soaked in carnage, sad and
still Culloden lay;
Far away the rosy sunset saw the Firth's broad
waters toss,
And lightly tinged the dark blue glory of the noble
hills of Ross;
On the moorland of Drumrossie, tumbled in the
budding heather,
Scotland's best and bravest hearted lay in gory rest
together,
For vainly courage and devotion in unequal strife
had stood,
And the royal Rose of Scotland drooped her snowy
leaves in blood.

Still amid the purple heather, many a long up-
swelling cairn
Marks the graves of Highland heroes in the shadow
of Strathnairn;
Still in many a ferny hollow, still in many a wood-
land nook,
Linger dark and dreadful legends, telling of the
Butcher Duke.
And the wayfarer benighted sudden hears the
muskets rattle,
Hears the clash and hurlyburly, charge and rally
of the battle,
While the pibroch wildly wailing tells how all was
lost and won
When upon that April evening slow and sadly sank
the sun.

In the gleamy April evening for a hundred weary
years,
On the day that loyal Scotland sacred holds for
prayers and tears,
Still, men say, a ghostly army flits across the
moorland wide,
Cumberland, and traitor Campbell, cruel Hawley at
their side,
English, Lowlanders, and Hessians, all who did
their bloody work,
Gliding grisly o'er Culloden, till at stroke of midnight mirk,
When with shrill remorseful wailing, the pale ranks
in gloom are lost:
Now God save the wanderer meeting, at such scene
so grim a host.

'LES GANTS GLACÉS.'

(AN ANECDOTE OF THE FRONDE, 1650.)

WRAPPED in smoke stood the towers of Rethel,
The battle surged fierce by the town,
On terror, and struggle, and turmoil,
The sweet skies of Champagne looked down.
Far away smiled the beautiful uplands,
The blue Vosges lay solemn beyond ;
Well France knew such discord of colour
In the terrible days of the Fronde.

At the breach in the ramparts of Rethel
Each stone was bought dearly by blood,
For Du Praslin was leading the stormers,
And Turenne on the battlements stood.

Again and again closed the conflict,
The madness of strife upon all,
Right well fought the ranks of the marshal,
Yet twice they fell back from the wall.

Twice, thrice, repulsed, baffled, and beaten,
They glared, where in gallant array,
Brave in gilding, and 'broidery, and feather,
The Guards, in reserve, watched the fray.
'En avant les gants glacés !' they shouted,
As sullenly rearward they bore,
The gaps deep and wide in their columns,
The lilies all dripping in gore.

' En avant les gants glacés !' and laughing
At the challenge, the Household Brigade
Dressed ranks, floated standards, blew trumpets,
And flashed out each glittering blade ;
And carelessly, as to a banquet,
And joyously, as to a dance,
Where the Frondeurs in triumph were gathered,
Went the best blood of Scotland and France.

The gay plumes were shorn as in tempest,
The gay scarves stained crimson and black,
Storm of bullet and broadsword closed o'er them,
Yet never one proud foot turned back.
Though half of their number lay silent,
On the breach their last effort had won,
King Louis was master of Rethel
Ere the day and its story was done.

And the fierce taunting cry grew a proverb,
Ere revolt and its horrors were past;
For men knew, ere o'er France's fair valleys
Peace waved her white banner at last,

That the softest of tones in the boudoir,
The lightest of steps in the 'ronde,'
Was theirs, whose keen swords bit the deepest
In the terrible days of the Fronde.

GOING SOFTLY.

She makes no moan above her faded flowers,
  She will not vainly strive against her lot,
Patient she wears away the slow, sad hours,
  As if the ray they had were quite forgot;
While stronger fingers snatch away the sword,
  And lighter footsteps pass her on the ways,
Yielding submissive to the stern award
  That said, she must go softly all her days.

She knows the pulse is beating quickly yet,
  She knows the dream is sweet and subtle still,
That struggling from the cloud of past regret,
  Ready for conflict live Hope, Joy, and Will;
So soon, so soon to veil the eager eyes,
  To dull the throbbing ear to blame or praise,
So soon to crush rewakening sympathies,
  And teach them she goes softly all her days.

She will not speak or move beneath the doom,
  She knows she had her day, and flung her cast,
The loser scarce the laurel may assume,
  Nor evening think the noonday glow can last.
Only, oh youth and love, as in your pride
  Of joyous triumph your gay notes you raise,
Throw one kind glance and word where, at your
      side,
  She creeps, who must go softly all her days.

THE UNKNOWN SEAS.

WHAT do they bring to us, through time and tide,
The ships still sailing on the unknown seas;
Whose oars by mighty viewless hands are plied,
Whose sails are filling by no earthly breeze;
What do they bring to us? who, all unknowing,
Sport by the verge and gather rosy shells,
And watch the great waves in their ebb and flowing,
Uncaring what their solemn music tells.

What do they bring to us? Our dreams we dream,
Our castles do we build and deck them fair,
We shed around our hopes a rosy gleam,
We light the onward path with all things rare;
We talk of love enduring, joys attained,
We rest in fearless faith, in careless ease;
And all the while another league is gained
By the barks nearing us o'er unknown seas.

There may be sorrow in the coming ships,
There may be gain unthought of, conquest great,
There may be cups of bliss for longing lips,
Or strange unlooked-for blow from lurking fate;
There may be shame or glory, life or death,
There may be some wild tale of sin or madness,
There may be slander's subtle Upas breath
To quench the tender rays of household gladness.

Who knows? who knows? We linger on the shore,
We hear the long waves in the distance breaking;
We pluck the rose, and sigh that June is o'er,
We sleep sweet sleeps, and dread the certain waking.
Only one thing is real; to clasp, to hold,
To make our shield in whirling thoughts like these,

This one great Truth is true to mortals told,
There is a Pilot on the unknown seas.

SAFE.

Safe? the battle-field of life
· Seldom knows a pause in strife.
Every path is set with snares,
Every joy is crossed by cares.
Brightest morn has darkest night,
Fairest bloom has quickest blight.
Hope has but a transient gleam,
Love is but a passing dream,
Trust is Folly's helpless waif;
Who dare call their dearest safe?

But thou, though peril loom afar,
What hast thou to do with war?
Let the wild stream flood its brink,
There's no bark of thine to sink.
Let Falsehood weave its subtle net,
Thou art done with vain regret.
Let fortune frown, and friends grow strange,
Thou hast passed the doom of change.
We plan and struggle, mourn and chafe—
Safe, my Darling, dead, and safe!

IN THE GERM.

What do they dream of, hidden away, where the
    snow piles soft and deep,
The roots that lie in the rich dark mould, lapped in
    their winter sleep?

Do they feel the pulse's beating?   Do they think
the hours are long,
The primrose fair, the violet sweet, the crocus gallant and strong?
Would the snowdrop fain ring her tiny bell to bid
the flowers awake?
Does the hyacinth long to the wooing air her luscious
scent to shake?

Have they visions of lush green grasses, or birds
upon darting wings,
And sunny showers to bead their leaves, till they
glitter like diamond strings?
Do they yearn to star the copses, and jewel the
sheltered lanes,
Or fling their glories free and far, over sweeping
upland plains?
Do they fancy gay voices to hail them, and white
fingers to caress,
When they and April arouse to deck the earth in
their loveliness?

Or do they nestle dreamlessly, as maiden fancies
may,
In the heart of a sleeping infant, or in childhood's
bosom gay,
Lying with all their passionate powers, for love,
hope, wrath, or wrong,
To dye the cheek and tone the lip, and sway the
life ere long!
Well innocent is the baby mirth, and smooth lie the
virgin snows,
But love and sorrow are near akin—by the hemlock
springs the rose.

IN THE SPRING.

I⊤ is spring, laughs the blue hepatica, as it gems
　　the garden bed;
It is spring, breathes the modest primrose, as it
　　rears its virgin head;
It is spring, says the pure anemone, amid the vivid
　　grass,
That waves beneath the merry winds, and glitters as
　　we pass.

The wild birds hail the spring-time, as they mate,
　　and sing and build,
The whole great sweep of earth and sky with
　　spring's gay smile is thrilled,
Young lambs in sunlit pastures, young chickens in
　　the croft,
Renew the lovely miracle that Nature sees so oft.

And something in my heart revives, that silent, sad,
　　and strong,
Fades all the early blooms for me, and jars the
　　thrushes' song,
The life that throbs in April's heart wakes every
　　mortal thing,
And grief, with birds, and buds, and flowers, stirs
　　freshly in the spring.

THE CHRISTENING OF THE FLOWERS.

W⊦o christened the flowers? the darlings of hearth,
　　and home, and song.
·Who made them the glory of lay and story? who
　　gave them for ages long

The names that make them human, in their touching
  of joy or grief,
That blend troth and plight, with the petals bright,
  and hope with the tender leaf?

We take from the hand of the gracious God, the
  best gift man can receive,
And our star of morn, pledge of love new born, we
  kiss, and greet her, Eve ;
We hail the 'man child' from the Lord, and as our
  fancies soar
To victories won, and high deeds done, we name
  him, Theodore.

We bless our pretty Maries, as we wish them the
  Virgin's grace,
Violet, and May, and Rose, we say, have types in
  each budding face ;
For George, we claim frank Saxon truth, for John,
  loyal stainless faith,
Keep Guy and Clare for the brave young heir, vow
  Alban to calm till death.

But with never allusion or culture, the field-flowers'
  names were won,
By river ledges, and clustering hedges, and hill-tops
  gilt by the sun,
Where 'speed-well' shimmers, and 'traveller's joy'
  spreads hoary o'er 'love lies bleeding';
Where 'forget-me-not' lights the fern-draped grot,
  and the 'blue-bell' rings unheeding.

Angel, or Fairy, or Dryad, something pitiful of us
  here,
We mortals who strive, toil, dream and live, each
  through the allotted sphere ;

Remembering how about our paths the season's
    jewels were strown,
Read the 'shepherd's clock,' saw the 'man's faith'
    mock, and made them all our own.

Baptized for us 'primrose' and 'immortelle,' and bade
    us trust the spell,
And people valley and meadow, with the lore we
    love so well;
And pluck the 'myrtle' for our brides, the 'cowslip'
    for babes to tread,
Crown our victors with 'laurel' and 'bay,' wreathe
    'ivy' for our dead.

And so make Nature chime to us, in our pæans of
    hope and joy,
And in flower and leaf, for fear or grief, find some-
    what of alloy;
For the blossoms never fail us, the snowdrop lives in
    the snow,
And April gleams and August beams make lilies
    and roses blow.

THE HARBINGERS.

DEEP in the sunny copses, thick in the sheltered
    lanes,
Gallantly decking the wind-swept turf out on the
    breezy plains,
Gemming the quiet hedge-rows, clustering by the
    stream,
Blossoming on the great hill-sides where the golden
    gorses gleam;

Blue and rosy, purple and white, 'mid the grasses
glistening,
They show, 'neath April shadow and shine, the harbingers of Spring.

Stern the Winter's sway has been, bitter and fierce
and long,
And still o'er the sea the black east wind is singing
his dying song;
But primrose, snowdrop, and violet join in the old
sweet strain,
' The frost is over, the snow is gone, we are coming
again, again;'
And from mating bird, and budding bough, and
wakening nature swelling,
Comes the echo of the joyous news the harbingers
are telling.

And youth springs out to hail them on happy kindred feet,
And sobered life and tranquil age give welcome grave
and sweet;
Only sorrow raising heavy eyes beside the cold
white cross,
Says, ' Here is what returns no more, no spring-tide
for my loss.'
Yet by that Cross the God of Love the sign to Faith
has given,
Of Him who came the harbinger of deathless joys
in Heaven.

IN JUNE.

THE elm and the oak full-foliaged swung about the
old grey house,
The thrushes' song rang all day long deep in the
world of boughs,

The roses flushed the lattices, the honeysuckle flung
Her perfume rare on the wooing air that round her
    played and clung,
As I listened the low sweet whisper that blent
    with the wild birds' tune,
In the days when all of life was love, and all of
    earth was June.

The lime could scarce support his blooms, though
    the woodbine climbed to help ;
The buttercups' glow lit the meadows below, 'mid
    the feathery spray of the kelp ;
The noonday's golden glory changed to the evening's
    flush,
The voice of the river, for ever and ever, thrilled
    through the living hush ;
And slowly over the dreaming Two closed the
    witchery of the moon,
In the days when all of life was love, and all of
    earth was June.

Ah, the trees renew their loveliness, the summer's
    flashing smile
Lights meads and flowers, and birds and bowers,
    bright as it did erewhile ;
But the silence of one voice for me, jars the music
    of the stream,
For his eyes' lost light, hot, fierce, and bright, must
    the mocking sun-rays seem.
O prize the cloudless days, young hearts ; too soon,
    alas, too soon,
Will you learn how loss replaces love, and memory
    darkens June.

AUTUMN HEDGES.

SEE the purple vetches climb
  Through the lush green grasses;
Hear the bluebell's fairy chime
  As the light wind passes;
The poppy, like a scarlet flame,
  By snowy starwort blazes;
The buttercup its golden head
  By rosy campion raises;
The bramble in its lavish bloom
  A fruitful future pledges;
The elder's glossy berries droop
  O'er the autumn hedges.

The bindweed flings her graceful wreath
  Where soft green nuts are darkening;
The fern leaves bow their lovely fronds,
  The thrushes' gurgle hearkening;
There the tall campanula
  Its lilac bloom is showing;
Subtle fragrance tells us where
  The purple clover's blowing;
Soft and hoar, the briony
  Hangs from rocky ledges,
Where tansy's rugged royalty
  Rules the autumn hedges.

The lordly foxgloves, side by side,
  Guard the creeping mosses;
The thistle to the wooing air
  Its thorny circlets tosses;
The crowsfoot glitters like a gem
  Where golden-rod waves thickest,

Where the orchis studs the green,
  Where money-wort runs quickest;
The rush-flower and the yellow flag
  Bloom amid the sedges,
Where the bonny becks dance down
  By the autumn hedges.

With a beauty all his own
  Reigns Winter, keen and hoary;
Sweet the Springtide's vivid smile,
  Sweet the Summer's glory;
But the Autumn's bounteous hand,
  In the cloudless weather,
Brings flower, fruit, and harvest-home
  To the world together.
So lovely dreams, bard-born in May,
  A brooding fancy fledges
To life as lavish, rich, and bright
  As glows in autumn hedges.

THE HOLLY.

The holly brightens every hedgerow brown,
  The scarlet berries light the drifted snow;
Amid the gaunt old oak-tree's withered crown
  Gleams the pale emerald of the mistletoe.
The fierce north-easter takes a joyous tone,
  As, sweeping landward from the northern main,
It hears on purple moor and valley lone
  The holly call, ' 'Tis Christmas come again!'

We twine the holly for the hearth and home,
  We twine the holly for the cherished grave;
For love and memory, joy and sorrow, come,
  To blend in Him, born once to die and save.

Alike on golden braid and marble cross,
  Alike where youth may smile or age may sigh,
Alike in yearning, hoping, gain or loss,
  The holly glistens 'neath the Christmas sky.

Fling down the yule log on the ruddy blaze,
  Spice furmety and fill the goblet up,
Summon the gladness of the bygone days,
  Drain to the memory of dear friends the cup;
Put cold estrangement and neglect aside,
  And while the morris-dancers claim the floor,
Let frank hands clasp, forgetting wrath or pride,
  And 'neath the holly join old ties once more.

Hark how the waits sing through the frosty air,
  'Good tidings of great joy to all mankind!'
Through smiling tears we see the vacant chair,
  And think his voice is with our songs combined;
For O, though wistful yearning tones our mirth,
  The Christmas holly this sweet thought has given,
While love and charity bring peace on earth,
  He, with the angels, keeps our feast in heaven.

ME AND MY MATE.

A WHITBY STORY.

Mates? ay, we've been mates together
  These threescore years and more:
Lord, how we used to lake and cuff
  In t' caves down there on t' shore!

Will, he were as bad as orphaned,
  His father were drowned at sea,
And his mother, poor fond dateless soul.
  Could do nought with such as he.

So my father, as were a kindly man,
  Though slow in his speech and stern,
Sent us both off to the whalery,
  Our bit and sup to earn.

And we were mates in the cold and the toil,
  And mates o'er a cheery glass,
Till we parted, as better men have done,
  For we'd words about a lass.

Poor Nance!—her red lips and bright blue eyes,
  And her smiles for one and another,
I wot those pretty ways of hers,
  Came betwixt us, friend and brother.

And she wouldn't have neither him nor me,
  But took up with an inland chap
As daren't step in a boat nor haul a rope;
  But he'd brass—we hadn't a rap.

Still, for all we heard her wedding bells,
  Changed blows are bitter coin :
We're hard to part, we Yorkshire folk,
  But we're harder yet to join.

Well, it were dree work to meet on t' pier,
  Nor once 'Well, mate' to say;
And one to start with the lifeboat crew,
  And the other to turn away.

To go alone for the Sunday walk,
  To smoke one's pipe alone;
For while we shunned each other like,
  We'd go with never a one.

Only when the herring got agate,
  And the lobster-pots were set,

We were partners in the *Nance*, you see,
  So we went together yet.

Together, but never a word we spoke
  Out on the dancing waves,
Under sunlight, or moonlight, or great white stars,
  As silent as men in their graves.

I tell you, we've sate as sullen as aught,
  One at t' sheet and one at t' helm,
Till the very ripples seemed to call,
  'Shame! shame!' in the sound of them.

Silent we pulled the fish aboard;
  Silent we turned her head,
And steered her home, and leaped ashore,
  And never a word we said.

The very bairns stood back afeard
  As we came glooming in,
And ever and aye I knew my heart
  Grew heavier in its sin.

One day the sky showed coarse and wild,
  And the wind kept shifting like,
As a man that has planned a murder,
  And doesn't know where to strike.

'Best stay ashore, and leave the pots;
  There's mischief brewing there;'
So spoke old Sam as could read the clouds;
  But I had an oath to swear,

And I muttered, 'Cowards might bide at home,
  As I glanced at Will the while;
And he swung himself aboard the *Nance*,
  With one queer quiet smile.

Out ran the rope, up went the sail,
  She shot across the bar,
And flew like a bird right through the surf
  As was whitening all the Scar.

We reached the pots, and Will stretched out
  To draw the bladder near;
I looked astern, and there wellnigh broke
  From my lips a cry of fear.

For, flying over the crested waves,
  Terrible, swift, and black,
I saw the squall come sweeping on;
  All round us closed the wrack.

The boat heeled over to the blast,
  The thunder filled the air,
Great seas came crashing over us,
  Scarce time to think a prayer.

But 'mid the foam that blinded us,
  And the turmoil of the sea,
I saw Will seize the bladder up
  And heave it right to me.

Can you understand, you landsmen?
  It was all the chance he had;
Ay, thou mayst growl thy fill out there,
  But I 'll tell the truth, old lad!

It was all the chance he 'd got, I say,
  And he gave it to his mate;
I 'd one hand on it, and one in his hair,
  When they found us, nigh too late.

For Sam had sent the lifeboat out,
  And they pulled us both aboard;

There was not a plank of the *Nance* afloat;
  But I 've got the bladder stored.

And whenever I 'm vext, or things go wrong,
  If Will should not be nigh,
I light my pipe, and sit nigh hand
  Where it hangs there safe and dry.

And I know through good and evil
  We are mates on to the end,
For the Book says, there is no greater love
  Than to give one's life for one's friend.

OUT ON THE SCAR.

Gold flashes back to the glowing west
From the headland crowned with gorses,
Silver gleams out from the sea's broad breast
In the manes of the wild 'white horses.'
Like sapphire shines each clear rock pool,
Where brown, and crimson, and rose,
The sea-flowers, shy, and scentless, and cool,
Are wooed by the winds to unclose;
And the billows, like warriors ranking for war,
Steady and regular, sweep-to the Scar.

Gray and jagged and cruel and strong
The rocks lie under the head,
While the breakers sing their mighty song,
The dirge for the mariners dead;
For thick I ween do the sailors lie
Down in the ocean deep,
With the wind's low sob, and the seamew's cry,
For lullaby o'er their sleep;
Little they reck of the moan at the bar,
Or the fierce surf ' calling ' out on the Scar.

Many a token of storm and of death
Must lurk in those rocky caves,
Left, when the foam hides all beneath,
And tossed by the furious waves,
The gallant ship strikes hard and fast,
And the blue lights burn in vain,
And the rocket hisses athwart the blast,
And the fearless fishermen strain
To force the life-boat, where crash and jar
Tell how timbers are parting out on the Scar.

But calm to-night as a babe's repose
Do the tides and their whispers come,
Murmuring aye through the ebbs and flows
With their lips of creamy foam,
Murmuring on 'neath the rose-flushed sky,
Through the lovely gloaming of May;
Till the happy smile creeps to heart and eye,
Sunning all cares away;
And fret and turmoil fade faint and far,
From the heart of the dreamer out on the Scar.

SONG.

Let the grasses grow
  Where the sweet dreams sleep,
Let the violets blow
  And the mosses creep;
Let the wild birds sing
  Where the willows wave,
And the bluebells ring
  Requiems o'er the grave.

Seek not to reanimate
  What is gone for ever;

By the tomb stand Time and Fate,
  Murmuring their 'Never.'
All you could awaken,
  But a pallid ghost,
From all purpose shaken,
  To all beauty lost.

Feign no idle sorrow,
  Speak no useless words,
Do not seek to borrow
  From the shattered chords
Music, such as filled you
  With a vague delight
When its presence thrilled you,
  Clouding sense and sight.

Life is full and eager,
  With work for head and hand;
Pale and cold and meagre
  Would youth's fair fancies stand,
If, starting from their slumber,
  Where the quivering aspens bend,
They came to haunt and cumber
  Our pathway to the end.

Yet because the glory
  Of their brief bright reign,
Wrote on our hearts a story
  We shall not read again,
Let no step intruding
  Break in upon their rest,
Where Memory's dove sits brooding
  Upon her lonely nest.

Pass, with step revering,
  Pass, with bended head;

Hush both sight and hearing
From all things but the dead.
Then back where full and flowing,
Life rushes to the deep,
And leave the violets blowing
Where the sweet dreams sleep.

IN THE EVENING.

ALL day the wind had howled along the leas,
All day the wind had swept across the plain,
All day on rustling grass, and waving trees,
Had fallen 'the useful trouble of the rain,'
All day beneath the low-hung dreary sky
The dripping earth had cowered sullenly.

At last the wind had sobbed itself to rest,
At last to weary calmness sank the storm,
A crimson line gleamed sudden in the west,
Where golden flecks rose wavering into form:
A hushed revival heralded the night,
And with the evening time awoke the light.

The rosy colour flushed the long gray waves;
The rosy colour tinged the mountains' brown;
And where the old church watched the village graves.
Wooed to a passing blush the yew-tree's frown:
Bird, beast, and flower relenting nature knew,
And one pale star rose shimmering in the blue.

So, to a life long crushed in heavy grief,
So, to a path long darkened by despair,
The slow sad hours bring touches of relief,
Whispers of hope, and strength of trustful prayer.
'Tarry His leisure,' God of love and might,
And with the evening time there will be light !

URE.

Glinting in her sunny shallows,
Rolling through the long green fallows,
Glittering under old gray bridges,
Fretting 'neath her willowed ridges;
Whispering to the mosses keeping
Vigil o'er the violets sleeping;
Flashing, laughing, dancing, gleaming,
With the sunshine o'er her streaming;
Rippling to the moonlight shining,
The spirit of her rays divining;
Giving back the glories given,
By rose dawn and golden even;
As age serene, as girlhood pure,
Softly seaward murmurs Ure.

From the moorland, fierce and strong,
Bearing whirling logs along,
Foam-flecks thick upon her breast,
Rousing sleepers from their rest;
Swol'n and brown with autumn showers,
Roaring past the old gray towers,
Rushing under great oak shadows,
Swirling over flooded meadows,
Tossing in her tiger play
The harvest's garnered gain away:
Calling through the woodlands sere
How she must 'have her life' each year;
Making her dread tribute sure,
Angry seaward thunders Ure.

We, who by our river dwell,
Know her changeful beauty well;

Love her, with a love allied
Half to fear and half to pride.
If Yorkshire lips triumphant claim
Storied honours for her name,
Many a saddened homestead knows
The years her stream in 'freshet' rose;
When strength and courage helpless stood.
To watch the work of Ure in flood.
So, glory of our northern dales,
So, terror of our northern tales,
Through rocky dell and purple moor,
Fierce, bright, and lovely, flashes Ure.

MY GHOSTS.

They never float along the corridors,
  Nor rustle 'neath the tapestry on the wall.
Nor drag old fetters clanking on the floors,
  Nor from the donjon tower cry and call;
My ghosts keep no traditions, own no rules,
Break every law of superstition's schools.

Where careless chatterers circle round the hearth.
  Or dancing feet fly round the lighted room,
Where merry sunlight floods the morning mirth,
  Or happy whisperers seek the twilight gloom,
Silent and sad, unseen by all but me,
My ghosts glide through the household revelry.

They lurk among the flowers the children bring,
  Up from the poet's golden page they start,
They echo back the sweetest songs you sing,
  They throw their shadow o'er the painter's art;
With fear, and hope, and dream, and joy they blend,
Haunt kindred greeting, mix as friend with friend.

O'er Dreamland undisputed sway they seize,
   Last thought ere sleeping, first in waking theirs,
If follies vex, and petty troubles tease,
   They hold their own amid the earthliest cares;
Their low reminder how One helped such pain,
Making it sting with fourfold pangs again.

Come round me, then, dearer than things I know,
   Come, make my sense, and heart, and thought
      your own;
Come, in the guise I loved so long ago,
   Come, in the glamour time has round you thrown;
Ghosts, born of love and memory, reared by Faith.
Come, mould the life, and tone the call of death.

THE POWER OF SONG.

THROUGH the long aisles her clear voice rose and rang,
   Thrilling above us to the vaulted roof,
   Dying in fretted niches far aloof;
Borne on its wings our fancies heavenward sprang.

The loiterer on the sunny morning leas
   Starts as a bird springs sudden at his feet;
   Hears the fresh air awake to music sweet,
And turning dazzled eyes above him, sees

The brown wings flutter, hears the rippling notes.
   Till bird and strain both vanish in the blue;
   Then, from the fair world, bathed in light and dew.
His silent praise up with the cadence floats.

And through the day's full hours, hot, hard, and long.
   The magic of sweet sounds lulls brain and heart,
   Haunting the court, the camp, the street, the mart,
With rare faint echoes of remembered song.

AFTER THE BATTLE.

JULY THE 3RD, 1644.

THE poor old banner! give it here, I say;
Though king and church are toppling to their fall,
I saved it from the Roundheads any way,
When black Long Marston made an end of all.
Why could not Rupert keep his squadrons back?
Unbreathed, they might have broken Cromwell's line,
But scattered far on flying Leslie's track!
Ah, stanch and true it stood, that troop of mine!

What boots it now, when every oak is down,
And even the great seal ring my father gave
Melted with all the rest to help the Crown;
The old man willed it, speaking from his grave.
Thank God, that I have neither wife nor son
To perish in the ruin we have wrought.
Poor Katie! waiting till the game is won!
Well, here's her flag, from its last battle brought.

Her deft hands broidered it, blood-stained and rent
It hangs about the staff. Why, who could guess
How gallantly to the gay breeze it bent
All gold and glitter, when, amid the press
Of shouting Cavaliers, I flung it forth,
And Katie clapped her little hands to see
How bravely the battalions of the North
Around her banner marched to victory.

To victory! the Ouse runs swol'n and red,
Sullenly sweeping to the angry main,
With the best blood of bonnie Yorkshire fed,
For on her banks knights fell like Autumn grain.

Well, life will scarce be long, or axe and block,
Or starving 'mid the Frenchmen, which were best?
Oh comrades, slain in fiery battle shock,
I would my time were come to join your rest.

So, to the vaults. I 'll leave my flag in trust,
To all our long line, wrapt in dreamless sleep.
I shall not lie amid ancestral dust,
Nor kin nor vassal live my rites to keep,
And better so. I 'll place my treasure close
Beneath my sire's blazoned coffin-lid,
And when, anon, the rebels sack our house,
They 'll miss, perchance, a prize so grimly hid.

There 's just one diamond left that claspt my plume;
Take it to my bright lady's feet, and tell,
I leave her banner in my father's tomb,
I leave my heart to her, and so, farewell.
Whether to die 'mid clashing bow and bill,
Or rot in prison, like some noisome thing;
Or make my last short shrift on Tower Hill:
Who knows, who cares. Not I. God save the king!

THE RETURN FROM COURT.

A.D. 1660.

The times are changed, girl; take away my sword:
  Hang it up yonder by the old torn flag:
One useless as the other nowadays,
  The battered, blunted steel, and blood-stained rag.
Up at Whitehall they stared and jeered to see
  The fashion of this trusty blade of mine,
My grandsire's gift; it served me well enow,
  When down from Naseby heights we charged in
      line.

The King, the King?—women are gossips all !
　I 've naught to tell thee of the sights at Court.
'Spin and be virtuous,' girl; thou scarce shalt hear
　Of Portsmouth's flashing eyes, or Sedley's sport.
Wouldst see a king? look at the Martyr there,
　Whose sad proud smile great Vandyke limned for
　　　　me ;
And for whose noble sake his son shall have
　All that his cause has left me—sword and knee.

O ay, he called me by my name; he spoke
　With his rare courtly grace of bygone days:
Spoke of my boy, who saved him at Dunbar;
　Spoke of Black Don, the horse he used to praise.
He puzzled somewhat—Rupert set him right—
　Of Charlie's death, the night of Worcester field;
Some quip of Rochester's was said too near,
　Or Castlemaine's low laugh too lightly pealed.

No more of Courts for me.　I 'll to the fields ;
　I 've none too many acres left to plough.
There 's richer dowry for a pedlar's wench
　Than I can give my line's last rosebud now.
Thou 'rt like thy mother too; just so she looked
　The day we gathered in Northampton town,
The day she bade us never heed the bode,
　When the wild wind had blown the standard down.

'Live for the King; die for the King!' she said.
　I 'll do her bidding duly, first and last.
I am but peevish, girl; old men forget
　The glorious summer of their prime is past.
And he was gracious, but he needs, you see,
　A readier tongue than mine—a quicker wit.
I 'll bide at home, and take the spade, and try
　To weight thy pretty hand with gold by it.

Broad lands and lordships!—never droop for them;
  We gave them frankly; we'll not grudge them, lass.
I would he'd not forgotten Charlie's end;
  But he is kind at heart—there, let it pass.
My brave boy laughed, and bade God bless the King,
  Just as the Roundhead gave the firing word.
I'd do it all again—pshaw, girl, no tears;
  The times are changed, I say; hang up the sword!

WITHIN AND WITHOUT.

THE Christmas-bells were ringing from the church
  upon the hill,
Where the gravestones in the twilight were gleaming
  white and chill;
The trees stood gaunt and leafless beneath the steely
  sky,
And clashed their bare arms drearily as the wind
  went moaning by.

Below, amid the stately oaks and uplands of the
  park,
The great ancestral towers of the hall lay grim and
  dark!
But the long range of windows with light were all
  aglow,
And all the while the church-bells were ringing o'er
  the snow.

Within, two sate together, in the warm luxurious
  room,
The ruddy firelight flashing far amid the pleasant
  gloom;
With the thrill of girlish laughter, and whispers low
  and soft,
Telling the sweet old story we never hear too oft.

Without, upon the terrace, outside the joyous flood
Of the light that filled the oriel, where the clustered
    flowers stood,
A woman crouched with wild blue eyes, and lips set
    stern and white;
And all the while the church-bells were ringing
    through the night.

Ah! hard to see that merry blaze, yet lie there in the
    cold,
And hard to hear that light laugh ring and guess the
    joy it told;
But harder far to see the head that she had loved
    too well,
Bent fondly o'er another of his fresh false vows to
    tell.

'Did a shadow cross the window?' 'Nay, darling,
    it was naught,
Just a light cloud swept across the stars, or a breeze
    the ivy caught.'
And from the rosy parted lips the passing fear he
    kissed:
And all the while the church-bells were ringing
    through the mist.

And when the glittering morning o'er the old gray
    towers broke,
From sunny dreams of plighted love the happy girl
    awoke;
And not one pang of late remorse had troubled his
    repose,
Who hastened in his triumph hour to greet his
    Christmas rose.

But on the sullen river, the ice was struck apart,
And ere it closed again above a broken human heart,
From its black depths a corpse they drew, whose
dreary race was run;
And all the while the Christmas-bells were ringing
'neath the sun.

MOTHER.

As the bonnie beck goes singing
Through the leafy land in June;
As the waves beneath the headland
Murmur aye their joyous tune;
As the wild birds' ceaseless chirping
Calls the woodland to rejoice,
The perpetual 'Mother, Mother'
Babbles from the baby voice.

Thrilling through the happy homestead,
As to some sweet recurrent strain
After every measured cadence
Singers sound a loved refrain,
Soothing every passing turmoil,
Shaming every passing strife,
The incessant 'Mother, Mother'
Keeps the sunshine of the life.

Mother, Mother! baby gladness
Needs must have her share his bliss;
Mother, Mother! baby trouble
Wants the curing of her kiss;
Merry waking, rosy sleeping,
Restless task and eager play,
Still the note of 'Mother, Mother'
Rounds the guarded infant day.

Surely some especial blessing
Son and Mother love may claim,
The only earthly bond our Saviour
Gave the glory of His name.
Oh, when life and work is over,
May we, by the Great White Throne,
In the call of Mother, Mother,
Hear our boys take back their own.

FIRST LOVE IN THE NURSERY.

ALREADY, already, oh bright brown eyes,
Heavy with hot love tears!
  Oh rose-red dewy lips I kiss,
  Too young to quiver with grief like this,
Let it come with the coming years.

I knew what fate had in store for me,
When my boy's romance begun:
  That I, whose part in the drama was o'er,
  Would sigh and tremble and thrill once more,
With the heart of my first-born son.

I thought of it oft with a rueful smile;
For never a mortal yet
  But, in passionate sorrow or passionate gladness,
  The fret and the fever of love's brief madness,
Has paid the human debt.

But I dreamt the 'bairn-time' was all my own,
My calm sweet pasture-land;
  With baby troubles that I could cure,
  And baby pleasures that, fresh and pure,
All flowed from the mother's hand.

Yet my face is wet with my boy's quick tears,
As he sobbed in my arms to say
  How his little Love with her rosy cheeks,
  And dimples that deepen whenever she speaks.
Refused ' to be married to-day '!

    Ah, well, with the drops all kissed away,
He shouts in his sport again.
  With wee warm eager fingers tight
  Round crimson flowers and bonbons bright,
What recks he of parted pain ?

    Alas and alas, my bonnie boy,
That ever the day should come,
  When the tears that start for a maiden's ' nay '
  Are too keen for a mother to soothe away
With a rose or a sugar-plum !

CHILDHOOD'S PLAYMATES.

  ARE the flowers comrades meet
  For my dainty lady ?
  Do the cowslips talk to her,
  Where the lanes are shady ?
  Does the crab-tree shower down
  Perfumed snow for treading ?
  Does the bonnie speed-well keep
  Turquoise gems for shedding ?
  Have the hedges' vetches wreathed,
  And moonlight coloured May,
  To woo my darling's dancing feet,
  And eager hands to stay ?

    Seek the woods, my little Queen,
    There lily-bells are ringing;

And violets and anemonies
Among the moss are springing ;
And down the dells the hyacinths
Flash living blue around,
As if a little bit of sky
Had fallen to the ground ;
And primroses are lingering,
As loth to pass away
From the bright world where sun and flowers
And children hail the May.

See where ragged-robin peeps
'Mid the pink-tipped daisies ;
See the gallant buttercup
By modest starwort blazes.
Creep down to the sparkling beck,
Through the budding clover ;
Gather fair forget-me-nots,
Ere their pride is over.
Has not Spring a lavish store,
Fit for fairy fingers ;
Though not a wild rose blushes yet,
Though not a snowdrop lingers.

Ask the wee wise pimpernel
Whether rain is coming,
To make her close her scarlet lips,
And stop my baby's roaming.
Seek the graceful celandine,
Pluck iris' sturdy head,
Ask the dandelion clock,
How long ere 'time for bed.'
Ah, but for wings to fly down south,
And make one May-day's hours

A peaceful bright idyllic dream,
With Dena and the flowers!

GROWING UP.

Oh to keep them still around us, baby darlings, fresh
and pure,
'Mother's' smile their pleasures' crowning, 'mother's'
kiss their sorrows' cure ;
Oh to keep the waxen touches, sunny curls, and
radiant eyes,
Pattering feet, and eager prattle —all young life's lost
Paradise !

One bright head above the other, tiny hands that
clung and clasped,
Little forms, that close enfolding, all of Love's best
gifts were grasped ;
Sporting in the summer sunshine, glancing round the
winter hearth,
Bidding all the bright world echo with their fearless,
careless mirth.

Oh to keep them ; how they gladdened all the path
from day to day,
What gay dreams we fashioned of them, as in rosy
sleep they lay ;
How each broken word was welcomed, how each
struggling thought was hailed,
As each bark went floating seaward, love-bedecked
and fancy-sailed !

Gliding from our jealous watching, gliding from our
clinging hold,
Lo ! the brave leaves bloom and burgeon ; lo ! the
shy sweet buds unfold ;

Fast to lip and cheek and tresses steals the maiden's
    bashful joy;
Fast the frank bold man's assertion tones the accents
    of the boy.

Neither love nor longing keeps them; soon in other
    shape than ours
Those young hands will seize their weapons, build
    their castles, plant their flowers;
Soon a fresher hope will brighten the dear eyes we
    trained to see;
Soon a closer love than ours in those wakening
    hearts will be.

So it is, and well it is so; fast the river nears the
    main,
Backward yearnings are but idle; dawning never
    glows again;
Slow and sure the distance deepens, slow and sure
    the links are rent;
Let us pluck our autumn roses, with their sober
    bloom content.

Let us see them springing round us, with a blessing
    and a prayer,
Let the memory of our loving breathe around them
    in the air,
Let us in our sons' protection, in our girls' sweet
    tendance blest
Look back in quiet gratitude, and smiling say, 'so
    best.'

ON THE THRESHOLD.

STANDING on the threshold, with her wakening heart
  and mind,
Standing on the threshold, with her childhood left
  behind;
The woman softness blending with the look of sweet
  surprise,
For life and all its marvels, that lights the clear blue
  eyes.

Standing on the threshold, with light foot and fearless hand,
As the young knight by his armour in a minster
  nave might stand;
The fresh red lip just touching youth's ruddy rap-
  turous wine,
The eager heart all brave pure hope, O happy
  child of mine!

I could guard the helpless infant that nestled in my
  arms ;
I could save the prattler's golden head from petty
  baby harms;
I could brighten childhood's gladness, and comfort
  childhood's tears,
But I cannot cross the threshold with the step of
  riper years.

For hopes, and joys, and maiden dreams are waiting
  for her there,
Where girlhood's fancies bud and bloom in April's
  golden air;

And passionate love, and passionate grief, and pas-
    sionate gladness lie
Among the crimson flowers that spring as youth
    goes fluttering by.

Ah! on those rosy pathways is no place for sobered
    feet,
My tired eyes have naught of strength such fervid
    glow to meet;
My voice is all too sad to sound amid the joyous
    notes,
Of the music that through charmèd air for opening
    girlhood floats.

Yet thorns amid the leaves may lurk, and thunder-
    clouds may lower,
And death, or change, or falsehood blight the
    jasmine in thy bower;
May God avert the woe, my child, but oh! should
    tempest come,
Remember, by the threshold waits the patient love
    of home!

MY PICTURES.

They gleam upon me from the silent walls,
    These mute companions of my darkened life.
Within, the fitful firelight leaps and falls;
    Without, the March winds meet in stormy strife.
Over the dazzling page the strained eyes ache,
    The pen drops listless from the weary hand,
The spirits of my pictures slowly wake,
    And wrapt in memory's halo, round me stand.

There the wild waves crash on the rocky beach;
    I gaze upon them till I hear once more

The thunder music on the hollow reach,
  E'en as we listened, lingering on the shore ;
Here, through the country hush I hear the swell,
  I breathe the sea's keen breath through land-locked
      air,
And see the feathery spray I love so well,
  Light 'mid the heather on the headland there.

That battle scene ! I recollect we bent,
  To read its tale in Froissart's roll of glory ;
Gathering the bright accessories that lent
  The flash and glitter to chivalric story.
There, through the bleak east wind, and London
      smoke,
  He brought the eastern tint, the crimson quiver,
As, picturing the scenes of which he spoke,
  He drew yon long low banks and mighty river.

There float the angels, each seraphic face
  In calm reproving sweetness stilling woe;
There smile the woodland paths our steps would
      trace,
  In the old happy time so long ago.
And there, the yearning sorrow to beguile,
  From the chill mists that round my vigil rise,
I see our boy's bright curls and joyous smile,
  The wistful beauty of our girl's blue eyes.

O, Heaven-sent Art ! Death's icy shadow rests
  On Nature's spring-like smile and kindred love,
Only Art's voice its mighty power attests,
  Still memory's pulse and memory's life to prove.
Yet from his pictures breathes the olden charm,
  Speaking the bliss that was—that yet shall be,
When earth, and life, and grief, and loss, and harm,
  Fade in the full glow of eternity.

LOVE'S DANGER.

A sudden glance, a hint no others guess,
The sweet soft subtle cadence of a word,
And all the surface of a life is stirred
To the light rippling waves of happiness.

A jarring jest, an act unseen or slighted,
A shy allusion missed, a mocking smile;
And joy and hope and peace so glad erewhile,
Shrink back like April buds by east winds blighted.

Ah, mighty arbiters of heart and life,
Ye loved ones ! know your sceptre's boundless sway ;
Nor in a careless hour fling gems away,
Whose worth would buckler you through storm and
    strife.

The flowers of joy as fragile are, as fair ;
The leaves may wither, though the roots endure ;
Let Love's strong hand their first bright bloom secure,
Or dread to lose the tender glory there.

AFTER THE GALE.

No longer in their reckless mood all earth and sky
    defying,
Soft as an infant's breath the winds across the sea
    are sighing ;
As if for all their wrath has done in penitence
    atoning,
Along the hollow shore the waves upon the sands
    are moaning.

No more the fitful sunlight glints the wild white
    crests to gild,
No more by ocean's mighty voice the weary air is
    filled,
The great gray sky stoops sullenly over the great
    gray sea,
And through the hush the curlew's call pipes shrill
    and eerily.

And tossing on the heaving main the drifting
    wreckage lies,
Telling wild tales of all the gale wrought 'neath the
    angry skies,
While staggering landward, crushed and beat, the
    storm-bound cobles come,
Bringing just lives, lives barely saved, to the yearning
    hearts at home.

Just lives ! and oh, though children spring the rescued
    men to meet,
Though wives and mothers by the hearth give
    welcome warm and sweet,
Black ruin marks the homestead upon our rock-girt
    coast,
When brave bronzed lips tell falteringly how ' nets
    and gear are lost.'

Ah, life upon our seaboard here, is full, and grave,
    and stern,
Deep need have we the help of faith, the strength
    of trust to learn ;
For, seeing all a gale can do, what have we but to
    rest
On Him who rules the seas and winds, on Him
    whose ' ways ' are best.

THE DEEP-SEA FISHING.

Up with the flags, white, purple, and red,
Flutter them out from the tall mast-head,
Let the broad brown sail be bravely spread,
For wives and children must be fed,
Though wintry winds wail wearily.
Though the great waves crash on the rocky shore,
Though the ominous foam on the sand lies hoar,
And over the reef where the breakers roar
The sea-fret's wreathing drearily.

The mother bids her children pray
For him who sails for them far away;
The widow shrinks from the light of day,
And shudders as cheering words they say:
For darkly the storm-clouds gather,
And her one bold boy has gone with the rest,
Where the long lines toss on the billows' crest,
O'er the pitiless sea whose 'wandering' breast,
Long years since took his father.

Up with the flag, while the sail is set,
Labour and danger must needs be met,
For fire and bread are hard to get;
Better than hunger, or cold, or debt,
The squall o'er the wild waves sweeping.
Up with the flag and away to the goal,
Where for fathoms deep the blue seas roll,
Where the dog-fish dart round the herring shoal,
And the skate and the cod are leaping.

Up with the flag, there is money to make,
Where the sails in the fierce north-easter shake;

Look to gear and tackle, away for the sake
Of the women at home, who will watch and wake
In the town 'neath the tall cliffs lying;
God speed the brave hearts in their toil afar,
Till their boats come home 'neath the evening star,
Till they steer their loads o'er the harbour bar,
Where the crimson flag is flying.

THE COBLE.

THE eye was filled by the heave and the flash,
  The ear was filled by the roar,
As the great wind blew from the wild north-west,
  And the great waves crashed on the shore;
The sky hung black and angry,
  Over the raging sea,
And away, where the mighty billows rolled,
  And the spray flew fast and free,
The broad brown sail of the coble
  Quivered, and filled, and shook;
And out on the pier the fishermen
  Stood stern and pale to look.

The eye was filled by the heave and the flash,
  The ear was filled by the roar,
The coble tossed, and veered, and tacked,
  As she strove to make the shore;
Ready with rope and rocket
  The stalwart coastguard stood.
And ever and ever fiercer rose
The fierce North Sea at the flood;
And the sail of the home-bound coble
  Still fluttered, true and brave,
Amid the howl of the rising wind
  And the crash of the rising wave.

At last she fetched the harbour,
   And rode o'er the foaming bar,
While the cheer of the eager watchers blent
   With the thunder on the Scar;
And I thought, just so, 'mid the turmoil,
   The fret and the fever of life,
A heart fares, striving and straining,
   'Gainst the currents of earthly strife.
Ah, let us keep sail and compass,
   Hope's star, and the anchor of Faith,
And so, glide to the haven where we would be,
   O'er the last long wave of Death!

MAD LUCE.

Along the hollow reaches where the ripples curve
   on the sand,
Or float the crimson sea-weeds that wreathe on the
   rocky strand;
Over the frowning headlands, when the heather is
   all aglow,
And the breakers crash 'neath the rugged cliffs, as
   the great tides come and go;
Out on the pier when the thundering surf thrills all
   the startled air,
She wanders, the woman with wild blue eyes, wan
   face, and grizzled hair.

Passing amid the merry groups, where the happy
   children play,
Passing where sturdy fishermen push their cobles
   out through the spray,

Passing where round the lighthouse the gathering
    sailors watch
The gleam on the warning crest of the Nab, or the
    tossing barque to catch ;
And still to the wondering questioner the fisher folk
    will use
To answer quickly and carelessly, 'It is only old
    Mad Luce !'

Should a pitying stranger ask of her, for ever the
    pale lips say,
While all the while the weary eyes are gazing over
    the bay :
'The sea ! I always loved it, since a bairn by its
    side I played,
Since down there by the Lecta Rock I and my Willie
    strayed ;
I said I would never have a home but stood on the
    sounding shore,
Nor eat nor sleep nor work nor live where I could
    not hear its roar.

' "Thou 'lt have to pay thy tribute, lass," I mind my
    mother said ;
Aye, I told him, as we kissed and laughed, the day
    that we were wed.
He said he 'd strive to earn it ; but a costlier fee, I
    wot,
Than all his wage was my good man's life, that the
    great sea sought and got.
I sate with our baby at my breast by his headstone
    up on the hill,
And heard the waves who kept his wake, and yet I
    loved them still.

' I wrought, and hard, for our bonnie bairn, and
　　　whenever the day was passed,
We'd creep where the sea lay rosy bright as sunset
　　　shadows were cast;
And we'd listen to hear his dadda call, amid the
　　　calling surf,
And fling him the pink-tipped daisies, that grew on
　　　the churchyard turf;
And I thought we might wait together, till life and
　　　its tasks were done,
But the sea would have its dues in full, and it took
　　　my bold one son.

' For he was never easy till the men would take
　　　him afloat;
I think they brought me back his cap, when they
　　　found the broken boat.
But I cannot tell; the fever got hold of my brain
　　　and me,
Yet I hear him talk with Willie in the whispering of
　　　the sea;
And when the foam is flying fast, and fierce north-
　　　easters blow,
I wait to hear them summon me, that am so fain
　　　to go.

' I daren't lie down in its arms and die, for I know
　　　the priest has said,
" They who will not wait God's time on earth, in
　　　Heaven must seek their dead."
But I've never murmured or complained of the sea
　　　I've loved so long,
And I let it take its tribute, and never thought of a
　　　wrong;

And may be some day its soft white surf, just for
    my patience' sake,
Will lap me round and waft me away, with Willie
    and George to wake.'

And so, along the sounding shore, and under the
    beetling cliffs,
While the soft wind ruffles the sea's broad breast
    and speeds the glancing skiffs,
With yearning gaze on the long bright heave, or the
    wave that gathers and breaks,
Her lonely way with her desolate hope, the weary
    wanderer takes ;
And still in the calm indifference, that is born of
    wont and use,
The idlers look, and smile, and say, ' It is only old
    Mad Luce !'

THE NORTHERN LIGHTS.

A NORSE SUPERSTITION.

' Nay, mother, nay ; the pictured coal is glowing,
Dully and redly on the hearthstone there ;
Yon was no flame of careless idlers' throwing,
Nor rocket flashing through the startled air ;
'Twas but the gleaming of the Northern Lights ;
Ah, there again, they reddened Huntcliff heights.

' So, let me raise you softly on the pillow,
See, how the crimson lustre flares and dies,
Tinging to rose the long heave of the billow,
And the great arch of all the starless skies ;
The fishers say such beauty bodes them sorrow,
Telling of storm, and wind to blow to-morrow.'

' No, child, the busy wife may bait her lines,
And net and gear lie ready for the morning,
No presage in that wavering glory shines,
No doom in the rich hues the clouds adorning;
They do but say the lingering hours are past,
The gates, the golden gates, unclose at last.

'Won the long hill so steep and drear to climb,
Done the long task so bitter hard in learning;
The tears are shed, and garnered up by time,
The heart beats, freed from all its lonely yearning;
The bar swings back, and flooding seas and skies,
Burst out the deathless lights of Paradise.

' See, see, by the great valves of pearl they stand,
Friends, children, husband; see glad hands out-
    reaching !
For me, for me, the undiscovered land,
Its promise in that roseate signal teaching;
Aye, kiss me, child, the lips will soon be dumb,
That yet in earthly words can say, " I come." '

Again the banner of the Northern Lights
Waved broad and bright across the face of heaven;
And in the cottage on the rugged heights,
The passing radiance by their glory given,
Showed a pale orphan weeping by the bed,
And the calm smiling of the happy dead.

LOVE.

A FRAGILE girl, who droops and pales
  Like a flower in sudden frost,
  Clasping her wailing infant tight,
  Shrinking away from her fellows' sight

Like a wounded bird from the noonday light,
Its plumage all smirched and tossed.

Why? and they whisper of sin and shame,
And falsehood spoken in Love's pure name.

A gray old grange, with the ivy wreaths
Far floating from the wall;
The thick dust drifting its floors to heap,
The spider across its doors to creep,
The flag-staff rotting upon the keep,
As the banners within the hall.

Why ? and they speak of a forfeit pledge,
And their lord, who fell on his sabre's edge.

A youth, in the genius-peopled room,
That once his kingdom made,
His pencil broken, his canvas blurred,
And the music that once the heart-strings stirred,
Dashed right across with a passionate word,
Like the blood from a heart betrayed.

Why? and a common story was told,
Of troth-plight broken for sheen of gold.

A little child, with frank blue eyes,
And lips like flowers in dew,
Who wondered amid his childish play
Why some should frown, some turn away,
While those who blessing words would say,
Wept 'mid their kisses too.

Why ? the passion was past, the charm was spent,
The poison was left for the innocent.

A wailing cry 'neath the sombre yew,
A sob by a lonely hearth,

Bright buds flung down upon quiet graves,
Where lush and green the long grass waves,
And the river's ceaseless requiem craves
God's pity for His earth.

Why? ah, who knows not how life is marred,
Where Death's strong hand strikes cold and hard?

Love. Love forgotten, betrayed, forsworn,
Crushed beneath Death and Time.
A clue to every secret wrong,
A note life's sadness to prolong ;
A key, keen, magical, and strong,
To sorrow, or care, or crime.

Yet priest and poet unite to prove
That 'Love is Heaven, and Heaven is Love.'

THE WHEEL OF WORK AND WORRY.

The wheel is turning, turning,
Through summer and winter days ;
Shadow and shine on its spokes are cast,
Sunlight and moonlight, zephyr and blast,
But, revolving slow or whirling fast,
Nor for power or prayer it stays.

The wheel is turning, turning,
In the marvellous stream of time ;
Joy brightens to silver each sparkling jet,
Fear darkens to tempest its foam and fret,
Grief sighs in its ripple, but never yet
Does the current cease its chime.

The wheel is turning, turning ;
What does it boot to dream?

To lie 'mid the lilies beside the brink
And let our spirits 'mid visions sink,
And to fair false fancies of 'resting' link
The murmuring of the stream.

For the wheel is turning, turning,
And for each and all will come
Work and worry and cross and care,
Baffled longing, ungranted prayer,
For the 'trail of the serpent' is everywhere,
From the cradle to the tomb.

Watch the wheel in turning, turning,
With brave bright patient eyes;
Take what it brings with a stedfast heart,
Striving to play a hero's part,
For He, whose Hand draws every chart,
Rules wave and wheel from the skies.

Is there life in its turning, turning?
Then do our best with the gift.
Is there sorrow? buds blossom beneath the rain;
Is there trial? frost strengthens the waiting grain;
Is there Death? 'tis the door to the last great gain,
When the shadows for ever lift.

'IF ONLY.'

If we had but known, if we had but known,
  Those summer days together,
That one would stand next year alone,
  In the blazing July weather!
Why, we trifled away the golden hours,
  With gladness, and beauty, and calm,

Watching the glory of blossoming flowers,
  Breathing the warm air's balm;
Seeing the children like sunbeams play
  In the glades of the long cool wood;
Hearing the wild bird's carol gay,
  And the song of the murmuring flood.
Rich gems to Time's pitiless river thrown,
If we had but known, if we had but known!

If we had but known, if we had but known,
  Those winter nights together,
How one would sit by the hearth alone,
  In the next December weather;
Why, we sped those last hours, each for each,
  With music, and games, and talk,
The careless, bright, delicious speech,
  With no doubt or fear to balk.
Touching on all things, grave and gay,
  With the freedom of two in one,
Yet leaving, as happy people may,
  So much unsaid, undone.
Ah, priceless hours for ever flown,
If we had but known, if we had but known!

If we had but known, if we had but known,
  While yet we stood together,
How a thoughtless look, a slighting tone,
  Would sting and jar for ever!
Cold lies the turf for the burning kiss,
  The cross stands deaf to cries,
Dull, as the wall of silence is,
  Are the gray unanswering skies!
We can never unsay a thing we said,
  While the weary life drags past;

We never can stanch the wound that bled,
  Where a chance stroke struck it last.
Oh, the patient love 'neath the heavy stone,
If we had but known, if we had but known!

If we had but known, if we had but known!
  We had climbed the hill together;
The path before us seemed all our own,
  And the glorious autumn weather.
We had sown: the harvest was there to reap.
  We had worked: lo! the wages ready.
Who was to guess that the last long sleep
  Was closing round one already?
With never a warning, sharp and strong,
  Came the bitter wrench of doom,
And love, and sorrow, and yearning, long
  May wail by the lonely tomb.
Oh, keenest of pangs 'mid the mourner's moan,
If we had but known, if we had but known!

THE LAST WISH.

This is all, is it much, my darling?   You must follow
  your path in life,
Have a head for its complex windings, a hand for
  its sudden strife;
The sun will shine, the flowers will bloom, though
  my course 'mid them all is o'er,
I would not that those dear living eyes should light
  in their joy no more;
Only just for the sake of the happy past, and the
  golden days that have been,
By the love we have loved, and the hopes we have
  hoped, will you have my grave kept green?

Just a moment in the morning, in the eager flush of
    the day,
To pluck some creeping weed perchance, or train
    the white rose spray ;
Just a moment to shade my violets from the glare
    of the noontide heat,
Just a tear and a prayer in the gloaming, ere you
    leave me with lingering feet.
Ah ! it is weak and foolish, but I think that in
    God's serene,
I shall know, and love to know, mine own, that you
    keep my grave so green.

I would fain, when the drops are plashing against
    your window-pane,
That you should be thinking wistfully of my grasses
    out in the rain ;
That when the winter veil is spread o'er the fair
    white world below,
Your tender hands twine the holly wreaths that
    mark my rest in the snow.
My clasp on life and life's rich gifts grows faint
    and cold I ween,
Yet oh ! I would hold it to the last—the trust of
    my grave kept green.

Because it is by such little signs the heart and its
    faith are read ;
Because the natural man must shrink ere he joins
    the forgotten dead ;
The Heavenly hope is bright and pure, and calm is
    the Heavenly rest,
Yet the human love clings yearningly to all it has
    prized the best.

We have been so happy, darling, and the parting
   pang is keen,
Ah ! soothe it by this last vow to me—you will
   watch that my grave keeps green.

BY THE HEARTH.

DEAD eyes are gazing on her from the pictures on
   the wall,
Dead voices in the wailing winds that sweep the
   uplands call,
Dead feet seem pattering round her as the raindrops
   lash the pane,
Till she stretches hands of greeting, dumb hands that
   yearn in vain.

Like one in fairy legend, like one in dreamland lost,
At every turn by dead men's steps her onward way
   is crossed,
The very flowers whisper, of who plucked them long
   ago,
The very birds have echoes in their trillings soft
   and low.

The chords she touches breathe for her the music
   of the past,
On every page the shadow of old memories is cast,
The 'brooding sense of something' gone falls solemn
   all around,
Making the common paths of life her hushed heart's
   holy ground.

On the table-ground of middle life, the dull and dreary
   land,
Where shadowless as sunless lies the stretch of beaten
   sand,

She stands alone and listens, all behind her veiled
  in mist,
In front dim hills beyond the vale, their summits
  promise kissed.

Sob on, O wind! sigh on, O rain! sweet faces form
  and die,
There, where amid the caverned coals the fairy
  fancies lie,
For in sleeping as in waking, till she crosses the
  dark stream,
The sunshine of her lonely heart from the peopled
  past must gleam.

AT SCARBOROUGH.

A GRAY sky and a gray sea,
All in the wild March weather;
A wind that bore down the storm-tossed shore,
Snowflake and spray together.
A wreck's jagged timbers, sharp and brown,
That shivered and swayed as the tide went down;
Red roofs, high piled in the quaint old town,
A headland grim with a castled crown,
'Mid a waste of withered heather.

A gray sky and a gray sea,
And a sound like rolling thunder,
As the foam flew fast on the bitter blast,
That tore the waves asunder.
A golden sand reach, long and low,
Black rocks, that through ages of ebb and flow,
Guard the beautiful bay where long ago
Came ships, with the Raven flag at their prow,
For slaughter, fire, and plunder.

A gray sky and a gray sea,
And two, who stood together,
With hands close clasped, as hands are grasped,
That parting, part for ever.
Two, whose pale lips quivered to say,
The words the world hears every day;
As for all we struggle, and weep and pray,
Young hearts must break in life's fever play,
And links are light to sever.

A gray sky and a gray sea,
Where white gulls stooped to hover,
Their broad wings flashed, as the great waves dashed,
Where by lover lingered lover;
Those two may never more meet again,
But the wild March wind with its fret and strain,
Will for aye recall the passionate pain
Of that farewell tryst by the stormy main,
When first love's dream was over.

HUSH!

Hush, hush, my darling, my darling,
  See where the pale light creeps up through the sky;
Soon the long ache of the night will be over,
  The night that has lingered so wearily by.

Hush, hush love, try to forget it,
  Let me bathe the hot forehead and smoothe the
      tossed hair;
Let me kiss the poor lips, whose delirious raving
  Mingle murmurs of passion, and anguish, and prayer.

Hush, hush, it is over, dear, over,
  Nothing can waken life's gladness again;

Nothing can give the crushed flower its freshness.
  Let us turn from the past, it is impotent pain.

Hush, hush; nay, *I* do not mock you,
  With the words that so often to mourners are
      said,
That one would not, if power to do so were given,
  Call back from their rest or their glory the Dead.

Aye, child, it is Nature's defiance :
  Though wrong, rash or selfish, whatever the cost,
What heart, in its hours of lonely despairing,
  But would call, an it could, from their Heaven,
      its lost ?

Hush, hush, the law is unbroken :
  Deep as the grave is and mighty as death,
Falsehood and treason the sweet dream have buried,
  Words to revive it were mere idle breath.

Hush, hush, my darling, my darling,
  I cannot avenge you, or rescue, or aid ;
I only can watch through the long, fevered hours,
  And mourn o'er the wreck one wild tempest has
      made.

Love, love, what has it brought you?
  Sorrow and suffering, struggle and fall ;
Turn to the quiet affection of kindred,
  To the fondness the first, as the last of it all.

Child, child, it will not fail you :
  It woke with your being, and lives in your life ;
Patient it waits through neglect and desertion,
  Silent in sunshine, and faithful in strife.

Deep, deep, the current is flowing
  Though the cataract flashes, in hurry and rush,
The bark shall yet safely glide into the harbour,
  Light comes in the eventide ; hush, darling, hush !

LAUNCHED.

'Neath a smiling sun and a wooing gale,
I set my feather-boats to sail,
By one, by two, by three.
One was laden with First Love's vow,
One had Fortune's flag at her prow,
One, Fame had freighted for me.

Never a weather sign I scanned,
As my gay bark left the flowery land
On a merry morn of May.
Down swept a squall of Doubt and Chance,
And wrecked on the shoal of Circumstance,
My first fair venture lay.

Gravely I looked to rigging and rope,
Ere, bathed in the lustre of golden hope,
My next to the open bore.
But fierce and treacherous rose the waves,
More ships than mine found fathomless graves,
Ere the noontide storm was o'er.

To the lulling whispers of Art and Song,
I framed my last boat true and strong,
And decked her with joyous dreams.
And sent her forth with a rosy smile,
Tinging her silken sails the while,
Caught from the sunset's gleams.

But oh, she never returned again,
O'er the wild waste waters my sad eyes strain,
In the sickness of hope deferred.
And I think sometimes, should she yet come back,
With the world's slow plaudits loud on her track,
Will the grass on my grave be stirred?

SHIPWRECK.

On the smiling sea was never a curl,
On the bright sky never a frown;
Never an omen of coming fate,
When my beautiful bark, with her costly freight,
In the glory of noon went down.

Boldly launched from a quiet shore;
Well framed with storms to cope;
By Youth and Courage nobly manned;
The sails were woven by Love's own hand,
The rudder was held by Hope.

The merciless sun shone full and fair,
The pitiless waves were calm.
No whisper of woe in the wooing breeze,
The gulls poised over the sleeping seas,
The treacherous air was balm.

With happy laughter, with joyous dreams,
We glided in fearless faith;
Then—the sullen jar on the sunken rock;
The grinding crash, the horrible shock;
The headlong plunge to death.

A moment's whirl of boiling foam,
A shriek through the slumberous day,

Then, smooth blue waters and calm blue skies,
And the startled birds with their keen dark eyes,
Intent on their darting prey.

The bright sea dimpled, the bright sun shone,
With nor cloud nor white crest flecked;
A thousand barks sailed gaily past,
A thousand flags light shadows cast,
Where my beautiful boat was wrecked.

Wrecked, with its hopes, its loves, its trusts,
Sunk deep to the sea-weeds brown;
The great world turns and the great waves break;
What should either heed of the moan we make,
When a life or a ship goes down?

NULLA DIES SINE LINEÂ.

(LUTHER'S MAXIM.)

Nulla dies sine lineâ;
Happy childhood, listen,
Some little kindness kindly wrought,
Some gentle word, some tender thought,
May win for April's primrose crown
A golden sun-ray, glinting down,
To heavenly life to glisten.

Hear it, on your eager start,
Youth, hopeful and undaunted;
Well for you, if every day,
On your glorious upward way,
By some tempting bait resigned,
Honour won, or truth defined,
As by sweet dream be haunted.

Hear it, arid middle age.
Hope and joy are over;
Yet open hand and pitying heart,
Still may play their healing part;
Every life has ample need,
Every field has springing seed,
Tired eyes may best discover.

Hear it, frail and feeble age.
Even for failing fingers,
At every tottering footstep lurk
Room for help and room for work;
And even on the dying bed
For prayer of faith in patience said
Reverent fondness lingers.

Nulla dies sine lineâ;
Speaking from his rest,
Luther bids us, each and all,
Hearken to his trumpet call;
In word, thought, action, prompt and true,
Every day, O brothers, do
Something of our best.

OUT OF THE MOUTH OF BABES, ETC.

Across the valley at our feet
  Swept April sun and shade;
Where Spring's green mantle, soft and sweet,
  Decked every wooded glade.
Pale primrose, pure anemone,
  Spread jewels everywhere;
On sky and sea, in flower and tree,
  The broad earth pranked her fair.

The light wind tossed the larch's buds,
  And stirred the lily's bells;
The wild birds nestled o'er their broods,
  Down in the leafy dells.
And the little child, 'neath the flowering thorn,
  Sang on the steep hill side,
'To save the world our Lord was born,
  To save the world He died.'

Upon the terrace where we sate,
  Heaped books and papers lay;
Treasures of learning, matters of State,
  Forgot for the laughing day.
We turned from our happy idleness
  To study the page of life;
No brooding charm in the eager 'Press,'
  No lull in the keen world's strife.
But Art and Science upward soared,
  Through baffling mist and bar;
Here, Statecraft o'er its meshes pored,
  There, loomed the cloud of War.
And the little child, 'neath the flowering thorn,
  Sang on the steep hill side,
'To save the world our Lord was born,
  To save the world He died.'

And we saw, how under Religion's cloak
  The bitterest anger lurked;
For it, the hardest laws men spoke,
  The sternest deeds they worked;
For it, the life-blood fastest flowed,
  For it, the gravest loss;
And every rival banner showed
  The symbol of the Cross.

Yet, no polemics the Master taught,
    As He stood on the Eastern Mount ;
With never a drop of poison fraught,
    Ran the stream from the Living Fount.
And the little child, 'neath the flowering thorn,
    Sang on the steep hill side,
' To save the world our Lord was born,
    To save the world He died.'

And we thought, the fact the baby sings,
    Our all of truth and worth,
With the infinite Love and pure Hope it brings
    To brighten the paths of earth.
Should it not quiet this restless roar,
    And hush those battle cries,
And make men trust a little more
    To the one Great Sacrifice ?
Ah, Brothers, let us meekly strive,
    To do our daily tasks ;
To keep sweet Charity's flame alive,
    Naught else the Gospel asks.
And the buds blow thick on the roughest thorn,
    The sun gilds the steep hill side ;
And to save the world our Lord was born,
    To save the world He died.

THE WORLD OF BOOKS.

Full fraught with fret, and weariness, and strife,
    Heavy with labour, burthened sore with woes,
Many long days of this our mortal life
    Drag sadly, from their dawning to their close.
Each counted hour, as it lingers by,
    Bringing fresh task-work, deepened fear or pain ;

And when kind Slumber seals the tired eye,
　Fancy enacts it all in dreams again.

Behind the swiftest horseman care will ride ;
　Up to the idlest lounger troubles creep ;
The spectre glowers by the banquet's side ;
　The terror mutters by the infant's sleep.
The proudest victor, in his hour of glory,
　Hears the hushed footstep of his treacherous foe ;
The happiest lover, whispering Hope's sweet story,
　Sees the thorn lurking 'neath the rose's glow.

Yet one fair world is left us, still secure
　From all the phantoms that beset our way ;
Where Joy is fearless, Love is strong and pure,
　And Faith knows naught of challenge or decay ;
Where Courage wakes old Chivalry to dare,
　Where Fancy weaves her airy web of light,
Where Learning cuts her gems for setting rare,
　And Science brings her mystic stores to sight.

In that great world—the world our books have
　　　made,
　E'en Death itself its grisly front must veil.
Before its steady sun the grave-lights fade ;
　Low music breathes for us beyond the pale.
In its deep lore vexations we forget.
　O'er its gay humour Sorrow learns to smile ;
And where its Master's vivid seals are set
　We linger, charmed and happy for a while.

Nature may jar or fail us, oftentimes
　The sunshine hurts, the tempest deepens gloom ;
Music has mockery in its sweetest chimes,
　And Memory poisons flowers and perfume.

But, sad or angry, lonely, fearful, worn,
  Come as you will, our world has room for each.
Or old, or young, birth-blighted, travel-torn;
  For books can charm, inspire, help, soothe, or
    teach.

WHAT DOES IT MEAN?

'I THOUGHT,'—how lightly we say it,
As touching a common thing,
Yet with mighty questions, unsounded depths,
The plain words throb and sting.
Who can tell why the sound of a song,
Sung by an idler, passing along,
Can thrill to the heart, with a sharp old pain
We fancied it never could feel again?
Why a scent on the summer breezes borne,
Or a poppy flaring amid the corn,
Can send the memory flying back,
To search on a long abandoned track
For a dream that is dreamt, for a joy that has been?
Yet, such things are, and what do they mean?

I thought—that the sky would be gloomier,
Or the wind would sink perchance;
Yet, fate was shaping, all the while,
The lot, from the circumstance.
That quick word spoken may prove a scourge,
To madness the impotent grief to urge;
That rose, gay token from careless hand,
Grow a treasure no future will understand;
That robin's sweet pathetic note,
Be a music through parted years to float;
That hour, forgotten, may dumbly sleep
Long months, then sudden to life to leap

To life, strong, bitter, and clear and keen ;
Aye, such things are, and what do they mean ?

I thought—that all had a purpose,
And actions a righteous law,
And oh ! it is well for the daily path,
The soothing code to draw ;
Only, while reason and memory lie,
A fathomless sea 'neath an iron sky,
While the chords each passing hand can touch,
Or in echo or silence reveal so much,
While a sunset, a flower, the crash of a wave
Can joy, or sadden, or help, or save ;
We can but bow our heads and trust
In something holy, and great, and just ;
For only when passing at last the screen,
Shall we see or know what it all may mean.

A LESSON.

I SAID, my life is a beautiful thing,
I will crown me with its flowers,
I will sing of its glory all day long,
For my harp is young, and sweet, and strong,
And the passionate power in my song
Shall thrill all the golden hours.
And over the sand and over the stone,
For ever and ever the waves rolled on.

I said, my life is a terrible thing,
All ruined, and lost, and crushed.
I will heap its ashes upon my head,
I will wail for my joy and my darling dead,
Till the dreary dirge for the days that are fled
Stirs faint through the dull dumb dust.

And over the sand and over the stone,
For ever and ever the waves rolled on.

I said, I was proud in my hour of mirth,
And mad in my first despair.
Now, I know nor earth, nor sky, nor sea,
Has heed or helping for one like me,
The doom or the boon comes, let it be.
For us, we can but bear.
And over the sand and over the stone,
For ever and ever the waves rolled on.

And I thought they sang, 'We laugh to the sun;
We shimmer to moon or star;
We foam to the lash of the furious blast;
We rage, when the rain falls, fierce and fast;
But we do our day's work, and at last
We sweep o'er the harbour-bar.'
And I learnt my lesson 'mid sand and stone,
As ever and ever the waves rolled on.

AFLOAT AND ASHORE.

Two wives sate by the ingle side,
  In the cottage upon the shore;
They heard the wild wind sweeping by,
  They heard the breakers roar.

One bent to kiss the baby
  That slumbered upon her knee;
'We must pray ere we go to our rest, mother;
  Pray for our men at sea.'

'Aye, we're ready, I and father,
  Though he's hale and hearty still;
But thou, with the little one nestled there,
  Thou'st need to pray for Will.

'Hark, how the surf is calling!
  But a man must do his work,
And God can guide the barque to port,
  In sunshine or midnight murk.

'Come, lass, never heed yon thunder,
  They are far enough by this;
But I say, God help a sailor's wife,
  For an anxious end it is.'

Two men stood calm together,
  The sky was one iron frown,
The sea was rolling, mast-head high,
  The ship was settling down.

'Here's a bad job, my lad,' said one,
  'Or ever the morn will come,
Two widows will be waiting us,
  By the kindly hearth at home.'

The young man's face was flushed and wild,
  The old man's set and gray,
And ever the ship was nearing doom,
  In fatal Biscay Bay.

And as a long, wild, wailing shriek
  Rang through the shuddering air,
Two women away in England
  Knelt for their morning prayer.

Knelt down to plead for their safety,
  Who were lying fathoms deep,
Where the coral wreathes and the fishes dart
  Over the seaman's sleep.

Two women who were widows,
  Were kneeling side by side;

And one was a gray-haired matron,
    And one was a year-old bride.

And their call rose up to Heaven,
    With that terrible drowning cry;
Did the Angel weep who bore them blent
    To the mercy-seat on high?

LOADED WAINS.

FROM the broad fields, their golden glory shorn,
And sunny uplands, of their beauty reft,
Through the still sunlight of the autumn morn,
And hedgerows, with their lingering jewels left,
By the brown river, through the leafy lanes,
On to the farmsteads move the loaded wains.

The stalwart reaper bears his brightened scythe.
Or tracks the course the great machine has made,
And bonnie lass and lad, sunburnt and lithe,
Round whose straw hats woodbine and poppies fade,
Wake all the meadow land with harvest strains,
Clustering and laughing round the loaded wains.

'Tis soft September nature's harvest yields,
But all through life our ripening fruit we reap,
Now storing violets from sweet April fields,
Now roses that bright July sunshines steep,
Now garnering gray October's sober gains,
Now Christmas hollies pile our loaded wains.

Ah me! how fast the fair spring flowers die,
How summer blossoms perish at the touch,
And Hope and Love in useless sympathy,
Weep for the Faith that gave and lost so much!

From half our sheaves drop out the golden grains,
Small is our portion in the loaded wains.

Yet, ere the mighty Reaper takes it all,
Fling out the seed, and tend it rood by rood;
One ear is full, though hundreds round it fall,
One acre 'mid a mildewed upland good;
Eternity will rear on heavenly plains
The smallest treasure won from loaded wains.

THE OLD BROWN SHAWL.

The Past, it clings, it clings; so the sweet singer
    sings,
  The singer around whose waving locks the vice-
    crown's glories fall;
And I thought of his words to-night, as I stood in
    the gloaming light,
  Smoothing with slow fond touches the folds of the
    Old Brown Shawl.

The Past, it clings, it clings, round the mute inani-
    mate things,
  That wake the chord of memory into vivid breath-
    ing life,
Till we people the vacant chair, crown with rosebuds
    the severed hair,
  And feel the desolate chamber with bright move-
    ment and laughters rife.

The Past, it clings, it clings; the sudden tear-rain
    springs
  To the waft of a hidden perfume, the leaf of a
    wayside weed;

By the jar of an idle word the dull sleeping depths
    are stirred ;
  At the stroke of a careless finger the old scared
    wounds will bleed.

The Past, it clings, it clings; forgotten music rings;
  About the lonely watch I keep, long-silenced foot-
    steps fall,
Sweet faces flash through the gloom, and the pre-
    sence that fills the room
  Moulds to familiar use and wont the draping of
    the shawl.

The Past, it clings, it clings : the rosy hue it flings,
  Of the days when on its spreading wide the Baby
    rolled and played,
And we drew it close and soft round her fragile
    figure oft,
  When too far into the woodland her tender wan-
    derings strayed.

The Past, it clings, it clings : a passionate longing
    stings,
  Through the helpless acquiescence, to submission
    dignified,
While the yearning empty arms the well-known
    texture warms,
  As they cling around the foldings that wrapped
    Him ere he died.

The Past, it clings, it clings : and the Indian warpage
    brings
  Troops of pale flitting phantoms, at thoughts' un-
    witting call,

Till the lost life lives again, and its hope, fear, joy,
    and pain,
All throb, and thrill, and dazzle, round the thread-
    bare Old Brown Shawl.

THE TAPESTRY ROOM.

To you, just nothing but four square walls
  Hung with an arras screen,
And windows that look on a purling brook,
  That runs by a bowling green.
Where blackbird and thrush on the shaven sward
  Twitter, and hop, and search,
And the yew-tree hedge makes impervious edge,
  'Neath the shelter of elm and birch.

To me, why, could I embody them,
  The shadows that around me crowd,
Should I not want both altar and font,
  White veil and funeral shroud?
The bride stood, busked for the bridal,
  There where yon ferns are grown,
Here the babe heir slept, as his state he kept,
  There the widow wailed, alone.

And just where to-day we gather
  Each glittering wedding gift,
I knelt, I remember, one dark November,
  The cloth from a face to lift,
When I 'd fain press a kiss at parting
  On the awful, beautiful lips,
Where the calm smile resting, seemed souls' protesting,
  Against Death's blank eclipse.

With blush and whisper and laughter
  Youth flutters across the floors,
But for me the ghost of a bright life lost
  Glides in at the open doors;
A silent Presence fills the air,
  And spreads a solemn gloom,
Where 'mid sun and flowers the golden hours
  Flit through the tapestry room.

GRANTED.

HIGH in air hung the flower,
The beautiful bloom of May;
I longed for it through my joys and my cares,
I thought how blest who such treasure wears,
I wearied Heaven with ceaseless prayers,
  Through hot night and fevered day;
I clasped the blossom, at last mine own,
And the sharp thorns pierced me to the bone.

Burnished and brave the laurel,
  Fain would I win its wreath;
Sense and will to the quest I vowed,
Love and rest at its shrine I bowed,
Let me gain but this, I said aloud,
  Then, welcome wrong, grief, or death.
I wore my bays, and the poison pain
Seared to its core the tired brain.

'Give me but this for my darling,
  The dream I have dreamt for her;
Let her sweet hopes rest in the castle I build,
Let her fair hand wear the ring I gild,
Let her life by the music I wake be thrilled,
  My fancy her minister.'

And I saw her step on the path I made,
And her love was blighted, her trust betrayed.

'Give him the crown of the victor;
　Make a hero of my boy;
Let his stroke be true and his arm be strong,
Let him save the feeble and right the wrong,
Let the voice of the poor his praise prolong,
　His glory shall be my joy.'

In the front of the battle I saw him stand,
Misjudged, crushed, baffled, heart, head, and hand.

At last I hushed my pleading,
　I silenced my rebel voice;
Amid thwarted aims and high hopes dead,
I bowed in awe my humbled head;
'Lord, let Thy will be done,' I said,
　'Hush thou my wilful choice.'

And Peace lit the quiet ways I trod,
And their sunshine fell from the smile of God.

BETWEEN THE LINES.

Sing the song of the singer, merrily ring the rhymes,
Light is the lay they tell us, light as its echoed
　　chimes;
Sing the song of the singer, mocking at doubt and
　　fear,
Catch the joy of its melody, let its daring beauty
　　cheer;
Well that the mellow music may bear no hidden
　　signs
Of the broken heart of the poet, written between
　　the lines.

Watch the part of the player, bravely and deftly
    done,
See the difficult height attained, the loud applauses
    won ;
Weep with his passionate sorrow, thrill to his pas-
    sionate bliss,
Blending your joyous laughter with that happy laugh
    of his ;
Well that his marvellous acting, dazzles, wins, refines ;
Who thinks of the desperate effort, written between
    the lines ?

See the work of the painter, in colouring rare and
    rich,
Give it its well-won homage, choose it the choicest
    niche ;
Hang it where it may render, as an artist's best can do,
Companionship in its beauty, delicate, pure, and true !
Well that its silent loveliness, softness and thought
    combines ;
None read the bitter baffling strife, written between
    the lines.

Watch the path of the prosperous, sunny, and smooth,
    and bright,
Health and wealth to give it its full of sweetness and
    light ;
See how the easy future is planned for the careless
    feet,
Given each slight desire, flattered each vague conceit.
Well that the outward surface, gladness and peace
    enshrines ;
Who knows the tale of the skeleton, written between
    the lines ?

If the singer dies in solitude, his songs sigh on as
    sweetly ;
If the statesman has a hearth disgraced, does he
    face the world less meetly?
So the artist's touch is fine and sure, who heeds the
    hand that guides it?
Does the player feel a fading life? his miming, mask-
    ing, hides it.
Cypress, and rose, and laurel, Fate's reckless hand
    entwines ;
Life reads the printed story—Death writes between
    the lines.

GERMAN LEGEND.

God bade His angel dye the flowers.
Creation's work was done,
Like jewels, blossoms, buds and bowers
Flashed 'neath the new-born sun ;
The violet, like a sapphire gleamed,
Deep set in the emerald grass ;
Roses, like topaz and ruby beamed,
As they felt the white wings pass;
Jasmine and lily, like pure pearls strewn,
Shimmered beneath his hand,
Crocus and musk and marigold shone
Like gold o'er the joyous land ;
The messenger paused o'er his task to rejoice,
When lo, from a river grot,
Rose up a pitiful pleading voice;
' And I—forget me not ! '

Down where upon the sparkling beck
The broad-leaved lilies lay,
Catching the random shadow and fleck
Of the sunshine's fitful play,
Down where the feathery rushes shook
All in the golden weather,
And silvery willows by the brook
Swayed their lithe boughs together,
The pale, dim, colourless petals stood;
The angel stole the green
For the fragile leaves from a birch's bud;
For the blossoms that peeped between,
He chose the faint sweet stainless blue,
Of Heaven's own smile begot,
And so, divine in grace and hue,
Woke the Forget-me-not.

Ah, take the lesson home, my heart;
Life may seem dark and drear,
Never a help in the long hard part,
Never a word to cheer;
With emptied arms by the vacant hearth,
We may stand in our woe alone,
While there is not a voice on the happy earth,
But jars us in its tone;
And life around us, day by day,
Showing rich, and full, and sweet,
Till the very contrast makes the way
Still worse for the tired feet:
Oh, just when darkest seems the night,
And heaviest weighs the lot,
Let the quaint old legend show the light,
'My God forgets me not.'

AS THE HEART HEARS.

I know that I never can hear it, never on earth any
    more,
I know the music of my life with that silenced voice
    is o'er;
Yet I tell you, that never across the fells the wild
    west wind can moan,
Nor my sad heart hear, close, true, and clear, the
    thrill of his earnest tone.

I know that I never can listen, with these mortal
    ears of mine,
To the step that meant joy and gladness, in the
    days of auld lang syne;
Yet I tell you the long waves never break in the
    hollows of the cove,
But they mimic in their rise and fall the tread I
    used to love.

I know the melody that you sing, with its delicate
    memoried words,
Is nothing but measured language, well set sweet to
    music's chords;
Yet I tell you, as you breathe it, my dead life
    wakes again,
I laugh to its passionate gladness, I weep to its
    passionate pain.

I know the beck that tinkles beside the forget-me-
    nots there,
Is nothing but water rippling where the willows
    shimmer fair;

Yet I tell you, for me it murmurs, the very words
    he said,
When We, and the Year, and Love were fresh, in
    the golden day that is dead.

Aye, Youth is proud, and gay, and bold; still this
    is left for us,
Who sit 'neath the yellowing tree leaves, and listen
    to silence thus;
It has life in its April glory, it has hope with its
    smiles and tears,
We live alone with Nature and Time, and hear, as
    the hush'd heart hears.

SEEN AT THE EBB.

SEE how the wavelets kiss the shelving shore,
Where 'twixt its headlands sleeps the quiet bay,
Outside upon the rocks the breakers roar,
Outside the wild white horses champ and play;
Here, soft as moonlight lies the silver sea,
Here, hush'd as slumber flows the harmless tide,
And while the west wind whispers harmony,
The ferns grow greenly at the water's side.

Aye, but when once the fierce north-easter wakes,
And sweeps in anger 'tween its guardians grim,
Each feeble land-grown leaf in terror shakes,
As crested billows rise to welcome him;
And all the little bay is flash and foam,
And women 'mid crushed flowerets standing pale,
Watch the brown sails, half furled, come staggering
    home,
And pray for love and life amid the gale.

And as the sea reluctant ebbs, sharp reefs
'Mid slime and tangle show their treacherous might:
Just so this life of ours has secret griefs,
And ways and wills hid from the passing sight.
Full many a lip smiles as on summer seas,
While fear and doubt and danger lurk beneath;
Full many a life has bitter mysteries,
Unveiled when time ebbs from the touch of death.

'FEY.'

I'm no way 'superstitious,' as the parson called our
    Mat,
When he'd none sail with the herring fleet, 'cause
    he met old Susie's cat.
There's none can say I heeded, though a hare has
    crossed my road,
Nor burnt my nets as venomed, where a woman's
    foot had trod.

And though it's mebby wisest to hearken when they
    tell,
The sea-maids shriek their warning, from the reef
    beside the bell;
Seeing I reckon one hears them, when the wind
    has a northerly set,
And at the lip of the Nab out there, the breakers
    rouse and fret;

Still I'm no way superstitious, but this I allis say,
You may get the coffin ready when once a man is
    fey.
Aye laugh, and call it folly, I see you glance aside,
Wait a bit until I tell you how poor Jem Dobson
    died.

We were mates, but he was master, and a cautious
    man was he,
For ever studying at the glass, and watching sky
    and sea;
I'se sure it ofens put me about, when the fish were
    as rank as aught,
And he'd none sail, for 'the wind was shy,' or 'the
    clouds were raffled,' he thought.

One day, an April morning, it was blowing east-nor'-
    east,
The call of the surf was on the Scar, the billows
    frothed like yeast;
Great foam-flakes rested on the sand, and the
    hollow sullen roar
Rose in the offing loud enow to bid us keep ashore.

Guess how the boldest among us stared when Jem
    came swinging down,
And bade me help to launch the Rose, with an
    oath and with a frown.
I was loath, but young and foolish, and shrank like
    from a sneer:
There's naught a frightened lad won't do to prove
    he has no fear.

There were plenty spoke to stop him, but he'd nor
    hear nor heed,
But sorted gear and hauled up sail, all in a strange
    dumb speed;
I tell you my heart leapt fit to burst, as we shot
    out in the bay,
For I met poor Jem's wild wandering eyes, and I
    knew the man was fey.

I said when I durst, 'There 's mischief there,' and I
  nodded where, right ahead,
The black squall lay on the water, the foe we
  mariners dread;
But he scarcely shifted the helm a point, as his eye
  o'er the distance ran,
But laughed and said, 'The breeze is like to wait
  for a sure-doomed man.'

Doomed, aye, for the squall burst on us, and he
  turned her broadside-to,
I sprang to the helm, but over late, the stout sheet
  strained and flew;
And as the Rose heeled over, and the seas broke
  fierce and grim,
I heard Jem saying quietly, 'Poor lad, it 's hard on
  him.'

Sam Lacy told me afterwards—he steered the life-
  boat then,
And their work was set to save me, those strong
  seafaring men,—
Jem just threw up his hands to heaven, and with
  never a cry or call,
Went down to the death he was bound to die, in
  the very face of them all.

So, though no way superstitious, I neither jest nor
  sneer,
When old wives talk of omens and signs they
  reckon should guide us here;
For it 's little we know of the world beyond, and I
  cannot forget the day
When I so nigh touched hands with Death, and
  poor old Jem was fey.

LITTLE WILLIE.

Such a day to leave him, laid in his lonely grave;
Hark how the north wind whistles through the
thunder of the wave;
Such a day to leave him, where the wild blast
sweeps and swirls,
With the cold rain plashing over him, and the sods
on his golden curls!

Just a short week since we watched him, down on
the sunny shore,
And smiled to hear his ringing laugh blend with the
breakers' roar;
Just one short week—a start, a cry, a crash from
the falling cliff,
Ah, pretty lips closed dumb and dead, light feet
laid still and stiff.

Such a day to leave him! How his blue eyes
danced and shone,
And the colour glowed in his round cool cheek but
one brief week agone;
Hard he fared, and cold he slept, yet his little life
was joy;
Sea, sand, and sunshine Nature gave to bless our
bonnie boy.

Such a day to leave him! What though the parson
blest
The black earth where we put him down, what does
the child with rest?
He loved his life, and light, and play—they were
all the boon he had;
Yet few the tears he ever shed, the bold and blithe-
some lad.

It had not been so hard perhaps the narrow grave
    to make,
If the sea-gulls had been floating where the waves
    showed like a lake ;
If the daisies had been springing, and the kindly
    sunlight warm,
And the green grass waiting for him like a mother's
    sheltering arm.

But while the whole air thrills and throbs with the
    great sea's angry thunder,
And the Churchyard Head looks grimly on the white
    surf boiling under,
With the pale rank grasses shivering 'neath stinging
    hail and snow,
Our joyous, happy darling—it is hard to leave him
    so.

Well, God took him in his merriment, our God
    whose ways are wise ;
He is safe from cold and hunger, in his home there
    in the skies ;
But, oh, that the wild winds and waves would hush
    them for an hour,
While up upon the Head we leave our early-gathered
    flower.

OUT OF SIGHT.

The drifting snow piles white and soft above them,
  The rain drips wearily on sodden clay,
The keen frost brings his sharpest darts to prove
    them,
  The east wind wails through all the lonely day ;
And yet, through bitter morn, and bitterer night,
The roots grow slow and surely—out of sight.

Chilled by indifference, drowned deep in tears,
  Withered by coldness, stung by subtle doubt,
Crushed by the counsel of world-hardened years,
  By poverty's armed cohorts put to rout,
Silent and shy, still forcing to the light,
The pure dumb love is growing—out of sight.

And sweetest of all darlings of the Spring,
  The violet nestled in the quickset hedge ;
And dearest is the mystic marriage-ring,
  Of hard-tried constancy triumphant pledge ;
The sunniest morning crowns the roughest night,
The richest treasures ripen—out of sight.

PICTURES IN THE FIRE.

PICTURES in the fire, we were wont to find them ;
Pictures with our own bright dreams nestling close
    behind them ;
Pictures of heroic forms, knights on chargers pranc-
    ing,
Queens enthroned on listed fields, plumes like snow-
    flakes dancing ;
Warriors pacing long arcades, vowed to deeds of
    daring,
Warriors keeping watch to save maidens half de-
    spairing ;
Shadows of the tales that lead young blood to aspire
To the gallant 'times' we saw pictured in the fire.

Fast the years sped onward, soft the fancies grew,
  Soon they held one face alone, a face that smiled
    like you ;

And you would blush confessing, how at gloaming
    gazing,
I came riding, clear and plain, 'mid the embers
    blazing ;
While I loved to whisper, I saw gay figures pass,
With maidens showering snowy buds on a church-
    yard grass ;
Till you struck the logs apart, scattering priest and
    spire,
Lest I dared to name the bride pictured in the fire.

Closer, closer, darling ; ah, we both remember,
How beside the bright home hearth, in that far
    December,
We two sate together, silent for a space,
Till we saw the caverned coals shape a baby face.
O sweet hope that perished, like the feathery flame ;
O fair dream that never to happy substance came ;
Yet spite the minor chord that wails from faithful
    memory's lyre,
Have we not a peaceful life to picture in the fire ?

We have nearly reached our goal ; we have had our
    day ;
Laughed beside our New Year's hearth, plucked our
    buds in May ;
Worn our July roses, stored our autumn wheat,
Shared our joys and griefs to know, each in sharing
    sweet.
Now let us in the fire trace our youth again,
All its eager pleasures, all its passionate pain ;
And, like the leaping blaze we watch, ever striving
    higher,
Pass, leaving Love to frame of us pictures in the
    fire.

'A LARL HELP 'S WORTH A DEAL OF PITY.'

THERE speaks the Yorkshire heart. The race may
　　lack
　The quick lip-sympathy, the fluent speech,
　Whose easy sweetness rankling wounds may reach,
And leave the surface smoother for its track ;
But when the blow strikes home, who finds them
　　slack
　Firm at the writhing sufferer's side to stand,
　With eager help, with full and flowing hand,
Tender and strong, putting expression back
　With the shy silent pride, the northern dower?
　Let those who will prefer the fair frail flower,
Sprung in an hour, an hour's life to keep ;
Mine be the roots that strike, strong, still, and deep,
　To nourish the grave bloom whose innate power,
　Bright in the sun, endures through shade and
　　shower.

THE CURLEWS.

WHAT are they saying the whole day long,
　Over the Snook at Seaton Carew ;
The curlews, who flit with their pitiful song
　O'er the sand's tossed gold and the sea's tossed
　　blue ?
Calling for ever, wild and strange,
　Where Tees sweeps into the Northern main,
And the glittering 'stells,' and the link's long range,
　Rosy with sea pinks, and yellow with grain.

Do they tell of the time when the Yorkshire hills
　Lay careless of treasure-trove under the heath ;

When, unsmirched in their purity, sparkling rills
  Swept down from their crests to the river beneath?
Ere the black smoke sullied the sunny sky,
  And the clash of the hammer the silence broke,
And the steam shriek blent with the curlews' cry,
  And all the fair valley from slumber awoke.

Do they tell wild tales of gallant ships
  That struck on the terrible Longscar rocks,
Ere the furnace opened its glowing lips,
  And the great hill heaved to the blasters' shocks?
Do they sing how the fishermen, simple and brave,
  Led lonely lives in the cots on the sand,
Ere earth her golden secrets gave,
  And labour and commerce annexed the land?

Flitting, flitting, the whole day through,
  Through sun and shadow, through cloud and
      gleam,
Over the Snook at Seaton Carew
  The curlews pipe through my noon-day dream.
For they prized the rest on the Durham shore,
  Ere work and wealth their royalty proved;
And I sigh with the curlews, 'No more, no more,'
  In the sea-side haunt that my childhood loved.

CARE.

She took her care to the country:
She dreamt she might leave it to rest
Where the virginal jewels of Spring gleamed bright,
Primrose and snowdrop and aconite,
On the glad earth's fresh green breast.

But her sorrow lay black and dreary,
Enwreathed with the silent flowers;

She heard its wail in the wild birds' song,
She saw it lurking the buds among
In the wild-rose scented bowers.

She took her care to the city,
To the whirl and the stir of men;
She said, 'I will plunge in the eager strife,
The pleasure and business and battle of life,
It scarce can haunt me then.'

But oh! 'mid the loudest clamour,
She heard its dull cold call;
Mid the thrill of music, the spell of art,
In the gayest hall, in the busiest mart,
Its empire seized on all.

She took her care to the ocean:
She said, 'I will strive no more
To loosen its grasp on my heart and me,
But wait by the side of the homeless sea
Till life and its load is o'er.'

And lo! alone by the restless tide,
Uncalled for, her solace came;
The long low musical chant of the waves,
Hushed the cry that rose from the grassy graves,
Hushed memory, chafe, and blame.

A solemn patience, a quiet faith,
She learnt from the ceaseless chime,
For it sang for ever, 'neath sun and stars,
'Ah, fret not life, 'gainst thy prison bars,
God's love has conquered Time!'

THE LOUIS XV. CABINET.

See on the tarnished silver ring, the tiny twisted
    keys,
Open the quaint old panelled doors—nay, dear,
    choose which you please.
This where the snowy lily-wreath from the royal
    azure glows?
Or that where the cherub faces smile from the pale
    Dubarri rose?

They are rusted, the gilded hinges, but they yield,
    like Time to Fate.
Now, what are the hoarded treasures hid behind the
    jealous gate?
What a subtle perfume steals around! it has lurked
    for centuries long,
To spring to life like a memory of a long-past grief
    or wrong.

See a faded sword-knot, a painted fan, a broken
    string of pearls,
A miniature of a fair proud face, and a mass of
    golden curls;
Some letters—'tis from their yellowing lines the scent
    you spoke of steals;
And a jewelled watch with a pictured front, snapped
    spring and useless wheels.

We might weave a story—might we not?—from the
    graceful flotsam left,
Hidden away after life's wild storm, all purpose and
    meaning reft!

Look, the ribbon has a crimson stain, blurring its
    silken sheen,
That knight, by his eyes, would guard full well a
    pledge he had won, I ween.

Who severed those waving curls of his, with kisses,
    and vows, and tears?
They are soft and bright, though the head they
    crowned has been dust for weary years.
Was it she who flung those idle gauds in her pas-
    sionate grief away,
When they brought her knot, with its blood-red
    brand, back from the fatal fray?

Knowing his hand was cold indeed when another
    held her token;
Knowing that like this pretty toy the spring of her
    life was broken.
There, heap the hair on the letters; let them keep
    each mouldering fold,
Let us search no deeper the records left of the sins
    and sorrows of old.

Another cycle, and unborn eyes will glance o'er
    relics of us,
And light white fingers toss and turn our sacred
    trifles thus!
So true, and real, and sad they seem—love, struggle,
    fight, and fall.
Another cycle, and laughing lips may guess a tale
    of it all.

Leave the picture, and the poor pale pearls. Hush!
    Was it a long low sigh?
It is but the larches on the hill as the light wind
    shivers by.

That scent is like one in a room of death—ay, jest
    at so idle a whim.
Come out on the terrace. Frank is there : ill fan-
    cies fly fast from him.

IN THE COTTAGE.

OUTSIDE, the noonday flooding the glittering Northern
    sea,
The gay wind from the moorland down sweeping
    fresh and free,
With the sunlight streams on the 'greening gleams,'
    where the sea-mews wheel and flit,
And the abbey fair on the Churchyard Head, by its
    steady radiance lit,
And the breakers under the beetling cliffs singing
    their ceaseless tune,
Frank Nature holding jubilee in the royalty of June.

Inside, the darkened breathless room, the watchers
    round the bed,
Where on the fevered couch for aye tosses the rest-
    less head ;
Poor pretty head ! the tangled curls pushed from
    the heated face,
Which e'en one shadow cannot rob of youth's pathetic
    grace ;
Poor maiden lips that pant apart o'er every laboured
    breath,
Poor sweet blue eyes that faintly look into the stare
    of Death.

Ah, keen north air, so pure and strong our languid
    blood to stir,
Has all your bright vitality no wakening pulse for
    her?

.Ah, bounteous June, all warmth and glow and lavish
    beauty giving,
Have you no voice to call her back to bloom among
    the living?
See, the soft eyes brighten in reply through the
    gathering last eclipse :
'I am glad to go to Jesus !' falter the dying lips.

Aye, glad to go to Jesus! loved, loving, young and
    fair,
Unsaddened yet by sorrow, unworn by cark and care,
She turns from all our fair life gives to the richer
    life beyond,
She hears the angels call, and feels her inmost heart
    respond.
Ah, glories of our glorious world, how must they
    pale and dim,
When through the opening gates we catch a glimpse
    of Heaven and Him !

THE SQUIRE'S FUNERAL.

THE bright May morning o'er the village broke,
The sunshine glittering downward from the hill
Flooded the uplands, rich in elm and oak,
And lit the willows by the sparkling rill.
The rill, through moor and meadow broadening on,
Till the long plain in the blue distance seen,
Felt the great river clasp her like a zone,
Flowing majestic hollow banks between.

But where, a tiny beck, it crossed the glade,
The old square tower in the churchyard kept
A solemn wardage, where, 'neath sun or shade,
The ' rude forefathers of the hamlet ' slept.

Green waved the grasses, softly blushed the flowers,
Where on 'God's Acre' Spring's sweet smile shone
    bright,
But close beneath the shadow of the towers,
One gloomy vault yawned open to the light.

The gay wind shook the poplar's hoary leaves,
And waved the tall laburnum's golden hair,
And crept beneath the elm-tree's rustling eaves,
And tossed the lime's rich perfume in the air.
Yet on the breezy morn a shadow lay,
A strange hushed tremor through the village ran ;
The very children stilled their wonted play,
Each woman wept, pale stood each stalwart man.

From the wide portals of the Manor-house,
Poured out a long procession, two by two,
Winding beneath the oak-trees' mighty rows,
And the quaint storied shapes of ancient yew.
And in the midst a chosen gray-haired band,
Bore a dark burthen draped in velvet pall,
While as it passed each trembling hand claspt hand,
And a low sob broke from the hearts of all.

And stroke by stroke high o'er the mourning crowd
Boomed the deep music of the passing bell,
Till the grave priest spoke solemnly aloud,
The glorious promise of our hope to tell.
'I am the resurrection and the life,'
Through breathing silence rang the noble words,
Arresting woe in its despairing strife,
Touching to trembling faith the stricken chords.

And so they laid ' the Squire ' to his rest,
While aged men who nursed him on their knee,

And babes still clinging to the mother's breast,
Bent o'er the vault, as if the last to see
Of him, whose kindly voice no more could cheer;
Of him, whose open hand was closed at last;
Of him, whose stainless name will linger here,
Honoured and loved while year by year rolls past.

Sleep 'mid thy fathers, sleep, O kindly dust,
Back to the earth from whence we come returned.
Soar, gentle spirit, to the Heaven we trust
Thy faithful love for Christ our Lord has earned.
The poor man's blessing long will crown thy name;
Thy friends revere thy memory, true and brave;
Thy kindred's yearning grief thy worth proclaim,
Undying flowers to wreathe thy quiet grave.

OUR VILLAGE.

Along the old accustomed paths with musing steps
    we go,
The green trees arch above our heads, and every
    branch we know;
The meadow has its tale for us, the lane its storied
    hour,
Companions in each hedge we hail, a friend in
    every flower.

The headstones by the grassy graves bear old
    familiar names,
Each, as we glance them idly o'er, its flash of
    memory claims,
There, a sweet touch of pathos wakes, here, loving
    laughter tells,
On some quaint long recorded trait the roused re-
    membrance dwells.

The little child that gazes up, with wide blue wistful
    eyes,
Unconscious of what charm for us in their soft lustre
    lies,
Will answer with her mother's smile, or in her
    father's voice,
And in the accent to whose ring our hearts can still
    rejoice.

The cottage doors are shut that ne'er closed to our
    steps of yore,
Beside the evening hearth they talk of us and ours
    no more,
Oh sad, and strange, and hard it seems, there are
    so few to greet,
As slow and silently we trace the winding village
    street!

Yet, half forgotten as we stand, amid the haunts of
    youth,
The golden past asserts for us its strength of love
    and truth,
Though other pathways woo us now, and other
    boons may bless,
The home that childhood's halo crowned claims
    separate tenderness.

THE OLD HOME.

THE roof-tree stands as ever it stood, the jasmine
    stars the wall,
The great Westeria's purple blooms o'er dark gray
    gables fall,

The roses that our mother loved blush 'neath her
    window sill,
And the clematis our father trained droops, as he
    taught it, still.

The August sunset lights the panes where we were
    wont to watch
Its rays of crimson and of gold on baby brows to
    catch,
On the wall where your first nest we found, the
    grand old ivy waves,
As when we chose a shoot to plant upon our
    sacred graves.

The thrushes that we paused to hear are dead long
    summers gone,
Yet the sweet rose thicket echoes now to the self-
    same ringing tone,
The flowers a fuller glory show, and the trees a
    deepened shade,
Naught else on Nature's face is changed, since here
    of yore we played.

Naught else on Nature's face. O life, can ever
    seasons pass
And leave our hearts renewed as fair and bright as
    meadow grass?
Death's icy shadow rests for us, on the home that
    once was ours,
We see through tears the bairns that sport among
    our childhood's flowers.

The stranger's shadow flits across our old familiar
    floors,
The stranger's footstep as of right seeks our old
    open doors,

With a dim sense of loss and wrong, like one from
    death returned,
We look on all for which for years our faithful fond-
    ness yearned.

Better to keep the fancy sketch of all it used to be,
Better than blurring by the truth the hues of memory!
Oh, earth has no abiding place, but the mighty Word
    is given,
No cloud, or care, or change will vex the countless
    homes of Heaven!

SONNET.

THIS facile faculty of ready rhyme,
This gift, if such a word were not too great,
That always finds a measured word to chime,
That always can beguile a weary time,
On every wilful mood content to wait;
They tell me I should hold it dear; in sooth,
I prize in age, just as I loved in youth,
The sweet companion of my lonely hours,
The voice that hails my joy and weeps my ruth,
The hand that twines my idle dreams with flowers;
Yet reading, as I paused to read to-night,
Clear set in noble words, a Master's thought,
I seemed, in sudden scorn, to judge aright
The feeble follies that myself had wrought.

And shall I therefore hush the chirp of song
That has so lightened life's rough road for me,
And care no more my fancies to prolong
In music, which if neither true nor strong,
Yet has some humble charm of melody?

Nay, shall no linnet twitter softly still,
Because the nightingale's rich warblings thrill
The passionate pulses in the hearts of all?
Because the eagle, clanging from his hill
Wakens world echoes with his royal call?
Through my own quiet woodland nook, apart,
Pleasing no ear but Love's, my lays shall rise,
Shaping each vague emotion of the heart,
Shrining each chance and change of earth and skies.

CONTENT.

FROM their raised seats above the mud and dust
The favoured darlings of the world look down,
Where the dense throng who live 'neath Fortune's
    frown
Press onward, footsore, wearied, baffled, crushed,
From the front ranks by stronger pilgrims thrust;
Look, wearing each the easy birthright crown,
Won by nor labour, genius, or renown,
Saying to tired strugglers, ' hope and trust,
Bear patiently the trials of the road:
We too, have thorns among our blushing flowers;
Fair seeming though the gifts by life bestowed,
There still are shadows on each path of ours;
Take such rare gleams as to your ways are sent,
And show through all the beauty of content!'

Content! O you who never feel or know
The frets and stings your poorer brethren bear,
You, with your lives all sweet, and full, and fair,
You, on whose guarded heads no winds may blow,
Pause, just a moment ere you counsel so.

You, with no need to plan, to save, to spare;
You, who can call the needy in to share;
You, who can raise the weak and heal the blow,
Nor ever miss the bounty you bestow;
Winning the blessing-prayers of all around
By the great luxury, lavish power to give;
Who, though some bitter in your cup is found,
Have all gold brings to grace each hour you live:
Wait till some fold of your rich robe is rent,
Ere you so glibly preach to us content!

BY THE RIVER.

ANGRY rushed the river, swollen high with rain,
Tossing on its mimic waves many a foam-flecked
    stain ;
Onward rushed the river, chafing in its course,
From tiny foss and tribute beck gathering depth and
    force ;
Through the quivering arches, 'neath the giant trees,
Past the gazing villages, by the golden leas,
Angry rushed the river to the northern seas.

Where beside the river frowns the gray old keep,
Watching long-forgotten graves, where its masters
    sleep ;
Gazing on the river sate the lonely lady,
Red gold hair and sad sweet lips, down-dropt eye-
    lids steady ;
Sable robes stirred languidly by the wailing breeze ;
What utterances hears she? what vision forms and
    flees
On the angry river, rushing to the seas?

Pictured on the river scenes of childhood pass,
The old home, lost for ever, smiles as once it was;
Whispering with the river tender voices speak,
Could she hear those tones indeed, Death's dumb
  laws must break!
Worn heart and tired spirit lulled to dreamful ease,
She sits beneath the odorous limes, with their swarm-
  ing bees,
Beside the angry river rushing to the seas.

O calm hour by the river, when do such moments
  last?
No lotus soothes us long away from the ' dreadful
  past';
The eyes that watch the river, tears dim their
  wistful smile,
No more spell of sound or sight Grief's hard claims
  beguile;
Like the heavy hearse-plumes wave the sombre trees,
Like the dirge above the dead sobs the autumn breeze,
Sweeping o'er the river rushing to the seas.

A SKETCH.

Our cottage crests the summit of a hill
  That rises o'er an old cathedral town.
There float through summer noontides, warm and
    still,
  Rare scents of heather from the purple down;
There the sweet April shadows glance and play,
  There autumn's glory glows from golden leas,
And the wild north winds of the winter's day
  Bring keen fresh waftings from the far-off seas.

Through the calm July evenings sunsets blush,
  Where the dark woods sweep round the glittering
      river,
Through the rich silence of the country hush,
  We hear the soft rain 'mid the grasses shiver.
Our little garden like a jewel gleams,
  Full, like a cup, of bright old homely flowers,
And through the breath of breeze-wooed roses streams
  The bells' faint clashing from the minster towers.

Lingering at nightfall by the lonely house,
  'Mid jasmine stars in dark-green foliage set,
And tall white lilies in majestic rows,
  And fragrant musk, and dewy mignonette,
In the deep valley, one by one, we see
  The humble town put out its lingering lights,
While the great towers that face us solemnly,
  Take up their brooding vigil with the night's.

We muse how every separate homestead bears
  Its separate crown of joy, or cross of sorrow,
Ere taking our own weight of hopes or cares,
  To court their brief oblivion till the morrow;
The morrow, which to cottage, grange, or hall,
  Brings twelve long hours, each fraught with weal
      or woe,
Ah! gather present peace, thank God for all:
  Most, that no future we are given to know.

SAINT BRIDGET'S WELL.

Down in the bosky hollow, by the old cathedral
    town
That stands with the hoary minster towers as its
    ancestral crown,

Down where amid the broad oak boughs and the
    shadow of the limes
Softly at morn and evensong float the sweet re-
    current chimes,
Where the steady drip we hear to-day through the
    bygone ages fell,
Half hid by fern and woodbine gleams Saint
    Bridget's blessèd well.

See where the steps of pilgrims have worn a mazy
    path
Through tangled brier and wreathing root, to the
    holy spring beneath;
See how the stony margin is wellnigh kissed
    away
By the pious lips of those who sought its grace in
    the elder day!
Ah, lovers whisper and children sport beside the
    waters now,
Saint Bridget hears no penitent and shrines no
    votary's vow.

We tell her tale and boast her deeds, we dwellers
    by the spot,
As those who know the ancient tale they prize but
    hallow not;
E'en as our mighty Wilfrid's fame still lingers
    round the towers
He made his own, when Yorkshire strength clashed
    with the Danish powers;
Float on above us, O sweet saints, keep gentle
    wardage yet
Round us the careless heirs of all we should not
    quite forget.

But there is one whose patient steps still haunt
    Saint Bridget's shrine,
With yearning eyes that seem to seek lost light they
    held divine;
The years have touched the sparse gray hair and
    thinned the hollow cheek,
Those poor pale lips are all unfit youth's rosy
    hopes to speak;
Why should she, through the April gleam, June
    glow, and autumn mist,
And Winter's bitter tempest come to keep her lonely
    tryst?

She dips her feeble fingers in the sparkling of the
    spring,
She gathers creeping ivy, round her grizzled locks
    to cling,
And ever more the weary eyes are gazing down
    the road,
Where in the glory of his prime the coming lover
    strode;
Ah since upon the winding way that eager footstep
    fell,
How many a season's shine and shade have passed
    Saint Bridget's well.

She does not heed the flying time; the merciful con-
    fusion
That swept o'er heart and brain maintains its sunny,
    sad illusion.
In every passing foot she hears the music that will
    come,
In every rustling sound she hails the accents that
    are dumb.

And when the violets spring to life, and the lark
    sings clear and strong,
Her heart beats welcome to the clasp for which it
    aches so long.

None know the maniac's story, none guess for whom
    she waits,
Where the lush grasses climb and weave round Saint
    Bridget's crumbling gates,
Nor question why she starts and weeps when through
    the boskage swells
The low melodious clangour of the minster's vesper
    bells,
But happy pairs, late lingering, ere the last farewell
    is kissed,
Will sigh and smile to watch her, as she keeps her
    faithful tryst.

THE CYCLAMEN.

Unloved, uncared for, young, and poor,
On the fair Italian plain,
The shepherd mourned for his wasted youth,
His baffled hope, his unsought truth,
His fancies ending in wrong or ruth,
His bright dreams, dreamed in vain.

'See,' said a pitying fairy,
'See this purple cyclamen,
Breathe its sweet breath, and wishes three
My mystic power shall give to thee;
Wilt thou come, joy-crowned, to say to me,
That the world is brighter then?'

The boy bent over the blossom;
'Let me be gay,' he said;

But a soulless, mirthless laughter rung
From the lips so dewy, and fresh, and young,
The spirit of joy shunned the noisy tongue,
The glory of joy was fled.

The boy turned angrily to the flower,
'Let me be loved,' he sighed;
And a golden head was upon his breast,
And soft tones murmured of passionate rest.
Yet, though Beauty gave her richest and best,
His want was unsupplied.

He dashed away the mocking wreath,
He turned from the surface smile;
'Ah, the cup of gladness is not for me,
Let others be loved, and happy, and free,
Let the poor and lonely be blessed,' said he,
'And I shall rejoice the while.'

And lo, the laugh rang sweet and clear,
O'er that patient wish of his;
Mirth hasted her harvest to unbind,
And love to him who loved his kind
Came pure and frank; so from self resigned
He won the self-less bliss.

FORGET ME NOT.

Forget me not, forget me not; great seas between
    us roll,
With absence like a broadening gulf, dividing soul
    from soul;
Our footsteps in each others' lives fade yet and yet
    more faint,
Each day must fancy harder strive each hourly task
    to paint;

New troubles jar the onward road, new customs shape
    the lot,
New sunbeams gild the stranger skies ; but still,
    forget me not.

Round separate poles, slow perfecting, the separate
    spheres revolve ;
I share not now your battle day, nor strengthen
    your resolve ;
New hands must pluck the sweet new blooms that
    grace my garden ground,
And I must wear the alien wreaths, or sit, alone,
    uncrowned ;
The slow diverging footsteps pass by every well-
    known spot,
The great world changes, plans, aspires ; but you,
    forget me not.

Because though Time's gray lichens creep, and hide,
    and moulder thus,
One spell its poison cannot reach lives strong and
    pure for us ;
For as for both the July glow fades into gray
    November,
To me, me only you can turn, with 'Dear, do you
    remember ?'
By April's haloing golden youth, defying rust or rot,
By memory's holy power I say, you shall forget me
    not !

THE BOATS.

A BOAT upon the margin of the waves,
With fluttering flag and ready cordage lies,
Waiting the tide that softly round her laves,
And the low winds that linger in the skies,

Waiting, to dance across the waters wide,
With snowy sails that, filling in the breeze,
Will bear her in her careless, joyous pride,
Like some glad living thing upon the seas.

Another, where dead weed and yellow foam,
Tell where the breakers pause, their goal attained,
With bulwarks stove just as she staggered home,
And canvas torn, and timbers rent and strained,
Lies, shattered from the perils she has passed,
Yet still her innate strength and power are there ;
Repaired, renewed, once more she 'll meet the blast,
Prompt her brave part through storm and strife to
        bear.

But oh, the third ! hauled where the sea-pinks grow,
And the dry rushes shiver in the sand;
Where the salt spray, when fierce north-easters blow,
Whirls in wild embassy across the land ;
Where sun-burnt babies roll upon the turf,
And climb about her, rots the poor old boat,
Never again to breast the snowy surf,
Or spread her broad brown wings and dart afloat.

O daring youth, all eager for the launch,
Who sees the sea so calm, the wind so sweet ;
O manhood, tossed and torn, yet true and staunch,
Ready, with fresh-healed wounds, new wars to meet ;
For both, for both, the years are flying fast,
To the hushed rest of age all footsteps tend.
Reap joy from sunshine, wisdom from the blast,
And so, in trust and patience, wait the end.

HER.

I STROVE, I did, to save her;
  Not a better ship could be,
Ere she had, what I reckon would wear us all,
  Twenty long years at sea.

We 've not much to love, we sailors,
  That live our lives afloat;
Dearer than many hold wife or bairns
  I loved the brave old boat.

Had you heard her striving and straining
  In the long Pacific wave;
I know my own heart felt a pang
  For every groan she gave.

Her timbers were half on 'em rotten,
  Her bolts had never a head ;
Her canvas hung like useless rags,
  Her cargo weighed like lead.

While sea and sky together
  Met in a whirling haze,
'Mid roaring waves and howling winds,
We could scarce tell nights from days.

She laboured, the poor old Betsy,
  While the mighty rollers swept
O'er gunwale, and helm, and dripping deck;
  'Twas a weary watch we kept.

I 'd fain, for sake of my mates and her,
  Just have done my best with a prayer;
Yet, as I strove to save her,
  I could not but wish out there

That they who 'd sent us all to die,
  The good old ship and her crew,
And sate at home and counted their gains,
  Had half our work to do.

Could know the desperate struggle,
  The hunger, and thirst, and cold.
Well, maybe things may be righted yet
  When the whole log comes to be told.

We! oh, we got us afloat on a raft;
  There were three who sank with her,
And Bill dropped off the freezing planks,
  With never a moan or stir.

And Jack died just as we rounded the Horn,
  And sighted a sail at last;
When they flung us a rope, we 'd hardlings strength
  To catch and hold it fast.

We left the Betsy where the bergs
  Take many an eerie shape,
Down in the depths of the angry seas
  That surge about the Cape.

I say it was by no 'act of God,'
  But by greed of man she were lost.
Aye, the spirits of many a murdered ship
  Rave stormily round the coast!

SING, SING.

Sing, sing, my darling, my darling;
  Sing in a voice like your father's of old;
Sing, with the light in the brown eyes awaking,
  Like his when they shone o'er the tale that he
    told.

Sing, sing, my darling, my darling;
  Sing in the glow of your glorious youth;
Sing, like the great silver trumpets that echo,
  For the battles of country, or honour, or truth.

Sing, sing the old ringing ballad
  That tells of the deeds of the chivalric days,
When men fought for a rosebud or died for a banner,
  And held life well lost for a pure woman's praise.

Sing, sing the sweet lover fancy,
  The song sung erewhile in the gloaming for me.
Ah, little the listener thought in her gladness
  How like a low death-bell that measure could be!

Sing, sing! What does youth with remembrance?
  It wears the wild rose while we cherish the yew.
But oh, in the autumn we prize the spring breezes:
  October may love what but April can do.

Sing, sing, my darling, my darling;
  And I—why, I turn from my sadness to heed,
While the happy young voice and the eager young
     fingers
  Soothe the heart that still rankles, the wounds that
     still bleed.

THE OLD ROOM.

Do the moonbeams glint through its windows now,
  Bright as they did of yore,
To light the cluster of lily-bells,
  The lilies I tend no more?
Does the jasmine climb round the casement yet,
  With one vagrant tendril peeping,

To see, deep sunk in her downy nest,
  The mistress who train'd it sleeping?
And oh, what hangs o'er the mantel now,
  Whence a calm proud face look'd down,
With lips that could smile so tenderly,
  With eyes that could flash or frown?

What volumes range on the oaken shelf,
  Where Tennyson sang of old,
Where Dickens stood with his genial laugh,
  Where Carlyle's grand thunder roll'd?
Does order rule on the table now,
  Where papers were wont to heap,
Mid fair quaint toys and open books,
  With a rosebud the place to keep?
And in the old gilded secrétaire
  Have they found in the hid recess
The token whose meaning, well I ween,
  There is none save I can guess?

Death's heavy hand struck sudden and strong
  All the links of a life to sever;
And we were parted, my room and I,
  Were parted, and oh, for ever!
It is all such a trifle; and there is enough,
  Too real, God knows, in the world;
No time to pause to snatch at a leaf,
  In the wild life-current hurl'd!
Only just sometimes, when I dream awhile,
  In the midnight when all is still,
I muse how my room is looking then,
  In the moonbeams weird and chill.

AMONG THE SAND-HILLS.

SILENCE among the sand-hills.
  Only the ceaseless roar,
The thundering roll of the sullen surge,
As lashed by the black north-easter's scourge,
  It crashes upon the shore.

Quiet among the sand-hills.
  Only the sea-mews fly,
Blending their shrill unceasing wail
With the ominous sob of the rising gale,
  Flitting 'twixt sea and sky.

Dreary among the sand-hills.
  The great gray sweep of waves,
As cold and as dull as the heavy sorrow,
That seems from the scene new strength to borrow,
  To reckon the past's thick graves.

Lonely among the sand-hills.
  In a helpless, hopeless woe,
While the wild birds cry and the wild winds moan,
And the white surf creeps over sand and stone,
  And the great tides ebb and flow.

THE DYING WRECKER.

THE parson needn't darken my door; there 's time
    enough for him
When my hand can lift the can no more, and my
    sight is waxing dim.
Just put a pillow beneath my head, and hold me up
    the glass;
For all that the sea keeps calling me, I 'll not die
    this bout, my lass.

Thou 'lt sit by me a bit to-night ?—'tis the tenth of
    March once more :
Hark how the wild winds wail and howl, and the
    great waves crash on the shore.
There might be a vessel out in the haze, where the
    reef lies under the foam ;
But there 's never a light in a lattice now, to wile
    the mariners home.

Give us hold of the watch and the golden case. I
    promised, to day 's a year,
I 'd tell their tale, so thou 'd stay and keep thy
    grandad company here.
It 's fit to scare a man, to sit by the drift-wood fire
    alone,
Till he hears the billows shriek for help, the gale for
    mercy moan.

'Twas a black and bitter night like this, just fifty
    years ago ;
The breakers churned and frothed like yeast, the wind
    was thick with snow.
We drove the old horse with his lantern out, and
    we cowered beneath the crags ;
And a brave ship drove on the cruel reef, where
    the white surf veils the jags.

Not a plank could live, I tell thee—we knew naught
    of lifeboats then—
We had bairns to keep, and bread to get ; we were
    hungry desperate men.
It didn't hurt them, dead and drowned, if we dragged
    their chests to land,
And fought and strove 'mid the angry sea for the
    prizes on the sand.

I thought he was gone—I hope I did; yet I never
    can sleep and dream
But I see his bold fair face, and watch his blue
    eyes' opening gleam;
And the wound in his breast ; I know I struck—I
    had snatch'd old Tommy's dirk;
And hearts were hot and hands were quick when
    the wreckers were at work.

His fingers were tight around the case : I hack'd
    them to get it free.
Don't open it, lass—it got stain'd with blood; and
    such stain will bide, dost see?
It 's only the picture of a girl; and Bill had a purse
    of gold;
And Black Jim had blue and yellow stones to stitch
    in his jersey's fold.

They all had better luck than I. I say the woman
    was dead,
When I caught the watch and push'd her back; if
    the water coloured red,
There were plenty torn 'mid the hard sharp rocks;
    and plenty as keen to keep
The harvest sown by the wild north blast for hands
    like ours to reap.

I 'll give thee case and watch, my wench, so thou 'lt
    swear to make my grave
Where never can come the call of the surf, nor the
    thunder of the wave;
I could not wait in my coffin, if I heard that choking
    cry
That in every tide, for fifty years, has rung to the
    gray March sky.

Shall I see them in the other place, where the parson
    says is rest;
Her with the bruise on her forehead, or him with
    the stab in his breast?
If I do, mayhap they'll forgive me; for a bitter
    penance I've done
Since, in the fierce March hurricane, the wrecker's
    prize was won.

WHITBY BELLS.

FULL and sweet, and clear and shrill,
  When the bright day breaks and the sun sinks
    down,
While the quaint old church on the windy hill;
  Looks solemnly over the little town,
Telling of weal and telling of woe,
  Calling to benison, praise and prayer,
While ever the great waves come and go,
  And their thunder booms through the summer air:
While the wild wind wails through the ruins gray,
The bells ring out over Whitby Bay.

When the breeze blows soft from the flowery land,
  Bringing us breath of the tedded hay,
And the foam creeps silently over the sand,
  The golden sand where the children play.
When the sea-gull floats on his idle wing,
  And the fishes dart through the clear green waves,
And the long brown sea-weeds wreathe and cling
  Round the rugged cliffs and the hollow caves,
'God bless the bride,' we smile and say,
As the glad peal echoes o'er Whitby Bay.

When the sun sinks down by the headland grim,
  And the great sea blushes his last good night;
When the Abbey arches stand pale and dim,
  And the ships at sea show a flickering light;
When we linger under the shadowy cliffs,
  While the gloaming darkens along the shore,
And count the sails of the home-bound skiffs,
  And hearken the long unceasing roar,
We know that a soul has passed away
For the death-bell tolls over Whitby Bay.

When the broad bright breast of the Northern Sea,
  Laughs in the light of the summer sun,
And the rippling wavelets dance in glee
  As they break on the shingle, one by one.
While up through the red roofs of the town,
  Like a long bright ribbon the people climb
Up the steep stone steps to the breezy down,
  Where the headstones gleam 'mid the purple thyme,
We know it is God's calm sabbath day
As the sweet chimes ring over Whitby Bay.

So clear and full their music swells
  As we listen and muse where the great waves foam,
Bringing us dreams of far-off bells
  That ring through the leafy lanes at home;
Of the old gray tower and winding walk,
  And the roses that grew by the river side,
Of the meadow stroll, and the Sunday talk,
  'Ere the cable was cut and the voyage tried;
Till the idle tears that for ever rise,
As the heart turns back to its earliest ties,
Dim the glory of sky and sea away
As the bells ring out over Whitby Bay.

ABSIT OMEN.

I KNEW the scent of the hawthorn,
As I loitered along the hedges;
I knew the breath of the violet,
From its nest in the mossy ledges;
I saw the flash of the marigold,
Down in the glistening sedges;
And as I looked and lingered, alone in the sunny field,
Over the uplands, clear and sad, the notes of a death-
bell pealed.

Over the emerald grasses
Crept the vivid green of spring;
April spoke in the bursting buds,
And shone in the darting wing:
'Life and the year are waking up,'
I heard the woodlark sing;
Each golden hour as it passed, token of hope re-
vealing,
Over the uplands clear and sad, the bell's deep note
was pealing.

As a sorrow all unthought of
Falls upon happy hours;
As a bitter blight at midnight,
Strikes on autumnal bowers;
As the forked head of the viper
Starts up 'mid heather flowers,
So, through the new-born gladness, flooding the
sunny field,
Sudden, distant, and ominous, the solemn death-bell
pealed.

Yet I turned not from the beauty
Of air, and sky, and earth,
Though fate, in ghastly majesty,
Glared warning on their mirth;
Snowdrops and pure pale primroses
Were springing from winter's dearth,
And God, who in His Only Son our great redemp-
tion sealed,
Types life to come in the sweet spring world o'er
which the death-bell pealed.

ON THE BALCONY.

THE great bow-window of my sunny room
    Hangs o'er the heights that guard the Northern Sea,
Where, through the noontide glow and midnight
        gloom,
    It sings its mighty mournful song to me;
Its aspect, ever glorious, ever grand,
    Suits each fresh mood that marks the lonely day,
Now rippling in bright dimples on the sand,
    Now rolling foam-fleck'd breakers up the bay.

From my low couch upon the balcony
    I watch the full tides as they ebb and flow;
I watch the other stream, humanity,
    Flood the broad terrace on the cliffs below:
There, while the music peals through gloaming's hour,
    And graceful robes go floating down the walk,
I catch the scent of many a summer flower
    And sweet low murmurings of happy talk.

Through my barr'd screen I see and hear it all,
    Blent with the wave's bright face and deepening
        voice,

Till the soft splendour of the evenfall
  Bids my dim vigil with the world rejoice;
My childhood lives in those bright darting elves,
  My girlhood lingers with each lingering pair;
Crush'd health and ruin'd hopes assert themselves,
  And claim affiance with the gay throngs there.

And through and over all the ocean says:
  'Ye mortals, come and go, and laugh and weep;
I, only I, the ancient of the days,
  My solemn, changeless, changing courses keep.
Your flowers spring to blossom on your graves,
  Your snows lie deep where fresh fruits fade away;
Hush, hush, and patience,' sing the eternal waves;
  'Death does but garner for the endless day.'

Forgetful of the iron bars that fate
  Has raised between me and yon joyous life,
My spirit sweeps aside the envious grate,
  To take its portion in the eager strife.
Ah, the cold metal jars the fever'd touch,
  Back to their bonds the rebel fancies shrink;
Yet do I thank the hour that gave so much,
  Even for one twilight sweet the mimic link.

THE LAST.

Never the patter of baby feet upon the shining
    floors;
Never the rustle of maidens' robes in the long rich
    corridors;
Never a bold boy's whistle to ring through the silent
    room;
Never the thrill of a girlish laugh, like a sun-ray in
    the gloom.

Nothing to break the order that reigns in the gilt
    saloon,
Through morning glimmer, or gloaming hush, or
    sultry haze of noon ;
Nothing to break the stillness of the great ancestral
    house,
That lies 'mid its statued terraces, smooth lawns, and
    oaken boughs.

In the proud painted gallery, the portraits hang on
    the wall,
You may trace the haughty smile on the lip, the
    dark eyes' glance in all.
Ah, lovely lady ! ah, gallant knight ! ah, beauty and
    valour free !
The last pale leaf hangs fluttering upon the moulder-
    ing tree.

He stormed the breach at Ascalon, at Cœur de
    Lion's side ;
He held a pass in Wensleydale against Cromwell in
    his pride ;
She saved her House's honour in a day of desperate
    fight,
For her fearless frown and wooing voice made every
    serf a knight.

Now, shut in the dim east parlour, fragile, and white,
    and old,
The one lone scion of their line waits till her hour
    is told ;
The flickering of the dying flame just shown in the
    chiselled face,
And the quiet pride of her low sweet tones, the Last
    of all her Race.

Do the spirits of the glorious past come whispering
    round her there?
Do they peep from the oriel's glowing glass, or lean
    on the tapestried chair?
Do they speak from the blazoned breviary, that lies
    at the lady's side?
Or hide by the hearth where the mighty logs pile
    in the chimney wide?

Or does there lurk in the pensive blue of the wist-
    ful childless eyes
A yearning for what she has never known, the
    sweet home-paradise,
For the husband's shelter, the household warmth,
    the clinging of childish hands,
The tender fireside gladness that true woman un-
    derstands?

Who knows? The daughters of her house made
    never public moan ;
Sorrow, or wrong, or bitterness, if they bore, they
    bore alone.
The wild winds moan around her towers, the snow
    heaps park and chase,
And there, in her stately solitude, sits the Last of
    all her Race.

FAIN.

The days in the golden meadows, where the cowslip
    and crowsfoot shone,
'Mid the falling fairy shadows of April's cloud and
    sun,

The walks by the vernal hedges, with orchis and
    speedwell gay,
And vetches that lit the hedges, that fringed the
    willows gray ;
Fain, fain would I roam again,
Where those flowers bloomed and that river rolled,
    But I am old.

The hours of joyous dreamings, beneath the twilight
    sky,
The sweet transparent seemings, hid smile, and down-
    cast eye ;
The eves of happy lingering, beneath the summer
    moon,
When Love's own hand was fingering the lute that
    breathed his tune ;
Fain, fain would I feel again,
How the pulse beat then, that throbs so cold,
    Now I am old.

The spell of glorious vision, of freedom and renown,
Of life in lands Elysian, pure law, and righteous
    crown ;
The charm of noble fancies, of courage and of fame,
The debonnaire romances, that rose around a name ;
Fain, fain would I build again
Those castles, that seemed all virgin gold ;
    But I am old.

The joyous noon-day glory pales to the eventide,
And from the thrilling story drops all the truth and
    pride ;
Youth did but dream his mission, love did but trust
    a myth,
And faith but framed a vision for joy to trifle with ;

Fain, fain would I hope again,
But the glamour is past, the tale is told,
   And I am old.

MAY LEAVES.

Sweet May leaves! fair May leaves,
   Stainless and bright in their vivid dress,
   Fresh in their pure young loveliness,
  Growing as gaily on oak-tree tall,
  As on violet roots 'neath the mossy wall,
  Decking the coigns of the lordly hall,
Like the lowly cottage eaves.

Glittering leaves, Spring's radiant crown,
   To wear a darker livery soon,
   For the parting smile of lingering June,
  To burgeon richer and fuller still,
  When August has his bounteous will,
  And of warmth and colour earth drinks her fill,
On dell and dale and down.

Sweet May leaves, on fairy stems,
   With the fitful sunlights upon their green,
   Like golden flecks on the emerald's sheen.
  To flash and deepen to gorgeous tints,
  When October's fiery sunset glints,
  On the mighty forests his finger prints
In hues like a monarch's crown.

Fresh young leaves, Spring's heralds shy,
   Alas, that a life so sweet is brief!
   The doom is on every fragile leaf.
  November's wailing winds will sweep,
  Their fading pride in a rustling heap,
  Ere winter's kindly snows drift deep,
'Neath the gaunt trees where they lie.

Yet, sweet May leaves, brave May leaves,
   Your dark days done, you blossom again,
   To gladden and glorify hill and plain.
  Our dead loves never fresh springs restore.
  Lost hopes, spent youth, may return no more,
  One pre-doomed round of his seasons four,
All man and his heart achieves.

MISSING, THE BARQUE 'LECTA' OF WHITBY, TEN HANDS ALL TOLD.

Missing, three weeks and more, missing from life
   and light,
The sea roars up through the bay, the dim suns rise
   and set;
Missing; the long days pass, the stars gleam out in
   the night,
Hot eyes strain over the Roads, no sign of the
   vessel yet.

The glass falls down and down, the big clouds pack
   in the west,
The fierce north-easter sweeps over the angry
   waves,
And ghastly dreams creep in to fever the mother's
   rest,
And wives and sisters shrink as the gale past the
   cottage raves.

Missing, three weeks and more; yet children must
   be fed,
Little they reck how fast the tears fall over the
   plate;

Will the sailor's strong brown hand yet pay for his
    babies' bread,
Or does it toss in the deep, a toy for the sole and
    the skate?

Ten hands; aye, Hal is there. Hal with his drowned
    father's eyes,
And Willie, so proud to pace the deck with a
    master's tread;
And George, whose sweetheart waits, tears fading
    her cheeks' rose dyes,
It is three weeks past already, the day they had
    fixed to wed.

Ten hands; and the curt phrase means just ten
    brave human lives;
Ten centres of household love, husband, brother and
    son,
Who each for his own at home suffers and dares
    and strives;
Hark! was it the echoing surf, or the boom of the
    minute gun?

Better almost to see the rocket leap from the land,
And the lifeboat shooting out amid the flash and the
    foam;
And the ship on the cruel reef, and clinging to spar
    and strand;
Men face to face with death, with death, so close to
    home.

Better almost to know the last long voyage over,
Done the danger and labour, struggle and tempest
    past;

That safe in God's quiet Haven rest husband, child,
    and lover,
While we wait on for a little to join them all at last;

Than to madden here in silence, while under the
    low, gray sky
The wild winds wail and moan, and the wild waves
    lash the shore;
To weep, and pray, and listen, while the long hours
    weary by,
And still the ship is missing, missing three weeks
    and more.

NAMELESS GRAVES.

Some one's heart is wearying for those who lie so still,
In the churchyard on the seaboard, in the shadow
    of the hill;
Some one's eyes are watching for those who will
    not come,
Some one's ears are aching for the tones for ever
    dumb.

Some one lying sleepless, in the watches of the
    night,
While the angry surf is calling below the beacon
    height,
Was praying in the sickness of a yearning hope
    deferred,
While the light wind o'er the nameless graves the
    birchen branches stirred.

Some one, through the hours of the long sweet sum-
    mer day,
Paused amid full life's busy fret, to gaze across the bay,

A sudden ship might loom in sight o'er the bright
    heave of the waves;
And the mocking sunlight glittered upon the name-
    less graves.

Some one thinks, if only she knew his place of rest,
If she could but shower kisses on the turf that
    marked his breast,
If she could but lose the horror of the haunting
    tossing deep;
And strange hands train the roses where the name-
    less lie asleep.

Some one watching languidly the sea-gull's swoop
    and flit,
And the dark blue rollers breaking to foaming silver
    lit ;
Never knows how they are telling her, how long ago
    they bore
The dead drowned sailor to his grave, upon a far-
    off shore.

Some one passing slowly to a desolate old age,
Will never read the characters on fate's mysterious
    page ;
Will never know how quietly in consecrated sod,
The loved and lost are lying to wait the call of God.

Some one, beyond the barrier, some day will see
    and know,
How a Power, wise and merciful, holds all the
    threads below ;
But oh, we waiting in the dusk, but watch while
    hearts are breaking,
While the lark above the nameless graves, his matin
    hymn is waking.

A TRUE STORY OF THE YORKSHIRE COAST.

'Beautiful!' melbby it be, bairn,
  Folk moastly präise t' sea;
But I'se lived nigh hand it ower lang,
  It's maän like a gräve to me.

Dost see yon cottage up on t' hauf,
  Where t' reek curls up to t' sky?
I'se bided there these fourscore year,
  An there I hoapes to die.

It wer a heartsome spot eneaf,
  For all it 's se dowly now,
When feyther fettled his nets at neet,
  And t' childer laked on t' brow.

Feyther,—well, he wer drouned, honey,
  I' t' year as I wer wed,
We put him a stean, for respect, you know,
  In t' Churchgarth up on t' head.

Muther,—she deed at oor awn fire side,
  As wer nobbut rect and due;
I addles ma bit an sup frev t' sea,
  Winter an summer through.

Ma Mairster säiled for Hartlypool,
  When t' mackerel wer agäte;
I'd ha liked to lig by ma poor auld man,
  He wer a trusty mäte.

But t' Parson niver blest his gräve,
  He rowls i' t' grate salt sea;
T' rudder yoake an a cassen net,
  Wer all that cam back to me.

I'd browt him first five stolart sons;
  Honey, when I lies dead,
But yan 'll hearken t' bidding bell,
  An stan at t' coffin head.

But yan I said. How dars I say 't?
  Will ever t' Noerth wind blaw,
An t' lifeboät launch mid t' boiling surf,
  Nor he be t' first to goa?

An I wadna stay him by a word,
  A man mun do his best,
When t' mariners strive wi t' sea an Death,
  And God mun heed t' rest,

Oor first-born sailed for t' Whälery;
  I know'd I'd na call ta pine,
We are all like to do oor wark,
  An it's better sune nor syne.

But many a winter's nect I cried,
  For oor lad sa far away,
As t' tide cam thunnering ower t' reef,
  An its roar roase up t' bay.

At last they sighted t' Amazon,
  I seed her flag afar;
They shouted on t' Pier, an tossed their caps,
  As she came ower t' harbour bar.

She 'd browt a wealth o' oil an bänes,
  As t' owner wer fain to see;
She 'd browt back many a muther's son,
  But niver ma boy to me.

She 'd none browt hame oor bonny lad,
  He wer left i' t' Greanland wäves;
Honey, dost think they 'll rise as wick
  As them i' t' Churchgarth gräves?

Oor Harry wer lost yan stormy neet,
  Off t' coast o' Elsinore;
I ofens thinks I hears his laugh,
  When t' gales t' loodest roar.

For he'd call it 'beautiful' an all,
  Yon sea sa cruel an strong,
Ma wark wer set to hinder him
  Frev t' watter all day long.

And t' others? Well, I'll tell the', bairn.
  'Twer an aternoon i' March,
An all frev t' Nab to Kettle Ness,
  Wer foäming white as t' starch.

'T' sky wer coarse, an t' swell wer fierce,
  An t' wind blew waur and waur,
When a cry roase up frev t' crouded staithes,
  That a brig wer fast on t' scaur.

They hauled t' lifeboät doun t' roäd,
  They'd naan te seak her crew,
T' Whitby lads are niver slack,
  Wi' parlous wark to do.

Oor boys wer there, oor George laughed out,
  As t' spräy dashed iv his face;
An Charlie shooted out ma näme,
  As he saw me in ma pläce.

His sweetheart stood agin me there
  She wer a grädely lass,
There wer none sa stern in all t' toun,
  But smiled to see her pass.

But she went däteless, poor fond thing,
  Or ever t' morning gray,
Rose ower t' sorrowful toun it left,
  That black and bitter day.

Thrice went t' boät thruf wind and wäve,
  And thrice she wonned her home,
Till every saul in two brave barks
  Wer snatched frev t' kingdom come.

Folk thronged aroond to treat t' lads,
  As wor spent wi' toil an drouth,
When thruf t' scud an mist they seed a ship
  Drive right past t' harbour's mouth.

There wer plenty there, sea-faring men,
  An naither weak nor nesh,
An keen to tak a part at last,
  An man t' boät afresh.

But t' crew wer wilful an ower wrowt,
  They leapt frev t' edge o' t' pier,
An pushed her off mid t' breakers there,
  With naither wit nor fear.

Up yonder i' t' hoos iv Hagalythe,
  I 'd wakkened a cheery low,
I knowed ma boys ud need a drop
  For t' wind wer thick wi' snow.

An time had quietened half ma fear,
  I reckoned as t' warst wer done ;
When I heerd a sudden fearful skrike,
  An t' grate crowd heaved an run.

I seed t' men dash amang t' surf,
  An t' women faant an flee,
I seed 'em rive t' capstan planks
  And fling 'em out tiv t' sea.

She 'd caught i' t' back sweep, close t'u t' bar,
  I 'll hardlings tell the' more,
There wer twelve brave lads as started her,
  They drew but yan t'u t' shore.

Whist, bairn, there 's trouble ower deep for words ;
  Lang sin I cried my fill ;
I went next day, when t' wind were lound,
  Where t' waves had wrowt their will.

I fund 'em lying side by side,
  I seed 'em at ma feet,
Their eyes were aupen, and fixed abuv,
  Their smile wer gräve and sweet.

I seed 'em, oor two bonny lads,
  I noorsed 'em at ma breast,
Ill främed these withered hands o' mine
  To streak 'em for their rest.

They said oor cry went thruf t' land,
  To t' Queen upon her throan,
Brass came eneaf to dry some tears,
  Ere t' gräves were owergroawn.

It didna dea much gude to me,
  I know'd ma sorrow mesel ;
I'se none sa fond o' seeking folk
  Of ma lonesome hearth to tell.

Oor John will mebby cloase ma eyes,
  A reet good son is he ;
But, bairn, if t' sea *be* ' beautiful,'
  Doan't threep on it to me.

ON THE OTHER SIDE.

I HAD a glorious coronal—emeralds, sapphires, and
    pearls ;
Brave was its glow on the frank young brow, 'mid
    the sheen of the clustering curls,

But the purest gem of the diadem was the first to
    drop away.
There are few to be told, 'mid the tarnished gold,
    round the tresses scant and gray.
Men ask for the jewels I wore erewhile:
'Over the river,' I say, and smile.

I had a wealth of beautiful buds, crimson and golden
    and blue;
Through the April hours my fair frail flowers nor
    change nor drooping knew;
But some shrunk and died in the summer's pride,
    some faded in autumn's rain:
The wild winds moan where I stand alone, on the
    arid leafless plain.
Where are the roses you cherished of late?
'Over the river,' I say, and wait.

I had a lute, whose music was the glory of life to me;
Love gave to each string its happy ring, hope woke
    its melody.
But the thrilling chords and the passionate words
    died into silence soon,
And my faint cold touch cannot wake so much as
    the ghost of a vanished tune.
Where is the measure you loved the best?
'Over the river, with all the rest.'

Fast as the fleeting moments, sure as the night to
    the day,
Our hopes and pleasures, our joys and treasures,
    glide from our clasp away;
Sudden and swift the dark clouds lift, the lightning
    flashes down,

Not an hour we know on our path below, if marked
    for the cross or the crown:
Yet God guides all to the perfect day;
Till we cross the river, love, trust, and pray.

AT THE ELECTION.

HIGH raged the party spirit
    In the quaint old seaport town;
'Spite new-wove veil of secresy,
    Each side threw gauntlets down.
Old watch-words flew from lip to lip,
    Of 'Church,' and 'Crown,' and 'State';
Here clamour of 'Economy,'
    There rancour 'gainst a 'Rate';
And all the while, by a sick man's side,
    A pale wife dreaded the falling tide.

The women left their hearths unswept,
    To join the tossing crowd,
The children caught the flying heat,
    And shouted cries aloud,
Each seeking scraps to deck its rags,
    Of orange or of blue;
And ever over the long gray waves
    The white-winged sea-gulls flew;
And softly and slowly ebbed the tide,
    And the wife wept on at the sick man's side.

With floods of frothy eloquence,
    With promise, view, and pledge,
Each eager champion of the hour
    Vaunted his sabre's edge.
Swayed to and fro, the fickle crowd

Listened with hiss or cheer,
And evermore the waves' low song
Chimed on for none to hear,
Save she, who shivered to hear the tide
Sob fainter yet, at the sick man's side.

And midnight hushed the surging throng,
The fight was lost and won;
Victor and vanquished pass away,
Their moment's glory done.
To-morrow, only bairns at play
Will call the faction names;
While old men over pipes and ale
Laugh at 'election games.'
And out on the sands moans the turning tide,
And a widow weeps by a dead man's side.

THE STILE.

SET deep in the hawthorn hedgerow stands the old
rustic stile;
Beyond it, the breezy uplands lie stretching many a
mile;
Above it, the pale wild roses spread fairy hands to
meet
Below it, the scarlet poppy flaunts, with the daisies
at its feet;
Beside it, the bright brown river stirs the lilies amid
the sedges,
And sings to the blue forget-me-nots that nestle on
willow ledges.

Over the hill, where the heather glowed to a purple
flush,
And the gorses flashed their lavish gold, 'mid the
pink of the bilberry bush,

Tracing the meadow pathway where the tedded hay
    was sweet,
Through waves of the bearded barley, and the soft
    cool green of wheat,
Graceful, and gay, and gallant, with the lover's eager
    smile,
He strode through the July sunshine, to keep his
    tryst at the stile.

Amid the fir boles glancing, her robe's white foldings
    showed,
The bluebell rang its prophet chime, by the winding
    way she trode;
The skylark poised above her, shook out his joyous
    song,
Butterflies, white, and blue, and gold, heralded her
    along;
On her cheek a wavering colour, on her lip a flutter-
    ing smile,
She stood in the July sunshine, keeping her tryst at
    the stile.

Flower and bird will fade and die, and summer to
    winter change,
Many a heavy doom may lie in the future's mystical
    range,
Many a glitter and glory the coming years may bring,
Many a wild and varying note from the great life-
    harp may ring,
But oh, those two young lovers, let fortune frown or
    smile,
Will scarce know an hour more purely sweet than
    the tryst they kept at the stile!

THE BIRTHDAY SONG OF THE FLOWERS.

WE are calling, we are calling;
Yorkshire skies are dull and gray,
Yorkshire winds are sharp and bitter
Yet we lift our heads to say,
From the slumber of the snowdrift,
From the weight of sodden clay,
We are waking, we are peeping
For our Lady's natal day.

We are calling, we are calling.
Nestling in the sheltered nook,
Bravely brightening breezy uplands,
Making mirrors in the brook,
Blossoming in lonely wood-walks,
By her customed tread forsook
Bordering all her laurel copses,
Waiting for our Lady's look.

We are calling, we are calling.
She has loved us well and long,
Sought us for her mute companions,
Hailed our praise in tale or song,
Loved us more than hot-house beauties,
Nature's nurslings, pure and strong,
Violet, crocus, primrose, snowdrop,
Say, her absence does them wrong.

We are calling, we are calling;
With our pleading sweet and dumb,
With our wealth of spring and promise,
Gathered in a vernal sum,

Flying through the budding shires,
To the London din we come,
In our birthday greeting breathing
'Ah our Lady, hasten home.'

MIDDLE AGE.

What is it, little one? Mother was dreaming;
    Dreaming a dream it was well you should break:
Wrapt in a vision of fancies Elysian,
    Whose colours all fled as she started awake.

Forgetting the wrinkles so deep on the forehead,
    Forgetting the silver so thick in the hair,
Forgetting how older, and sadder, and colder,
    The life and the world that once, once were so fair.

It is hard to remember, just hard for a moment,
    While the pulse throbs so full and the heart beats
        so fast,
That youth's golden hours, its sun and its flowers,
    Are all swept away to the pitiless past.

It is hard to remember, just hard for a moment,
    ' While dear hopes bewilder and lovely dreams thrill,
That the gray mist is round us, the gloaming has
        found us;
That the magic is broken, the embers are chill.

What is it, little one? Where is the trouble?
    Ah! the lash off the whip, and the paint off the toy!
Well, they can be mended, though sweet dreams are
        ended,
' Mother' still can work charms in the eyes of her boy.

IN VAIN.

UTTERLY in vain, utterly in vain,
The devotion of the heart and the labour of the brain ;
The honest work of the honest hand, the endless
    helpless strife,
The gallant mute endurance of a struggling baffled life ;
So hard the daily task-work, so far the glittering gain.
Utterly in vain, utterly in vain.

Utterly in vain, utterly in vain :
As the vessel swings at anchor the cable snaps in
    twain ;
To the love that clings the closest, comes treachery
    or death ;
For the step that climbs the highest, yawns the
    precipice beneath.
For the head that strives the hardest, waits genius'
    yearning pain.
Utterly in vain, utterly in vain.

Utterly in vain, utterly in vain :
Ay, to earth's common reading, the heavy text is
    plain ;
But, by the noble effort, and by the solemn trust,
By steadfast faith and fearless death, by all things
    pure and just,
'Spite frustrate aim, and failing hope, 'spite wrong
    and loss and stain,
No life that God has given is utterly in vain.

LAST WORDS.

Darling, 'tis all in vain,
No eager helping of the tender hands
Can ever knit again the failing strands
  The slow waves wash in twain.

Hush, love, no passionate prayer,
No wistful watching of the weary eyes,
Can bring noon's radiance back to winter skies,
  Spring's glow to autumn's air.

My little day is done,
The weakening pulse, the feeble fluttering heart,
Have nearly throbbed their last: we two must part
  We two, who were but one!

I will not say to-day,
'Would I had loved you better.' May be so;
But all my heart could give, it gave, I know.
  The last hours glide away.

And you—you shall not weep;
Tears cannot stay me, and I want to rest
My living head upon your loving breast.
  Time comes for woe, for sleep.

You will have time for sorrow
When the grave closes o'er my head for ever:
We may not watch the red sun sink together,
  Perchance, mine own, to-morrow.

Now while the world goes by,
While blossoms bloom and fade, fruits form and wither,
And winter's ice benumbs the summer river,
  Babes smile and old men die,

Unheeded and unheeding,
Let life, and time, and death their records leave;
While you and I, on this sweet autumn eve,
  Our last fair page are reading.

Talk of the past, my love,
Of the sweet days while yet you wooed your bride ;
Of gloaming lingerings at the dim seaside,
  Of walks through glen and grove.

Tell how the great waves crashed
In long low thunder music at our feet;
How far below our favourite woodland seat
  The bright beck danced and flashed.

Listen! I heard a clang,
Mellow and musical of far-off bells;
How softly through the golden air it swells!
  Just so the joy-peal rang

From the old tower at home,
When we two started on life's path—ah me!
'Twas well we had no prophet's eyes to see
  How soon the end would come.

Hush, hush, dear! had I known
Death lurked still closer, think you I had sought
For turn or stay? Nay: it is cheaply bought,
  Such year as ours, mine own.

Look at the pretty bird,
There mid the fallen rose-leaves—in my dreams,
When, shy and sweet as April's earliest gleams,
  Fresh hopes within me stirred;

I used to think, we two
Would love to show such pretty sights as those,
A bird, a butterfly, a crimson rose,
  To eyes of baby blue!

Well, it will soon be past:
And you will plant bright flowers uopn our earth,
I, and our wee bud blighted in its birth';
　　We gathered violets last.

　　Good-night, love. I am tired.
How the old hill, with all its forests crowned,
Smiles on the wealth of sweeping uplands round
　　By day's last glory fired!

ALL ELSE.

Soft flushes creep through the dawning,
　　Soft sun-glints dusk and shiver,
Where the snowdrops peep from their winter sleep
　　On the banks of the glittering river.
Soft hues gleam out on the branches
　　Where the tiny birch-buds wake ;
Soft shadows rest on the hill's broad breast,
　　Where the daisy blossoms shake.
But oh, there is never a stir of light
Where the grave lies green and the cross stands
　　　　white.

Low chirpings sound in the hedge-rows,
　　Where the wild birds mate and woo ;
Low twinkles the beck as 'mid sunshade and fleck
　　It hurries the woodlands through.
Low whisper the waves to the golden sand,
　　Saying, ' Spring is awake to-day ;'
While the ringing trills of child-laughter fills,
　　As with music, the sheltered bay.
But oh, there is never a joyous sound
Where the tall cross stands by the grassy mound.

Blue gleams the sky with its fleecy clouds;
  Golden, and purple, and red
Are the dells, and the lanes, and the long rich plains
  With crocus and violet spread.
Anemones flash through the mosses;
  Like moonlight pale primroses gleam;
And forget-me-nots shine, where the pale bindweeds
    twine,
  'Neath the willows that edge the stream.
But oh, there is nothing of colour or glow
Where the lonely cross guards the grave below.

Young hearts arouse to the spring time;
  Young fancies lightlier flow;
Shy hopes arise; and bright lips and eyes
  Catch a deeper and fuller glow.
Young lambs sport, snow-like, on emerald grass;
  Through the fresh buds fresh carols ring;
Even tired life, spite its fret and its strife,
  Owns the spell of the coming spring.
But nor light, nor glory, nor change may be
Where the white cross stands for my love and me.

AUTUMN.

THE year is dying, dying,
On fell, and plain, and hill;
Rich-robed in russet and gold he lies,
While his dirge swells up to the low gray skies,
In the wild wet wind that sobs and moans,
In the stream that frets o'er its troubled stones,
In the weary wail of the ceaseless rain,
On plashing wood-walk and sodden plain
Sad nature mourns her fill.

The year is dying, dying;
They are gathering round his grave
The grasses that shiver, and blanch, and die,
The leaves that float earthward silently,
The hollyhock bowing her stately head,
To the moist rich mould of the garden bed;
And bee and butterfly, folding their wings,
As they perish amid their wanderings,
Where the last rose petals wave.

The year is dying, dying;
And watching his bier, in sooth
'Tis as hard to believe in sun and flowers,
As for age to realise golden hours,
When hope, and joy, and trust arose,
As the violets waken from winter snows.
Ah! at April's call they return once more,
But never for us on the farther shore,
Dawns the morning of love and youth!

OUR SHIP.

When our ship comes in—when our ship comes in,
What a time of gladness shall begin!
Flowers that never shall fade or die,
   Cherries and peaches together;
Suns that shine on in a bright blue sky,
   As we play in the cloudless weather.
No rules to follow, no tasks to begin,
When our ship comes in—when our ship comes in.

When our ship comes in—when our ship comes in!
They talk of poverty as of sin!

Warnings and shadows crowd our way,
  Called up from the dull old Past.
Nay, droop not, darling; frown as they may,
  Time flies for us, free and fast.
Our fame and fortune are there to win,
When our ship comes in—when our ship comes in!

When our ship comes in—when our ship comes in!
Life and labour are close akin.
But the children around us are springing up,
  To renew our youth's sweet hours.
We may taste with our boys the loving cup,
  With our girls pick the spring's fresh flowers,
And wellnigh again the race begin,
When our ship comes in—when our ship comes in!

When our ship comes in—when our ship comes in!
We are wellnigh tired of life's loud din.
Friend and lover are gone before,
  Through the beautiful golden gates;
We have but to glide to the further shore,
  Where their eager welcome waits.
Ah! the richest boon it is ours to win,
When our ship comes in—when our ship comes in!

A SIMILE.

The boughs were crossing and lacing—black boughs
  against the blue,
And aye, as the wild winds tossed and chafed, glints
  of the sky peeped through;
Crossing and lacing ever, vexing the dreamy eye
That fain had dwelt in hushed content on the stainless depths of sky.

Closer I looked at the branches, all gaunt and black
    and bare,
And I saw, as the sunlight struck them, the pale
    buds sprouting there;
So, though life's quick cares and strivings trouble
    our upward sight,
Earth's joys are springing among them, and beyond
    is the heavenly light.

LE VENGEUR.

A LEGEND OF ROBIN HOOD.

Now lithe and listen, gentles all,
To a tale of bold Robin Hood,
How he held his own on the brave North Sea
As well as in gay greenwood.

The waves were dancing to the dawn
On a smiling summer's day,
When Robin steered his coble out
In beautiful Whitby Bay.

And with him four stout mariners
Set canvas to the breeze,
And away to reap the harvest
That grows in the deep blue seas.

England and France were grappling
In their life-long struggle then,
And King Philip loved the lusty thews
That mark the Yorkshire men.

So, when away in the offing
A vessel hove in sight,
Like sea-mews startled from their prey
The fishing-boats took flight.

Good need to haul the brown sail up,
Good need to ply the oar;
When the golden lilies flaunt so near,
The fishers were best ashore

Fast, fast they flew, but faster yet,
Was the frigate's swift advance;
Must the wives and babies starve at home,
While their men are slaves for France?

Nigher and nigher came the ship,
Her prize was wellnigh won,
It is ever in their desperate need,
The Many find the One.

'Down with the sail!' said Robin Hood,
And bind me to the mast;
I would stand steady, mates, to see
The Frenchman sail so fast;

'She bears a gallant steersman there,
A goodly mark is he,
If I sleep beneath the waves to-night,
Methinks he will lie with me.

'So away till you make the Abbey Head,
Then, rest on your oars awhile,
You can match the frigate at the worst,
If I buy you half a mile.'

Four boats fled onward to the land,
One at her anchor lay,
Watching how fast Le Vengeur swept
Upon her helpless prey.

Bold Robin proved his tough bow string.
Glanced grave at seas and skies,
Then counted the bolts in his baldric,
With a flash in his frank blue eyes.

The steersman smiled to see the fool
In his foemen's clutches rest,
Then staggered backward from the helm,
An arrow in his breast.

Twelve Frenchmen trod Le Vengeur's deck,
As she chased the fishing craft;
Twelve times across the heaving waves
Flew Robin's fatal shaft.

The cobles brought nought to the shouting beach
Of the booty they sailed to win,
But at the wake of Robin's boat
They towed Le Vengeur in !

THALATTA ! THALATTA !

Brave North Sea, bright North Sea,
Send your freshness and strength to greet
Us toilers beneath the inland heat.
The great trees droop with their weight of leaves,
The roses cluster on cottage eaves,
Jasmine, and myrtle, and mignonette,
And tall white lilies in order set,
Load the slow airs with their rich sweet scent.
And the lime, with its odorous branches bent
O'er its busy court of murmurous bees,
Pervades with its perfume the July breeze ;
We turn for succour and breath to thee,
To thy broad blue waters, O great North Sea.

Brave North Sea, bold North Sea,
He heard the call from the slumberous dales,
He heard the sigh from the fair hushed vales,
On the rocky coast, on the cliff-girt strand,
He flung his answer on dune and sand.

He tossed his crest, all glittering white,
In gay defiance to noon's keen light;
He dashed his breakers upon the shore,
He chanted in full resounding roar,
'Come to me, rest by me, plunge in my waves,
In the strong salt water that sains and saves,
There is cooling and help in my arms and me,'
Sang the Isles' bright girdle, the frank North Sea.

Ah, glorious sea, ah, grand North Sea,
Well may we gaze on thy sparkling breast,
Well may we hail thee as truest and best;
Best guardian for friend, best shield from foe,
Let the Island Empress her glory know.
Let the sufferer seek for healing there,
Let the mourner pause in the sobbing prayer,
And hear the solemn music sweep,
From the full-toned harp of the mighty deep,
Breathing, 'Hush, hush, sad human heart,
From my ebbing and flowing learn duty's part;
Wait His leisure who guides my strength and me,'
Sings the beautiful ocean, the brave North Sea.

FLOTSAM AND JETSAM.

The sea crashed over the grim gray rocks,
It thundered beneath the height,
It swept by reef and sandy dune,
It glittered beneath the harvest moon,
That bathed it in yellow light.

Shell, and seaweed, and sparkling stone,
It flung on the golden sand.
Strange relics torn from its deepest caves,
Sad trophies of wild victorious waves,
It scattered upon the strand.

Spars that had looked so strong and true,
When the gallant ship was launched,
Shattered and broken, flung to the shore,
While the tide in its deep triumphant roar
Rang the dirge for old wounds long stanched.

Petty trifles that love had brought
From many a foreign clime,
Snatched by the storm from the clinging clasp,
Of hands that the lonely will never grasp,
While the world yet counts by time.

Back, back to its depths went the ebbing tide,
Leaving its stores to rest,
Unsought and unseen in the silent bay,
To be gathered again ere close of day,
To the ocean's mighty breast.

Kinder than man art thou, O sea ;
Frankly we give our best,
Truth, and hope, and love, and faith,
Devotion that challenges time and death,
Its sterling worth to test.

We fling them down at our darling's feet,
Indifference leaves them there.
The careless footstep turns aside,
Weariness, changefulness, scorn, or pride,
Bring little of thought or care.

No tide of human feeling turns,
Once ebbed, love never flows ;
The pitiful wreckage of time and strife,
The flotsam and jetsam of human life,
No saving reflux knows.

GONE AWAY.

THE winter wears the old pure dress you used to
    love so well,
The snow lies dazzling in the sun, on moorland,
    hill, and fell;
Gay clad in silver tracery stands every leafless tree,
High pile the drifts of frozen white on meadow,
    land, and lea;
The robin that you always fed lights on the ivy
    spray,
Your dog lies wistful at your door, but you are gone
    away.

The yule-log crackles on the hearth; out in the
    moonlit snow
The waits are singing the same songs we echoed
    long ago;
With a pale mimicry of mirth, old customs, one by
    one,
Are followed through the Christmas hours as you
    would have them done;
The ancient feast the children hail, and play the
    ancient play,
But even through their laughter sigh that you are
    gone away.

Life will resume its quiet course, by cloud or sun-
    shine crossed,
And only for one heart remain 'the sense of some-
    thing lost;'
They will pass on, the dated days, close held in
    love's fond keeping,
And Spring will call on leaf and flower, to wake
    them from their sleeping.

You prized the yearly miracle that Nature works in
    May,
The buds will blow in England, dear; but you are
    gone away.

Gone from the happy intercourse of kindred heart
    and mind;
Gone from the daily round that used its joys in you
    to find ;
But from the longing, yearning love, the clinging
    thought and prayer,
The fond recurring reference, the tender thought
    and care,
From the dreaming of the lonely night, the memory
    of the day,
Dear, from all this, and more than this, you are not
    gone away.

AMONG THE GORSE.

The light wind swept across the sea,
    And woke the wild ' white horses,'
The warm wind reached the sunny hill,
    And tossed the golden gorses.
The soft wind heaved the purple bells
    That flushed the scented heather,
Where a dark-eyed lady lay and dreamed
    All in the cloudless weather.
The gay wind waved the chestnut curls
    That crowned the merry boy,
Whose mother smiled to watch his sport,
    And hear his shout of joy.

The wild wind roared across the sea,
    And woke its dormant forces;

The cold wind whirled the drifted snow
  About the dark green gorses.
The fierce wind swept the dreary moor,
  And shook the withered heather,
Where the curlew piped, and the brown snipe called,
  All in the hard black weather,
The bleak wind wailed above a grave,
  With some wintry blossoms strown;
And there, beside a tall white cross,
  Crouched a little child, alone.

THE GODS OF THE HEARTH.

Only a picture dimmed and smirched
By many a weary year;
Only a plant, with a rugged stem,
Its scant leaves frail and sere;
Only a book, its pages torn,
Its dainty binding stained;
Only a harp, its music jarred,
Its strings all dumb and strained,
Only a phrase, that strikes the ear,
As awkward, dull, and cold;
Only a ring, with its jewel flawed,
And loose in its tarnished gold.

Yet that portrait stirs one secret heart,
As no master's work can do;
Those flowers for one outbloom all buds
Of royal scent and hue;
No poet's golden utterance
Charms as those pages did;
No lute has melody half so sweet
In its measured cadence hid;

Those rough frank words—a courtly phrase
Sounds scarce so dear and true;
No sapphire shrines the glow that once
The poor pale turquoise knew.

The gods of the hearth, they reign supreme
On the altar of the heart.
Life flashes on its varying way,
Each takes his destined part;
The wheel revolves, the sunbeams glint,
Storms roar, and quick rains fall;
The thorns grow thick on the rose's stem,
Death strikes to end it all;
But oh, it is only his mighty hand
Can hurl them from their throne,
The gods that home, and heart, and hearth
In love unite to own.

' SI.'

' Si la jeunesse voulait,' at the dawn of day,
' Si la vieillesse pouvait,' when it dies away.

' Si la jeunesse voulait,' brightly glow the skies,
Fairly bloom the flowers, soft the zephyr sighs;
Upwards winds the pathway, to the dizzy height
Where the rocks of promise gleam in living light.
Needs a daring footstep, needs a steady hand,
Needs an eye unflinching on such point to stand;
Youth has all these riches in his golden day,
Lent, with hand unsparing, ta'en to fling away.

' Si la vieillesse pouvait,' slowly sinks the sun,
The shadows dusk the valley, the day is wellnigh
    done;

The sweetest flowers are closing, the gayest winds
    are hushed,
The richest fruits, o'er-ripened, are drooping to the
    dust;
The sad eyes see the glory that laughs upon the hill,
The foot is weak and weary, the blood runs slow
    and chill;
Age knows the game is waiting, age knows the
    prize is sweet,
But, to the strong is honour, the race is to the fleet.

'Si la jeunesse voulait,' when freshly lies the dew,
When the gaze is frank and fearless, the pulse beats
    strong and true;
'Si la vieillesse pouvait,' when the task is taught,
When it might use the knowledge the bitter race
    has brought;
Ah the world were other than we find it now,
More vintage for the storing, less foliage on the
    bough;
Yet, youth were scarce so sunny, did it do the all
    it could,
And age were scarce so holy, did it do the all it
    would.

'Si la jeunesse voulait,' at the dawn of day,
'Si la vieillesse pouvait,' when it dies away.

THE MERCY OF DREAMLAND.

Ask of the Dreamland its mercies;
  You are worn and weary here,
Life has not a gift that you care to lift,
  Time has not a promise to cheer;

The possible bliss of the future,
  Hides dim in the mystical skies,
Your hand is not pure, your hope is not sure,
  Its brightness flits and flies;
The sea you drift on has never a chart,
  Ask of the Dreamland O desolate heart.

Aye, the glories of the Dreamland,
  With morning will vanish away,
Its gold will crust and to common dust
  Fade its flowers fresh and gay:
But never a cloud of warning
  Darkens its smiling sky,
Not a dread to scare, not a cark or care,
  Not a murmur like 'change' or 'die':
And ere from its spell to life you start,
  There is peace in the Dreamland, desolate heart.

For its rosy empire never
  Shows us our darlings dead,
Though the marble cross marks the place of loss,
  Where we laid the cherished head;
In Dreamland the soft eyes shine for us,
  In Dreamland the sweet lips smile,
The low laughs ring, the soft arms cling
  Just as they wont erewhile:
Oh weary of acting the lone life part,
  Seek the mercies of Dreamland, desolate heart.

ANNIVERSARIES.

WHY do we mark them? The long road we travel
  Has little need of milestones on the way;
Since, or by mossy reach or grating gravel,
  The pilgrim must plod on from day to day.

For some, low waters whisper, sweet buds bloom;
  For some, keen dust-clouds sweep or gray mists lower;
But onward, from the cradle to the tomb,
  The road is trodden through each counted hour.

For each, at morning, noon, or gloaming-tide,
  The sudden death-bolt hurtles through the air;
For each, some fair dreams fade—some trust or pride
  Sinks into weakness, falsehood, or despair;
For each, some date stands out in dread relief,
  Through weary waiting, .woe, or fear renew'd;
For each, the impress of a great life-grief
  Holds empire solemn, sad, and unsubdued.

Better to sweep the record from the page;
  To fill the present with its ready work;
To drown, with the full voices of the age,
  The whispering memories that round us lurk.
'Last week,' 'last month,' 'last year,' 'so long ago,
  This very day,'—weak phrases are they all;
Enough our life and all its needs we know:
  What recks to raise the dead past's funeral pall?

So speaks the world, so echoes will and sense;
  And all the while the heart asserts its might,
And love, in sad sweet subtle eloquence,
  Peoples the busy day, the lonely night.
The last low words breathe in the thrilling ear;
  The faint fond glances meet the swimming eyes;
And through the glare and turmoil round us here
  The phantoms of our darlings softly rise.

Perhaps in the bright life that they have won,
  Safe on the far side of the mighty river,
Our loved may count the time as we have done,
  And own our dates without our human shiver;

And in calm knowledge of eternal life,
  Seeing the bliss to come, through mortal yearning
Say gently, through our care and fret and strife,
  'Soon *we* shall smile to know our day returning.'

THE SNOWDROP BULB.

OF its crown of glittering whiteness, of its clustering
    leaves bereft,
Unwarmed by sun, unfed by dew, the dry brown
    bulb is left,
Dull and inert, through summer's glow, and autumn's
    bounteous power,
Of all the golden year to know but its own little hour.
Lay it by in dust and darkness, the poor unlovely
    thing,
To wait, uncared for and unseen, the summons of
    the Spring.

Nay, Nature knows no idleness; we wonder, doubt,
    suspect,
But find no flaw in all His work, the Almighty
    Architect;
No useless item can exist in all His hand has wrought.
As the heart has aye its pulsing blood, the brain its
    ceaseless thought,
So in each tree, and flower, and root, through the
    seasons one by one,
Unseen and silent all the while, the appointed task
    is done.

Hid in the little bulb you hold, calyx and petal shape,
The soft green hood forms ready from its prison
    to escape;

The tender lines, the graceful curve, from day to
  day they grow,
Waiting the warm strong welcome of the mould
  beneath the snow,
When, at its aid, to life and light the tiny stem
  will burst,
And give the winter world its flower, the fairest and
  the first.

What use o'er storied wisdom of learned tomes to
  pore,
Why seek at need for help to faith at founts of
  earthly lore?
In Nature's yearly miracle, God writes His lesson
  plain,
Though heats may parch, and frosts may sear, each
  frail flower lives again,
And weary heart, and head inert, and dull unanswering mind,
In the story of the Snowdrop Bulb may hope and
  comfort find.

THAT WHICH ENDURES.

The broadsword loses its glitter
As it hangs in the ancient hall,
Rusted and blunt the keen-edged blade,
That once so gallant a champion made,
As it gleamed from the castle wall.

The jewel loses its lustre
As it lies in its velvet nest;
Dull and dim grows the good red gold,
That showed such a royal light of old,
As it flashed from a beauty's breast.

The blue eye loses its power
As age comes creeping on;
The fair form droops from its stately grace,
The roses fly from the care-worn face,
The charm from the trembling tone.

The colour fades from the canvas,
The magic from ringing rhyme,
Now, is there a joy in this world of ours,
Riches, or glories, or hopes, or flowers,
But dies at the touch of Time?

Ay, Love in his pure serenity
Can the pitiless spell defy,
For tears cannot drown, nor absence dim,
And death itself may not conquer him,
For true love never can die.

DALTON'S TRUST.

Out through bonny Wensleydale Rupert's summons
    rung;
Nortons, Scropes, and Powlets to the winds their
    banners flung;
Daltons, Marmions, and Fitzhughs swift to the chal-
    lenge sprung.

Masham, Marske, and Middleham sent their tale of men;
Thoresby, Hawes, and Sedbergh rose to battle then;
Wensleydale call'd soldiers out, well-told hundreds ten.

On to fatal Marston Moor, for 'Church and King and
    Crown,'
They marched by Tanfield's towers gray, they march'd
    by Norlaze down;
And the minster bells rang merrily as they pass'd
    through Ripon town.

'Great our King and true our cause,' Mabel Mowbray
      said;
'Yet my all of hope and joy rests on my father's head;
What were church and throne to me, if his life were
      sped?'

Dalton's boy had lingered there for a parting word;
Vassals own'd his brother's rule—his naught but steel
      and sword;
Yet gay and gallant as the best, young Frank of
      Sleningford.

'Trust him for me, lady mine, trust him all to me;
Heart is stout, and hand is strong; spent they both
      shall be
Ere the Mowbray's good gray head down 'mid the
      spears I see.'

By the flashing waves of Ure, youth and maiden stood;
Soft his wooing whisper blent with the murmuring flood;
Round them both the morning sun glow'd from Hack-
      fall wood.

'Mabel, one word ere I go.' The maiden smiled and
      blush'd,
The sweet lips moved; the lover's heart leapt to her
      low 'I trust.'
The charger wheel'd, the long white plume was lost
      in clouds of dust.

     *   *   *   *   *   *

Sullen to the Northern Sea swept the redden'd Ouse,
When the sun had set in clouds, content such sight to
      lose;
Royalty, to people's rights, had paid its deadly dues.

'Neath an old ancestral oak leant the maiden wearily;
Up the Ure the slow mist crept, wreathing chill and eerily;
Down the vale from Jervaulx pile clang of bells came
    drearily.

Suddenly she raised her head, sound of hoofs to heed;
Tramp of horses, hardly press'd, spurr'd to desperate
    speed;
Every stroke rang keen and clear, like cry of bitter need.

Clattering down the winding hill on two horsemen rode;
The crimson Mowbray cognisance o'er old Sir Hubert
    flowed;
Broken and stain'd, his comrade's helm a snowy
    feather show'd.

' He has brought thee back thy father, wench; the lad
    would have his way,
Else had I died 'mid England's best, nor mourned this
    fatal day;
He took a pikeman's thrust for me—What, Frank!
    hold up, I say!'

One flashing smile, one whisper'd phrase, 'My trust
    redeem'd,' the sound:
One kiss on the white hand that strove to stanch the
    gushing wound;
'Tis but her gallant lover's corpse upon the blood-
    stain'd ground.

    *   *   *   *   *   *

Old names decay, old stories die, as names and stories
    must;
But still the Dalton faith is known as steadfast, true,
    and just;
Still old men show that oak, and tell the tale of
    ' Dalton's Trust.'

THE RED CROSS ON THE BOLE.

BRAVELY 'burgeoned the mighty oak
In the heart of the good green wood,
His great arms stretching far and wide,
The sunbeams glinting his boughs beside,
The leafy crown on his hoary pride,
The forest's king he stood.

Under his shade the lovers met,
As the twilight around them stole;
The shy deer found safe covert there,
His nest the rook built, high in air,
Little they recked that the old oak bare
The red cross on his bole.

Little they recked how some dewy morn,
Strong men would pause at the sign;
The distance ta'en, the labour planned,
An echo of blows through the fair green land,
A mighty crash, and by man's strong hand
A ruin of work divine.

Ah, the gap in the lovely boskage,
Ah, the crush of flowers and moss,
But Nature's fingers are quick and deft
At filling the blanks in the picture left,
And the beauty she gives, for the glory reft,
Smiles down the sense of loss.

But for us, for us, who cannot fill
So soon the vacant place;
For us, whose wilful hearts will burn
For the darlings who never can return;
For us, who vainly long and yearn
For the look on a vanished face.

Is it not well for the clinging heart,
Well for the tender soul,
That, as our destined paths we tread,
No light on our mortal eyes is shed,
To show us with terrible prescient dread,
The red cross on the bole?

So sure, so full, the bright life seems,
So sudden falls the blow;
For the sign of doom there is none who sees,
Save the angel who carries the sword and keys;
It is best to ask upon our knees,
'O God, make us fit for woe!'

ST. MARTIN'S SUMMER.

THE genial sunshine floods the pale blue sky,
  The sullen river wakes to glint and flash,
The low winds whisper, tossing merrily
  The scarlet tassels of the mountain ash;
The lingering roses, pale and faint and sweet,
  Smile, opening to the warmth their fragrant breasts,
And 'mid the dead leaves nestling 'neath the feet
  The violets peep to light from sheltered nests.

Each mighty tree October's signet bears,
  Gleaming in hues of crimson, gold, and brown,
As some barbaric monarch, dying, wears
  His richest robes and dons his brightest crown.
A soft sad loveliness, a perfume rare,
  Seems round the Autumn's parting hours to cling;
A strange enchantment fills the brooding air,
  As through a dirge triumphant hope may ring.

So, in some lives, we watch with reverent love,
  After long trials borne, long sorrows past,

A hushed tranquillity awakes, to prove
  Patience has wrought her perfect work at last.
But once, to glad the hot world's restless strife,
  Comes childhood's April, youth's impassioned June;
The sweet serenity of waning life,
  St. Martin's Summer, is its dearest boon.

NATURE'S COMFORTING.

No, not to the April lilies,
Though fair be their moonlight sheen,
No, not to the July roses,
Though each be a radiant queen.
Not to the sweet spring loveliness,
Not to the summer glow,
Not to autumn's gorgeous parting smile,
Nor to winter's royal snow.
The world is rich in its varying dress,
Its seasons are full and fair,
It can brighten, gladden, or dream for us,
But O mourner, go not there!

The young leaves flaunt their fresh green life
Though they wave o'er the coffin-pall,
The young flowers blossom in beauty bright,
Though our heart-buds fade and fall.
The birds' gay carol jars the ear,
That thrills to the death-bell's note,
Drearily into the darkened room
Sweet scents of the jasmine float.
If our hopes are blighted, our prizes naught,
Are the fruits less rich and rare?
Wears the laughing sky one cloud for us?
Nay, mourner, look not there!

Who would have nature's comforting,
I rede them seek the shore,
Where ever and aye through sun and shade,
The great waves rise and roar.
The mighty thunderous music
Will lull the fevered brain,
The low melodious monotone
Breathe patience unto pain.
The whisper of the ebbing tide
Answer the passionate prayer,
With 'wait, hush! wait for a little while,'
O mourner, linger there!

The glorious, vast, unchanging sweep,
The long unceasing boom,
Carry the saddened spirit on
To the world beyond the tomb.
Nothing of fading and coming back,
In the great eternal waves,
Nothing of horrible contrast mocks,
Like flowers on tended graves.
Deep as love is, and solemn as faith,
Tender and strong as prayer,
The sea has solace for every mood,
Oh, mourner, seek it there!

THE EVERLASTING PITY.

As lies the blue behind the thunder-cloud,
  As lurk the snowdrops 'neath the drifted snow,
As the bright buds till April calls aloud
  Hide deep within the black and leafless bough,

So, despite care and sorrow, loss and fret,
　God's loving pity guards His children's .fates;
Oh, in our darkness let us trust Him yet,
　Whose Comforter each patient soul awaits.

Believe the rankling wound in love is sent,
　Believe the grief in chastening mercy comes,
And so the bitter 'why' to faith will melt,
　And sorrow smile among her darlings' tombs.
Watching the violets gem the grassy lane
　That late in desolate winter chill we trod,
Let the sweet flowers preach to the lonely pain
　The everlasting pity of our God.

THE FIRST TELEGRAPH.

For us, the black north-easter sweeps across
　The shuddering moorland and snow-crested hills;
For you, blue waves of tropic oceans toss,
　And balmy air the lazy canvas fills,
As mid warm Nature's wealth of sunniest smiles
The ship glides westward to the golden isles.

For us, the quiet days of wont and use
　Pass scarcely marked upon the chart of time;
For you, to charm, bewilder, and amuse,
　Strange aspects range from curious to sublime;
Each hour with something new takes separate form,
As broad seas change 'neath April's shine and storm.

Yet, dear, between us stretches, strong and fine,
　The quick electric wire of loving thought;
As each for each securely can divine
　The subtle links by parted friendship wrought,
At silence and at absence they can laugh
Whose frank affection works mind's telegraph.

Here, in the pauses of the tender talk,
  That bids the past's lost lustre live once more,
We seem to hear the footfall on the walk,
  And glance expectant at the opening door;
Then sighing, smiling, memory's lore renew,
And dedicate the gloaming hour to you.

There, as the water whispers round the keel,
  And strange bright fishes through the glitter dart,
The English hearth-lights mid your fancies steal,
  And the soft empress of the wanderer's heart,
With snowdrop face, sweet lips, and laughing eyes,
Outshines the glories of the tropic skies.

So 'here' and 'there' unite in that fair realm
  That mind creates and dream and fancy guard,
Nor time nor space the kingdom can o'erwhelm
    Where Trust holds sway and Faith keeps watchful
        ward,
And parting's pang scarce pains, when shared in half
To form the stations for Love's telegraph.

IN THE SICK ROOM.

Outside is the east wind blowing, sullen and fierce
    and black,
Bearing the breath of the great gray seas, to scatter
    upon his track;
Mocking the pale green buds that dare to peep through
    the shivering boughs,
Where honeysuckle and jasmine twine about the old
    red house;
Shaking the thin green grasses, where the snowdrifts
    lay so long,
And wailing across the uplands, like a Viking's
    dying song.

Inside, the fire flames flash and leap in the softly
    shadowed room,
Where love makes languor beautiful, with comfort
    and perfume ;
Where books lie open wooingly, best friends of solitude,
And pets and children's merry life to cheer the lighter
    mood,
And the whistle of the homeless wind outside the
    guarded pane
But bids the loiterer gratefully turn to the hearth again.

And yet ye droop your virgin heads, pale primrose,
    snowdrop white ;
You fade beneath your dark green leaves, O fragile
    aconite ;
Ah, pretty blue hepatica, was not the cold earth drear ?
Will you not flash your vernal hues 'mid warmth
    and shelter here ?
Nay, gallant crocus, violet sweet, no gleam is in the sky,

Cannot the fireside's mimic sun beguile you not to die?
Better they love unshackled air, though cold and
    keen it be,
The hardy children English Springs nurse on a
    Spartan knee ;
The living jewels that she wreathes, her April crown
    to gem,
Thrive on the dew the wild east wind wafts freshly
    iced for them ;
Then bring the hot-house dainty blooms, to brighten
    weary hours,
And to youth, and health, and nature, leave the
    happy early flowers.

KISSES.

'Are kisses spirits, mother?'
  Little Bertie asks,
Raising great dark earnest eyes,
To others, blue as summer's skies,
That brighten for her eager boy,
Through her life of hope and joy,
  And tender woman tasks.

Fearless little questioner,
  What knows he of kisses?
Save caresses soft and sweet,
Each fresh hour of life to greet;
Blessing kiss of sire and mother,
Clasp of sister, hug of brother;
  Thanks for baby blisses.

Happy cherished darling,
  He nor knows nor cares;
Of passionate lips that press in vain,
On those that cannot glow again;
Of wild despairing kisses pressed
On damp sods where our idols rest;
  'Mid sad unanswered prayers.

Can true-hearted childhood
  Guess such things can be,
As kiss 'tween secret foe and foe,
As hands that clasp o'er gulfs below,
As kisses with no loving leaven,
Coldly taken, idly given,
  In custom courtesy?

Can frank-hearted childhood
    Dream that kindred lips,
Lips that have met a thousand times,
Warm and true as poets' rhymes,
May for each other learn to frame
Scorn or hatred, mock or blame,
    Love's unwarned eclipse?

Dim not childhood's golden faith,
    With such lore as this is;
Let him trust the gladness round,
Trust the love as birthright found;
Soon, too soon, the world will teach,
Stings may lurk in honeyed speech,
    Treason hide in kisses.

A NOVEMBER EVENING.

ONLY the plash of the oar
Heard on the sleeping seas;
Only the low monotonous roar,
As the long waves broke on the hollow shore,
In the teeth of the western breeze.

The chill November light,
Reigned in the soft gray sky,
The pale mist born from the breath of night,
Crept, veiling dune and rock and height,
In a cloud of mystery.

Gleaming like eyes of fire,
Shone the lights from the little town,
From the huts on the hill side, high and higher,
And highest yet, like the crown of the pyre,
Flamed the beacon on the down.

The boat went drifting on;
With a strange half-ghostly thrill,
She thought of all that had come and gone,
The prizes missed, the victories won,
The days of good and ill.

Like something set apart,
Out on the sea she seemed;
Lost, fear, security, hope, or smart,
Like one, who dreams of a frozen heart,
Yet dreaming knew she dreamed.

Only the plash of the oar,
Only the moan of the waves,
Only a dull sense 'life is o'er,'
Then just 'November soft and hoar,
Dews the grass upon lonely graves.'

A PORTRAIT GALLERY.

It is not in the storied corridor
    Of the old ancestral hall,
Where the belted knight and the lady bright
    Smile from the tapestried wall;
Where a Guido's tender radiance shows
    By a Rubens' gorgeous hues,
Or the stately grace of a Vandyke face
    By the soft slow glance of a Greuze.

Drawn on no earthly canvas,
    By no mortal pencil limned,
Ne'er glorified by an age's pride,
    By no poet's pæan hymned:
By the quiet hush of the winter's hearth,
    Or the breathless nights of June,
Are my pictures seen by the firelight's sheen,
    Or framed by the silvery moon.

They rise around me, one by one,
  The lost, the changed, the dead;
I see the smile I knew erewhile
  On the sweet lips dewy red;
The soft dark eyes flash love for me,
  The soft curls gleam and wave,
Till I half forget how my life-sun set
  'Neath the yews by a lonely grave.

I see white robes and blushing flowers,
  And two close side by side;
Nor think how deep is the bridegroom's sleep,
  As I watch him clasp his bride.
I look in the gentle mother's face,
  Till her blessing is breathed again;
While the father's eyes, strong, true, and wise,
  Call counsel and calm to pain.

I seem to smooth the golden curls
  Tossed back from the child's pure brow,
And prize them as then, though the whirl of men
  Has smirched their glitter now.
The first friend's form moves joyously
  Out through the dusky air,
In its frank fresh truth, as when hope and youth
  Set a royal signet there.

Naught fades my portraits' living lines,
  No flecks or sun-stains fall;
No time corrodes, no thick dust loads
  Their beauty with its pall.
Painted by memory and love
  For my waiting life and me,
My pictures will shine till in light divine
  Their deathless types I see.

IN MEMORIAM.

May 26, 1873.

Late lingering, yet as lovely as of yore,
  Sweet summer wakens in the arms of spring,
Her laughter ripples on the sunny shore,
  Her footsteps through the western zephyrs ring.
Fairest of all fair Yorkshire's favoured haunts
  Lies Whitby, beautiful and grand as ever;
Old Whitby, blest in all that nature grants,
  Glory of sea, and sky, and golden weather.

Unchanged the wavelets 'curve in creamy spray';
  Unchanged the Esk through wooded banks is flowing;
The mighty headlands guard the noble bay,
  With gorse and heather on their summits glowing.
Grave, gray, and graceful, 'neath the cloudless sky,
  The Abbey ruins tower on the height;
Out from the harbour sails flit fairily,
  And on the Scar the blue waves flash to white.

Is naught then altered for accustomed eyes,
  O happy truants from the city's din,
O wanderers from hushed homes 'neath inland skies,
  Seeking the sea, its joy and strength to win?
Still on the busy Staithes the fishers meet,
  The idlers loiter on the breezy cliffs,
The jet wheel's whirr sounds in each narrow street,
  And merry groups crowd to the white-sailed skiffs.

Yet who could know and love our Whitby well,
  Nor miss One, summoned from its midst to-day;
One whose keen mark distinct and vivid fell,
  As in a darksome pass a noon-tide ray;

The eager eyes that lit the white worn face,
  The pleading, thrilling voice, the radiant smile,
The figure, watching helpless in its place,
  Prompt every passer to a pause to wile.

O tender spirit to his people's woes!
  O gallant heart triumphant over pain!
O steadfast faith, that through the mortal throes
  Held fast the promise of eternal gain!
O brilliant wit, that flashed through cross and care.
  O thought and culture polished for the strife!
Brave soul, so quick to see, so strong to dare,
  To bear the fragile, failing frame through life!

What though the arm might sometimes strike awry,
  What though the foot too fleetly tried the height;
The gaze was ever, fixed upon the sky,
  The heart was ever straining for the right.
Well may the memory of the good man gone,
  Help many a sufferer on his weary path;
Best tribute unto him, whose work is done,
  To own and emulate his patient faith.

THE WHIN AND THE WORKHOUSE.

' BETWEEN the whin and the workhouse,' so spoke the
    pretty child,
With eyes that glistened like April dews, with lips
    that had always smiled;
But as the light hand pointed across the golden furze,
The older gaze in the space she showed saw another
    sight than hers.

She saw where the riders gathered, from the forty
    minutes' run,
Young blood all dancing in their veins, the hour's
    triumph won;
With clustering hound and panting horse, bright girl
    and rosy lad,
A firm white hand for the well-won brush, a smile and
    blush for the pad.

Between the whin and the workhouse they pulled the
    old fox down,
Where the woods lie under the long low hill with its
    gray cathedral crown;
And the hunt and my gay companion went sweeping
    down the vale,
And between the whin and the workhouse, I though
    of the gap and its tale.

On one side budding gorses and the slumbering flowers
    of spring,
Snowdrop and primrose and aconite, all waiting their
    blossoming;
On the other, the bare, blank, ugly walls, where age,
    decrepit and poor,
Lingered in dreary patience, till death should knock
    at the door.

Between them, the rush and hurry, the joy and
    excitement of life,
Bold hand for its perilous chances, strong head for
    its sudden strife;
And over the whin and the workhouse, and over the
    gap between,
The sky hung low and gray and chill, like a hope
    that once had been.

But down from the distant moorlands, where the
　　drifted snow-wreaths lay,
A sighing wind swept softly, as the slow step turned
　　away,
And it said, over whin and workhouse, over man-
　　hood, and age, and youth,
Watches the God who made them all, and His names
　　are Love and Truth.

A NOVEL.

She tossed it aside, the third volume, impatient, half
　　sigh, half smile,
Finished the vague light interest, strong enow just
　　the hour to beguile,
As she glanced where, over the mantel, the picture
　　hung all the while.

The dark eyes looking down on her, with the calm
　　light they always shed,
The old still set of the placid lips, the old proud
　　pose of the head,
And as she looked she remembered, why he, like the
　　book, is dead.

He lived and loved and suffered, like the marionettes
　　in the tale,
Met the heat of the morning glory, the strength of
　　the noon-day gale,
And felt the chill of the evening, as the sky grew
　　cold and pale.

Aye, but the book lies quiet, just as she threw it aside,
He is gone from the life we live in, but he treads
　　the paths untried,
And holds, perhaps so, does he? the clue to us all
　　denied.

Perchance—for all is guesswork,—all but the one great
  truth
God's love, God's death, God's power, His infinite
  mercy and ruth,
For the rest, well just in the darkness, we grope
  from age to youth.

She gathers up her novel, she smooths the ruffled leaves,
After all, while the magic holds one, one laughs,
  fears, wonders, grieves;
Smile grave face over the mantel; art gives life its
  best reprieves.

A DEAD DAY'S GHOST.

Gliding up to the pillow, just as a happy dream
Was showing life as it used to be, in the rosy morning gleam,
Scaring the peaceful fancies, that were lapping the
  quiet head,
Ghastly and chill and terrible, the ghost of a dark
  day dead.

Creeping up to its victim, when beside the winter hearth
The crushed heart was re-opening to the fearless
  household mirth;
Till the laughter sank to a quivering wail, and to
  lip, and cheek, and eye
The gladness faded like morning dews beneath a
  noon-day sky.

Hiding amid the April buds, lurking in summer
  flowers,
Starting up grim amid the glow of April's laden bowers,
Crossing on every pathway, the weary foot may tread,
Silent, cold, and relentless, the ghost of a dark day
  dead.

Front it with reckless courage; mock it with bitter
    speech;
Seek for a depth it may not sound, a height it can-
    not reach;
Dig its grave with stern resolving; melt it with
    prayers and cries;
Seek pious counsel and solemn lore, its power to
    exorcise;

Never while throb the pulses in the heart it wrings
    and seres,
Never, while counted day on day pile to allotted years,
While smiles are smiled, and loves are lost, and idle
    tears are shed,
Will it vanish from the life it wrecks, that ghost of
    a dark day dead.

WYVIL'S HOUR.

AN INCIDENT OF THE CIVIL WAR.

'You must gain us an hour, my son, gain it at any cost;
Better our race end here and now, than King and
    cause be lost,
Lost on the first proud day his foot our threshold crossed.

We cannot raise our flag, as erst, defiant on our walls,
And bid our monarch rest secure mid loyal hearts
    and halls;
But boys and old men answer now, when Wyvil's
    trumpet calls.

But I swore by my dead lord's side—dead mid his
    gallant band,
The bullet deep in his heart, the sword in his strong
    cold hand,
To spare in the royal cause nor love, nor life, nor land.

Take all who can strike a blow, take all who have
    arms to wield;
Go, with your father's sword, my boy, to your first
    desperate field.
Ha! from yon valley-side the rebel trumpets pealed.

See how the spear-heads glance! they are fierce and
    eager foes;
But many's the pass in Wensleydale where bracken
    thickest grows,
And not a pass in Wensleydale but Hugh the forester
    knows.

I have barred the postern close, and flung the key
    in the fosse;
There is but the hill to mount and the level chase to
    cross,
And he's safe in the thick oak wood, yonder by
    Aysgarth moss.

Keep them an hour, my boy, ere the ford by Ure is
    won;
Gain but an hour, and then—my life's last task is
    done.
Can your father see me now?—O God, my son, my
    son!'

     *   *   *   *   *   *

Twice had the clock boomed out, as steady and strong
    as Fate,
Since the brave lad led his little band out of the
    castle-gate;
And the lady, silent, calm, alone, still stood to watch
    and wait.

Such vigils are woman's victories, she wins them day
    by day,   ,
Deeds all untold in stirring tale, unsung in minstrel's
    lay,
Yet harder than the fiery feats of many a foughten fray.

    *   *   *   *   *   *

Slowly up from the banks of Ure, under the old oak-
    boughs,
With regular soldier tramp that rang, the couching
    fawn to rouse,
Came the victor ranks of Ironsides, stern triumph on
    their brows.

And in the midst, on serried spears, a ghastly load
    they bare,
The blood-stains red on the proud young face, red
    on the bright brown hair,
And the old trees bent as in stately grief over the
    dying heir.

Slowly across the drawbridge, where were none to
    challenge or greet;
Slowly across the bannered hall, in silence grave and
    meet;
Till they laid him down, the gallant boy, down at
    his mother's feet.

Never a word she said to them,—she knelt her close
    to his side;
The blue eyes opened, asked—hers spoke, all pas-
    sionate woe and pride;
He smiled as she kissed his lips; he gasped, ' The
    hour is won !' and died.

Full twice a hundred counted years in varying course
    have rolled
Since that noble band of loyalists fell on the Yorkshire
    wold ;
But legends keep, like uncut gems, heroic deeds of old.

Rest by the bonny banks of Ure, 'mid the heather's
    purple flower ;
Speak to the stalwart countryman, of the hill and old
    gray tower,
And he 'll tell my tale, and show the ford, and call it
    ' Wyvil's Hour.'

ABSORBED.

Wars and rumours of wars,
Storm rising black in the east,
Warnings flashing down busy wires,
The speech of the Press that never tires,
Doubt and wonder and prophecy,
Lurid clouds in the wintry sky,
Grave words of statesman and priest.
And all the while by a lonely hearth
One yearned for the echo of children's mirth.

Flood and fear and famine,
The ruin of cyclone waves,
Homesteads close by the angry Thames
That a moment threatens and overwhelms,
Terrible tales from the iron shores
Where the great North Sea in her fury roars
Over her mariners' graves.
And all the while mid the stir and whirl
One dreamt of the smile of a fair young girl.

Care and trouble around her,
Anxiety, doubts, and fret ;

And amid the trifles that make our life,
Brighten its gladness, and darken its strife,
Claims, whose reality well she knew,
Duties, solemn and sweet and true,
With every hour she met.
Heart and head were willing their debt to pay,
Yet she thought 'is all joyous with her to-day?'

Is such a love the lover's?
Nay, he asks the answering touch.
Sisters seek brothers' guardian cares;
Friends, that friendship their burthen shares;
Husbands call on the wives they prize
For sweet hours of centred sympathies,
Nor deem they claim too much.
The passion hushed, deep, all else above,
Selfless, changeless, absorbing, is mothers' love.

MOTHERHOOD.

'HER lot is on you'—woman's lot she meant,
The singer who sang sweetly long ago;
And rose and yew and tender myrtle blent
To crown the harp that rang to love and woe.
Awake, O Poetess, and vow one strain
To sing of Motherhood, its joy, its pain.

What does it give to us, this mother love
In verse and tale and legend glorified,
Chosen by lips divine as type above
All other passions? Men have lived and died
For sisters, maiden queens, and cherished wives,
Yet, sealed by God, the one chief love survives.

Yet what is it it gives us? Shrinking dread,
Peril and pain and agony forgot,

Because we hold the ray of gladness shed,
    By the first cry from lips that know us not,
Worth all that has been paid, is yet to pay,
For the new worship, born and crowned that day.

Then nursing, teaching, training, self-denial,
    That never knows itself, so deep it lies,
The eager taking up of every trial,
    To smooth Spring's pathway, light her April skies;
Watching and. guiding, loving, longing, praying,
No coldness daunting, and no wrong dismaying.

And when the lovely bud to blossom wakes,
    And when the soft shy dawn-star flashes bright,
Another hand the perfect flower takes,
    Another wins the gladness of the light;
A sweet, soft, clinging, fond farewell is given,
Still a farewell, and then alone with Heaven.

With Heaven! Will He take the tired heart,
    The God who gave the child and formed the mother,
Who sees her strive to play her destined part,
    And, smiling, yield her darling to another?
Ay, on His cross He thought of Mary's woe;
He pities still the mothers left below.

THE CRY OF THE AGED.

Be pitiful, O ye children! life is so fair to you,
Its veins all thrilling melody, its pulses beating true;
The very hill before you, in morning's mystical glow,
Takes radiance that we cannot see, as we shiver
        down below;
Fresh flowers spring before your feet, as you hail
        the rising sun,
Be pitiful, O ye children! to us whose race is run.

Aye, we see doom and presage in the laughing
    noonday skies,
Looking up at them wearily, with strained and tear-
    dimmed eyes,
Aye, we hear wailing sorrow in the merry winds
    that blow,
For to our ears stern life has taught the minor chords
    of woe.
Then listen as the broken voice, that once as gaily
    rung,
Pleads to you in your fearless mirth, 'be pitiful, ye
    young.'

The hands that fail and falter now, your helpless
    wakings tended;
The tones so dully low to catch, with cradle laughter
    blended;
The lips so pale and cold to kiss were rosy warm
    of old,
When to your opening sense the tale of love and
    life they told.
Ah, but for gentle memory's sake, be pitiful to us,
Left in the arid flowerless waste, to call upon you
    thus.

A little while, a little while, and fret and fever over,
Our feeble claims will fret no more companion,
    friend, or lover;
And love, impatient chafing past, repentant tears will
    spare,
Kneeling beside the empty bed, watching the vacant
    chair.
Then just to spare from vain remorse warm heart
    and hasty tongue,
By all we lose and all you win, be pitiful, ye young.

IN THE MEADOW.

ONLY a great green meadow, with an old oak-tree
　　in the hedge,
Where the brambles were first to ripen, the sparrow
　　was first to fledge;
Only a broad brown river that swept between willow
　　ranks,
Where the tansy tangled the bindweed fair that
　　graced the sandy banks.

Just the meadow, and the river, and a lane that
　　joined the two,
And a marsh where marygolds glistened, by forget-
　　me-nots' virgin blue,
With the purple hills for a background, and a lark
　　that always sang,
Till the bright keen air around it with the melody
　　thrilled and rang.

It is thirty weary years ago. Through many a lovely
　　scene,
Through many a fair and storied haunt my tired
　　steps have been,
Yet, whenever from life and its lessons I turn, a sup-
　　pliant guest,
To the land where memory shines for us beauty
　　and joy and rest,

I know the scent of the tansy, crushed 'neath an eager
　　tread,
I know the note of the skylark, as it soared from
　　its lowly bed;

I see the oak-tree's mighty boughs, I hear the willows
  shiver,
I see the blue forget-me-nots that grew by the northern
  river.
Fancies have failed and hopes have fled, and the prize
  but mocks the strife.
Death and sorrow, with busy hands, have altered the
  course of life,
But as fair and fresh as when down its path the
  fearless footstep sprung,
Is the meadow beside the broad brown stream I loved
  when all was young.

THE HOME HEART.

The babe that nestled in my arms coos for me but
  in dreams ;
The prattler crowned with golden curls lives but in
  memory's gleams :
What marvel, then, that loving fear blends with the
  pride and joy
That watches, on his manhood's verge, the bold and
  bonnie boy ?

The happy smile of infancy still wreathes his rosy lips,
The fearless light of childhood's eyes knows nothing
  of eclipse ;
But firmer tread and stronger clasp attest the rolling
  years,
While growing daring thought and will awake the
  woman-fears.

My son, a wiser Hand than mine will shape the onward way,
A greater Power soothe the night and guide thee
  through the day.

So, in a patient impotence, I strive to stand apart,
Only praying, for thy father's sake, oh, keep the
    frank home heart!

Keep the pure unstinted charity, the trust in all things
    fair,
The hope that 'mid each earthly cloud still feels the
    sunshine there;
The faith in goodness, love, and truth, that, spite of
    fault and fall,
Looks on the bright world God has made, and
    owns His touch on all.

So shall the light foot spring unharmed along the
    perilous path,
So shall the brave hand clasp and keep the one im-
    mortal wreath.
By the yearning of the lonely life, whose chiefest joy
    thou art,
Oh, darling of our severed lives, keep still the fresh
    home heart!

THE DAY'S DARG.

A LITTLE more or a little less,
A little harder, a little lighter,
One day the yoke may hardly press,
Another draws the rein the tighter;
One hour the foot on flowers may fall,
And the kindly turf be green;
Another, the stones may hide it all,
And the thorns lurk sharp between;
But breast the brae be it short or long,
At last it ringeth to evensong.

The task is set us for good or ill,
No shrinking 'scapes the learning;
The aching foot must scale the hill
Where the beacon lamp is burning;
The wound must bear the ceaseless smart,
The bond must brook the straining,
The spirit play its destined part,
Through the long life's lonely paining;
Ah soul, be stedfast; ah heart, be strong:
At last it ringeth to evensong.

What boots to struggle upon the brink?
What recks the cry of the weeper?
No clasp can rivet the shattered link,
No wail can wake the sleeper.
The life's last hope, and the year's last rose,
They lie in decay together,
Can Autumn give us Spring's vernal shows?
Or December mock June's sweet weather?
It is all in the day's work—be true and strong,
At last we shall hear the evensong.

'LOST.'

Yes, yes, I know, the broad bright sun
Has smiled out the thunder frown;
The lark sings clear up there in the sky,
The gorses gleam as the breeze sweeps by,
The wavelets whisper and laugh as they break,
Where the sea-blooms in crystal pools awake;
The storm is over, and once again
Spring, life, and beauty assert their reign,
But ah, my ship's gone down.

Soft as a baby's touch
The white surf kisses the rocks;
Calm and sweet as an infant's rest
Lies the heaving swell of the ocean's breast;
And the 'greening gleams' where the sea-mews flit,
And the quiet shallows by sunset lit,
And the long blue sweep of the sheltered bay,
Are as hushed as they looked ere that dawning day
Reeled to the tempest shocks.

What does it all boot now?
There is many a bark on the main;
Many a bark with as costly a freight
As that which I stood on the shore to wait,
As bravely rigged, and as deftly sailed;
Ah, for safety, nor love nor prayer availed;
O'er the great bright waters the black squall swept,
Not a hope for me the horizon kept
When the sunlight shone again.

So, what avails the glory
Of earth, and sky, and sea?
When my ship went down, all sank with her
The dreams that gladden, the hopes that stir,
The trust to rest on, the faith that gave
Voice to the wild wind, and song to the wave;
Now the seasons change, and time's ebb and flow
Shapes the world, as the long days come and go;
But—what is all to me!

A FADED PHOTOGRAPH.

Only a faded photograph; forgotten
And cast aside with other worthless things;
Relics of idle dreams, grown ripe and rotten,
Dead flowers, locks of hair, and broken rings;

Who but has storage of such hoarded trifles,
That children prize, and careless girlhood rifles?

'See, that old fan will suit my fancy dress!
We'll make a doll's wig of those golden curls.
Why, here's a billet-doux—quaint tenderness,
All "Sir" and "Madam"!—look, the orient pearls
Left round this miniature, a fair proud face,
Would do that necklet clasp of yours to grace.'

And 'mid the flotsam of the long-ebbed past,
The photograph, some twenty summers old,
By idle hand among the 'rubbish' cast,
Lies with its later story too untold;
With sad dimmed eyes and wistful smile it seems
To ask a place amid those perished dreams.

Once dear as that fair face on ivory limned,
And prized as that poor tangled tress of hair,
By pleading won, by happy lover hymned,
Pledge of a troth foredoomed no fruit to bear;
Faded and faint as faith foresworn and lost,
On the bleak shore that Lethe washes tossed.

Well, place it softly mid the yellowing lines
Of those old letters with their subtle scent,
Bind them with the red sword-knot there, where shines
A glittering pebble still, a token sent
Perchance from some sweet blue-eyed rose-lipped
     child.
To him, who like yon haughty portrait smiled.

So, past and present, chivalry and science,
Relic of knight and lady, dead men's words,
And link of broken ties, in strange alliance,
Are left to moulder in our treasure-hoards;

And the next age may wonder, jest, and laugh,
O'er quaint love vows and faded photograph.

THE LEGEND OF SEAMER WATER.

At the base of mighty Addlebro', fair glimmers
　　Seamer Water,
Where the dales send many a stalwart son, and
　　many a soft-eyed daughter,
To linger 'neath the larches, and watch the bright
　　becks leap,
From Raydale and from Bardale, to their home in
　　Seamer deep.

From the crest of mighty Addlebro', out-stretching
　　far away,
The pilgrim sees through Seamerdale the Bain's
　　bright wavelets play;
At the top of mighty Addlebro' the massive cairn
　　still stands,
For the cists that lie on Stone Raise were framed
　　by Roman hands.

Deep in the heart of Wensleydale fair Seamer Water
　　lies,
Where the lark springs up to carol in the pale blue
　　northern skies,
Where the trout and bream are leaping, where the
　　silvery willows quiver,
Where long-haired birches wave their locks when
　　June's soft breezes shiver.

And yet, eight hundred years ago, ere ever Conan gave
The meadow lands where Byland monks built Jer-
　　vaulx' stately nave,

The traveller scaling Addlebro', gazed from the
    summit there,
On towers, and streets, and guarded walls, that girt
    a city fair.

One summer eve the sinking sun shone full on
    Whitefell Foss,
As an aged man strove wearily, the brawling stream
    to cross,
As through romantic Cragdale, he tottered feebly on,
And sought for rest and welcome from hearts that
    gave him none.

At priestly door, at serf's low hut, at baron's lordly
    hall,
He prayed for food and shelter, and prayed in vain
    to all,
Till old, and worn, and lonely, the cruel streets he left,
And crawled into a lowly cot hid in the mountain's
    cleft.

'For the sake of Christ, I pray you for charity,' he
    said.
The peasant brought his cup of milk, he brought his
    crust of bread,
And shared his scanty pittance with the wanderer who
    came
To ask for human mercy in the God of mercy's name.

The old man ate and drank, and lo, his form and
    aspect seemed
To change before the peasant's eyes, as unto one
    who dreamed;
Right royally he trod the floor, right royally he spoke,
'My blessing on the homestead where the bread of
    life I broke.'

Out on the steep hill-side he strode, he raised his
    staff on high,
He shook it where the sleeping town lay 'neath the
    evening sky,
' I call thee, Seamer Water, rise fast, rise deep, rise
    free,
'Whelm all, except the little house that fed and
    sheltered me!'

And fast rose Seamer Water in answer to his word.
From beck and foss and tribute stream the floods
    obedient poured,
And as the air seemed booming with a mighty funeral
    knell,
'Mid shriek and shout and frantic prayer, to earth
    the peasant fell.

And when at sunrise, painfully, he roused him from
    his swoon,
His cot stood safe, and from his side his awful guest
    had gone;
But where at eve the city proud stood busy, strong,
    and gay,
Fair Seamer Water glittered to hail the wakening day.

It is eight hundred years ago, and legends dim and
    fade,
But still, men say, at Hallowe'en, beneath the larches'
    shade,
Whoso in Seamer Water at sunset gazes down,
Sees tower, and street, and battlement—the shadow
    of the town.

ON THE TERRACE.

MAY 14, 1875.

IT was a May-Day of the Poets; bright
Upon the terrace blazed the royal sun;
The great red House, majestic in his light,
Showed the grand peace long centuries had won;
The oak and sycamore broad shadows made,
With birches' graceful locks and silvered stems,
And guarded by its carven balustrade
The ordered parterre flashed its clustered gems.

Rich in its wealth of greenery lay the park,
Alive with 'many-twinkling ear and tail';
Tall ferns in sheltered dells grew cool and dark,
Cowslip and crowfoot wooed the laughing gale;
The glittering river rolled through shade and shine,
Where water-lilies bloomed 'mid dancing flies,
And where white woodbine crept his banks to twine,
Forget-me-nots gleamed blue 'neath bluer skies.

As the soft wind breathed through the mighty boughs,
Where golden sunlight filtered through the green,
It brought rich scents to greet the ancient house,
And linger round the sombre yew hedge screen;
The balmy air was vocal with the ring
Of birds that chirped and warbled, cawed and cooed,
And the quick whirring of the pheasant's wing
Rose ever from the woodland solitude.

From the fair scene a happy satiate eye
I turned, to rest on One revered, beloved,
And lo, sweet Nature's lavish revelry,
To kindred gladness her pure soul had moved:

As sky and land awoke the May to grace,
Where storms had raved, and frost had bound his chain,
So, after heaviest griefs, her patient face
Wore God's serene 'clear shining after rain.'

A SEARCH.

SHE wandered among the Churches, she studied
    them one by one,
All who built their creed at the footstool of God
    and taught the name of His Son.
One was narrow and awful, one seethed in endless strife
For symbol and rite that showed so small 'mid the
    terrible needs of life;
One was vaguely wide, and of God's fair world one
    made just a thing to dread,
For it bade all human longings hush, all human
    ties lie dead.

She wandered among the Churches. Oh was not
    there one for her,
Beneath whose shadow calm and broad she might
    rest from chafe and stir?
One who would say to the yearning heart, 'Be still,
    for I am strong,'
One who could whisper the tired brain, 'Be patient,
    light comes ere long,'
One to preach peace and purity, to practise faith,
    work, and love,
One to show the aching eyes on earth the shimmer
    of gleams above.

She wandered among the Churches, till she weariedly
    turned from all
Before the 'great world's altar stairs' in her bitter
    need to fall,

To cry 'God, give me charity; God make me true,
    brave, and pure;
God help me to love through good and ill; God
    strengthen me to endure;
Till with His word to guide my steps, and lighten
    me on my path,
Free from the angry clashing of creeds, I pass to
    Him, through death.'

A SERMON.

In the fair temple built in name of Him
Who made for Love the mighty sacrifice,
Before whose altar hour by hour arise
From white-robed choristers the joyous hymn,
Unto whose honour, through the chancel dim,
Sweet incense floats, to panes whose gorgeous dyes
Fling stains like sunset in the western skies
On pillar, arch, and sculptured cherubim;
While the grand Liturgy of England's Church
Flow'd on through humble prayer and praise sublime
In words to thrill and comfort, soothe and search,
In holy words, saint-writ in elder time;
The thunder-music swelled and died—and then
A Priest stood up to speak of God to men.

He spoke—of judgment hard and sudden doom,
Of sleepless eye on swerve and stumble bent,
Of sentence swift and endless punishment,
Of narrow pathway, steep and wrapped in gloom;
All human griefs, as threatening warnings sent,
All human loves, as sweet temptations meant,
All Life's fair flowers, but nightshade on a tomb.

Now praise to Thy long-suffering, gracious God;
Thou see'st Thy children take and turn Thy creed,
Thou hear'st Thy servants mock Thee as they plead,
Yet, in the loving mercy still bestowed,
See'st through the erring speech, the earnest deed,
Nor doom'st the Doomster from his own fierce code.

'OHNE HAST, OHNE RAST.'

HASTEN not, O my child; since all too soon
The Present's hours before our footsteps glide,
The blushing morning brightens into noon,
The noonday glories pale to eventide;
Drop not the snowdrop, snatching at the rose,
Crush not the bloom, too eager for the fruit,
For trustful patience purest buds unclose,
Seed, undisturbed, grows to the choicest root.

Loiter not, O my Child; before us all
Lies the fair goal that heart and head can win,
And to the strong the richest prizes fall,
The fleetest foot bounds ever foremost in;
Stedfast and earnest use the powers given,
To take and keep the radiant laurel wreath,
The bays that gladden earth and enter Heaven,
The bays that live through pain, and conquer death.

Hasten not, loiter not, through shade and shine,
With ready sword and settled purpose go,
Not lingering where sweet poison leaves entwine;
Not springing rashly on imagined foe.
With charity and peace on either hand,
The heart all love, the soul sublime in truth,
Pass onward, O my child, to that fair land
Where strength and quiet blend eternal youth.

DEAD DREAMS.

WHERE the sunshine glistens and the aspens wave,
By the rippling rivulet, dig the dead dreams' grave;
Do not heap above them the heavy fruitful soil,
The things ne'er shaped by patience or sanctified
    by toil.
Toss above their slumbers with quick irreverent hand,
As light and yielding as themselves, the shifting
    golden sand,
And leave them to forgetfulness in summer's lulling air,
Dreams born of fickle fancy, of things that never were.

They have no sacred sadness to charm us to the last,
To wake visions of allegiance to the glories of the past,
They shrine no vanished faces, they breathe no
    silenced voice,
They cannot wake to life again the prize of young
    life's choice,
Like those that fill the vacant chair, and haunt the
    lonely hearth,
And make for some companionship that have none
    else on earth ;
Such bring the yearning heart relief, the restless
    spirit ease,
Such lull the troubled soul to rest, we bury none
    of these.

For the pretty fairy fancies we summon to beguile
The tired brain to slumber, the weary lip to smile ;
One touch of stern reality, they wither in our clasp ;
One breath of earnest longing, they flit before the
    grasp ;

With half a smile and half a sigh we lay them in
    their rest,
The toys so gaily welcomed, so carelessly caressed,
Since though they paled the future light, full many
    tedious hours
They sped with merry music, and wreathed with
    joyous flowers.

So ere we turn and leave them, oh smooth their
    rest aright,
And heap above them violets, the purple and the white,
The parting has been lighter for the meeting that
    they told,
The load we had to carry they transmuted into gold;
The bitter sense of failure, the baffled vain regret,
They lulled with happy whispers, of joys to crown us yet,
True we never met, the glint but mocked, the hopes
    were idle gleams,
Yet for sake of all that might have been, sleep
    soft, O gentle dreams !

THE BREAKWATER.

Aye, strike them down to the depths of earth,
The piles of iron-bound stone;
Do all that 'Time's long hours have taught,
That Science' search has known;
Bring the strength of well-skilled labour,
And the thought of well-trained head,
All that man, in this wondrous age of ours,
Has learnt, and found, and read;
Bring prince or peer to bless the work
That stands here, strong and fast,
And say 'The Sea her master owns,
Her waves are curbed at last.'

She will laugh round the mass of masonry
In her hour of summer calm;
She will whisper and sing round the mighty stones,
With kisses as soft as balm;
She will roll her long slow solemn tides
On its barrier, day by day;
She will thunder against its sullen strength
In clouds of snowy spray;
But smooth or angry, fierce or fair,
She will come there, hour by hour;
Man's work will yield to her hand at last,
Man's best will own her power.

Slowly and surely, day by day,
The sea her own reclaims,
Her might no magic has meekened yet,
Her strength no mortal tames;
The black north-easter calls on her,
As she lies in her coral caves,
Up, to the ring of his trumpet-call,
Up spring the crested waves,
The wild white horses toss their crests,
And on the rocky shore,
Wind, wave, and weather, all blent together,
They rush with a royal roar.

Breakwater, pier, and sea-wall,
A wonder each of its age,
They take their place in the daily talk,
Their line in the printed page,
Sure as the night succeeds the day
To time and the sea they fall,
The deep persistent quiet strength
O'ercoming each and all;

And only He who holds the sea,
In the hollow of His Hand,
The great 'no further' sentence speaks,
That guards the helpless land.

'ANOTHER WOMAN'S BAIRN.'

Just told in the daily paper; not mine, not mine, thank
　　God;
Not mine the bare black hideous gap in the church-
　　yard's daisied sod;
Not mine the hush in the darkened home, not mine
　　the vacant place,
Not mine the April flowers strewn on crossed hands
　　and waxen face;
Not mine lost step and silenced voice, wild prayer
　　and useless tears,
Nor the dumb forced submission of the yearning
　　childless years.

Not mine; but somewhere in the world, bereft a
　　woman weeps,
Where in the awful loveliness of death her bright
　　boy sleeps,
Her joy is past, her dreams are naught, her happy
　　hopes are crushed,
Her breathing budding darling called where dust is
　　given to dust,
Years may revolve and life may change, but time
　　and tide are done,
For her, that stranger woman, who has 'lost her
　　only son.'

And just because my bonnie boy shouts 'neath the
    sweet spring skies,
And just because I smile to look in the depths of
    laughing eyes,
Because I stooped to-night above · my sleeping
    treasure's head,
To smooth the ruffled curls away, and kiss the lips'
    young red,
Tears choked the words of thankful prayer in the
    happy watch I kept,
For I thought how by an empty couch that other
    woman wept.

TWO FACES.

Two faces—one that shone for her
  In the fairy days of youth,
With an idle glory of April love,
And faith, so easy to disprove,
And hope, that never won its crown,
And vows, that lightly crumbled down
  At the touch of time and truth.

And another, that never wore for her
  Aught but a loving look;
That, glad or grave, or eager or hushed,
Had always the smile that she could trust;
Whose grave, sweet, patient, earnest eyes
Gleamed on for her, as stars in the skies
  Shine down a wayward brook.

Ah, cold, proud heart, how dully
  It bowed to that mighty love;
How wilfully it turned again,
To yearn for the dream that brought naught but pain;

How slowly it yielded to the spell,
Ere, folding her hands, she said ' 'tis well,'
　　And took her treasure trove.

One face—she meets it in life's set ways,
　　And turns with clear cold laughter
From the glance that has lost its pristine power,
And the whisper that charmed a foolish hour;
But the other, late loved, soon lost, ah me,
Shall she ever be blessed enough to see
　　Its smile in the dim Hereafter?

IN THE GARDEN.

She sate and looked at the garden, the borders were
　　all aglow,
The sunshine glinted gaily back where the roses
　　blazed below,
Azure and crimson, and gold and white, like jewels
　　set in the grass,
And the wooing breeze above them paused, as loth
　　on its way to pass;
Yet 'mid all the lavish loveliness, her eyes with an
　　aching strain,
Fixed wilfully where 'mid the sunlight jarred the blood-
　　red flower of pain.

She sate and looked at the garden, petal and leaf
　　hung dying,
Where over the waste of frost-bound earth, the black
　　east wind was sighing;
And ever and aye the snowflakes came floating idly past,
To melt on the shuddering evergreens, or drift down
　　the icy blast;

Yet her happy eyes with the fearlessness that is born
    of love's sweet madness,
Fixed on the sheltered nook where bloomed the
    tender flower of gladness.

The flash that strikes one hearth with death, for
    another lights the feast,
For burial and for bridal rite speaks on the selfsame
    priest;
One passes carelessly the prize that another dies in
    losing,
Our nearest and dearest will not take the pleasures
    of our choosing.
And in this world of shadow and shine, with its
    strange, predestined fates,
Life piles her richest stores for one, where another
    sickens and waits.

THE DESERTED ROOM.

THE fire flames leapt about the logs,
    As in the days of old;
About the silent room they played
In chequer-work of gleam and shade,
The Persian carpet on the floor
Showed its dimmed beauty as of yore;
The portraits from the walls looked down,
And eye and lip in smile or frown,
    The tale she taught them told.

The fire flames leapt about the hearth,
    The cricket sang its song;
The ivory notes she loved so much,
Lay waiting for her wakening touch,

Her own, or sister flowers, drooped,
Where the great crimson curtains looped;
And by her chair her favourite book
Its place, mute pleading for her, took
   To rest, unopened long.

The fire flames leapt about the hearth;
   A sense of something gone
Hung heavy on the listening ear,
That wont her joyous voice to hear;
The echoes of the silent house
Wanting her flying foot to rouse;
It seemed as ghosts her brightness laid,
In the dull stillness woke and strayed,
   And long-lost empire won.

The fire flames leapt, and paled, and died,
   And in the eerie gloom,
Sad memories gathered round the hearth,
Where she brought joy, and youth, and mirth:
Sad fancies mingling with them said
Old tales of half-forgotten dead;
And baffled prayers and visions met,
With loss, and longing, and regret,
   In the deserted room.

BLUE ROSES.

Blue roses! Violets blossomed
Where my April wanderings led;
And forget-me-nots, clear as their kindred sky,
And anemones, fragile and fair and shy;
But I passed them all with a vacant eye,
 Seeking for ever fruitlessly
The bloom no spring dews fed.

Blue roses! In lavish loveliness
June roses woke gay and brave;
Roses golden, and pink, and white,
Blazing fearless in flooding light
Blushing as morning, dewy as night,
But I turned from them all in my own despite,
To seek what no summer gave.

Blue roses! Through bounteous autumn
I followed my wilful quest,
Heedless of August's gorgeous flowers,
And painted woodlands and rich green bowers;
Gathering, failing, through wasted hours
Of baffled hopes and waning powers
And purposeless unrest.

And now, when soft-eyed October
Its sweet pale blossoms shows,
I strive to welcome and cherish in vain,
For still, in a helpless yearning pain,
O'er the silent future my sad eyes strain,
As in fancy my darling prize I gain,
And clasp my one blue rose!

And I think that for aye, wherever
My lonely footsteps tend,
Through time and tide, through weal and woe,
I shall see in the distance my treasure grow,
And on through the mirage to reach it go,
Past wearying friend and smiling foe;
· Blue Roses' to the end.

CREEDS.

'THE creeds are nothing now,' she said;
'Twas the close of a stormy life,

Much of trouble and careless fret,
Much of sorrow and vague regret,
Death hushing care and strife.

What could it matter now to her?
The page was closing fast,
To meet the hour and leave the rest,
To do in patient faith one's best.
Time has not the soul to last.

Time has not the soul; Eternity
But faces a want like this,
Has space to watch and gauge it all,
Struggle and failure, flight and fall,
Can see life as it is.

Creeds are as nothing, let it be,
The 'Lord of the Sabbath' knows,
Can judge the doubt, and forgive the fear,
Can own how subtle, and strong, and near,
Close the spirit's deathly foes.

It is all as nothing; only this
Remains for the human need:
Christ died for us, Christ lives for us.
Knowing it, feeling it, trusting it thus,
What reck we of earthly creed?

THIRSTY.

We gather happy auguries
From the springs that return again;
From the flowers that lift their storm-bowed heads
Beneath soft April rain;

From the light that blushes in the west,
After the stormy day;
From the sea that laughs and gleams, while still
The shore is flecked with spray;
But what are such fancies to wild regret,
Sad souls, wrung hearts, are thirsty yet.

Tear-swollen eyes strain eagerly
Over the sacred Word,
Where sorrow turns for comfort,
In each holy promise stored;
Thank God for the noble teaching
Thank God for the patient love,
Thank God for the great redemption,
All other boons above.
But the human question is hardly met,
The human yearning is thirsty yet.

With the last look of the loving eyes,
The last touch of the hand,
They glide away, our darlings,
To the undiscovered land.
Faith says ' believe in patience,'
Hope whispers ' ye shall meet,'
And oh, the trust is true and pure,
And oh, the dream is sweet;
But doubt will chafe and wonder fret,
The breaking heart is thirsty yet.

The daisies star the quiet grave,
The blue sky gleams above it,
The woodlark sings as it was wont,
When he was here to love it.

Mute hangs the veil, mute stands the cross,
  And tasks and duties wait,
What use our unavailing cries
  Outside the golden gate?
God's mighty silent seal is set,
  On earth love must be thirsty yet.

OVER THE RIVER.

Over the river, where dully shiver
  The bleak gray winds of Death;
Through the mystical veil whose foldings pale
  Hide the secret of all beneath.
Gone, over the river, from life for ever,
  Another dear old friend.
They are gathering fast, for the meeting at last,
  Where earth and its questions end.
There is most of the sunny world we knew
  On the further side, I think;
For though day by day may bring flowerets new,
  Each severs some precious link.

Over the river. We start and shiver
  As the sullen plunge we hear;
For the waves look black, and the clue we lack
  That would teach us to hush the fear,
For we see in our awe, how never a law
  Governs the terrible call;
The young and the glad, the old and the sad,
  Death swoops upon each and all.
Leaving one to weary the hours away
  For the summons that will not come;
While another, whose life was all dear and gay,
  Lies wildly wept in the tomb.

Over the river.   The heart-strings quiver,
    To the deep bell's solemn tone ;
And the empty chair, from the threshold bare,
    Shows blank by the cold hearth-stone.
Yet the rapture of meetings, of low sweet greetings,
    On the other side awaits ;
Where all who are nearest, and truest, and dearest,
    Stand close to the golden gates.
For is not the heavy ransom paid,
    The costly passport signed ;
The path of the Cross on the stream is laid,
    The path that is free to find.

Over the river.   The flesh will quiver
    At the touch of the icy wave.
The cold wind sighs 'neath the gloaming skies,
    Where the yew boughs guard the grave.
The dumb dead wall, to the wail and call,
    Stands dark, and still, and cold,
Till the passionate cry sinks despairingly,
    And the tears drop deep in the mould.
Yet over the river the love-lights quiver,
    Through the gloom glints the Love's bright smile ;
And over the river the breeze sings ever,
    ' It is but for a little while.'

DYING.

Dying, dying.   Just shut your eyes,
    And think for a moment of it,
Of the mighty knowledge that somewhere lies,
    Unknown of poet or prophet ;
The things that were, the things that shall be,
The ' joys unspeakable' we shall see.

Well, he, the feeble slight old man,
　Who was nothing in this our life,
Blind where the keen eyes of science scan,
　Weak in the fiery strife;
An hour, a minute, and he will know
All that we hopelessly grope at below:

The 'why' of the 'wonderful ways' of God;
　The 'when' of the great world's scheme;
The flowers that spring in the churchyard sod;
　The start from the purest dream;
The 'where' and the 'how' when our darlings die,
And the light goes out in the broad bright sky.

Look at him gravely, tend him well
　In silent reverence;
That tired hand will break the spell
　That fetters us, heart and sense;
Darkly we gaze into infinite space,
To-morrow he 'll see God face to face.

'PARVA DOMUS—MAGNA QUIES.'

A narrow home, but very still it seemeth;
　A silent home, no stir or tumult here.
Who wins that pillow of no sorrow dreameth,
　No whirling echoes jar his sealèd ear;
The tired hand lies very calm and quiet,
　The weary foot no more hard paths will tread,
The great world may revolve in clash and riot,
　To its loud summons leaps nor heart nor head.

The violets bloom above the tranquil sleeper,
　The morning dews fall gently on the grass,
Amid the daisies kneels the lonely weeper;
　He knows not when her lingering footsteps pass.

The autumn winds sigh softly o'er his slumber,
  The winter piles the snow-drifts o'er his rest;
He does not care the flying years to number,
  The narrow home contents its silent guest.

No baffled hope can haunt, no doubt perplexes,
  No parted love the deep repose can chafe,
No petty care can irk, no trouble vexes;
  From misconstruction his hushed heart is safe.
Freed from the weariness of worldly fretting,
  From pain and failure, bootless toil and strife,
From the dull wretchedness of vain regretting
  He lies, whose course has passed away from life.

A narrow home, and far beyond it lieth
  The land whereof no mortal tongue can tell.
We strain our sad eyes as the spirit flieth,
  Our fancy loves on heaven's bright hills to dwell.
God shuts the door, no angel lip uncloses;
  They whom Christ raised no word of guidance said.
Only the Cross speaks where our dust reposes,
  'Trust Him who calls unto His rest our dead.'

'FORGOTTEN.'

'Forgotten, as a dead man out of mind.'
Nay, surely, when the royal Psalmist sang,
Some thought of Life's hard teaching, cold, unkind,
Like nightshade 'mid his pure white lilies sprang;
Love, like a champion armed at cry of need,
Rises beside each cherished grave to say,
'I live, I struggle, hide the wounds that bleed.
Never forget them for a single day.'

Back to the world the quiet mourners turn,
Striving the daily duty still to do,
To veil the eyes that stream, the hearts that yearn,
For them who made the life sweet, pure, and true;
In reverent jealousy their memories guarding,
'Gainst sneer or weariness from those around,
The prompt impatience of this world's awarding,
Where Grief, too faithful to the Past, is found.

Time's hand does stanch the wound, and draws above it
The decent robes of custom and of life,
The daily taskwork gives to all who prove it,
Strength for the hour, and courage for the strife.
Pale flowers spring up where once our roses bloomed,
Pale moonbeams glisten where our full suns shone,
And passing where our treasures lie entombed,
We learn, in patient hope, to labour on.

But, oh dead eyes, that watch us on our road,
Look on us, mark us, scan us through and through;
Bravely, although we strive to bear our load,
Love sees where sorrow takes her tribute due;
Some day, some day, long silent lips may tell,
The warfare past, the heavy arms resigned,
Together, in God's joy unspeakable,
'Darling, I never once was out of mind.'

'AND THERE CAME TWO ANGELS AT EVEN.'—GENESIS XIX.

Have they passed from us for ever,
    Those angel visitants?
Will they leave no more their happy skies
To blend with our human sympathies,
To give to our nature's wailing cries
    The lore for which it pants.

To bring us tidings of our Dead,
  One word of 'how it is.'
Ah! from her who mourned death's earliest prey,
To the countless lives, woe stricken to-day,
Spite every tutored word we say,
  Is not the heart-cry this?

Cold stands the cross, cold lies the turf,
  Cold stoops the low gray sky;
A fair vague hope, a clinging trust,
A faith in something true and just;
There is naught else for the sons of dust,
  Till the hour is come to die.

But men have looked on angels:
  All through the sacred page
Their white wings rustle, their voices teach,
O'er the great dumb gulf their strong hands reach,
As they glide with their gentle gracious speech,
  'Mid the men of the elder age.

Did they heed not then, of the loved and lost
  That no questioning word was said?
Was the Patriarch deadened by earthly stir,
As he walked at eve on the plains of Shur,
That he never asked of his visitor
  'How is it with our Dead!"

Had Lazarus no sweet solemn truth
  For Mary's duteous ear?
Did that one blest widow of all the earth,
In the joy of the marvellous second birth,
Never ask her boy of the holy mirth
  He had gone to heaven to hear?

Hush! Eve has borne it, so it is;
  This last worst pang must be;
Perchance the meeting of life and love,
Of a richer fuller bliss may prove
For the darkness through which we mourners move
  Striving in vain to see.

THE GREAT SILENCE.

He wept, ere He called her brother back,
  For Mary, at the grave;
He paused, as the widow's cry of pain
Rang through the silent streets of Nain,
And gave her her only son again,
  With the hand so strong to save.

He never jarred the father's woe,
  By counsel or reproof;
The heart of deep human sympathies,
And the voice that governed earth and skies,
Blent in the simple 'Maid, arise,'
  That thrilled the stricken roof.

He knew, the God who lived in man,
  How from weary age to age,
One little word of promise said
By the Lord of the living and the dead,
Had its divine effulgence shed
  On the future's gloomiest page.

He knew such pledge from sacred lips,
  Had taken for aye from grief
The terrible yearning, the aching doubt,
That no faith can quiet, no reason rout,
The question, that rings our sorrow about,
  With the 'if' that has no relief.

But to be sure, that yet again,
  We shall find them gone before,
That hands will clasp, and eyes will meet,
And our Darlings around the mercy-seat
Will spring to our happy arms to greet
  The loved who will part no more.

No glorified celestial things ;
  No saints, of saints' divining ;
But the voice our hungry hearts have missed,
The touch we knew, the face we kissed,
Why, woe were naught but a patient mist,
  Did we *know* such sun were shining.

But ah, the gracious lips were mute :
  The pitying eyes wept only ;
And in humility and awe,
We can but bow our heads and draw,
From the mercy and justice of His law,
  Strength for the lives left lonely.

And as our flowers one by one
  Droop to their earthly bed,
Make prophets of Autumn's bounteous day,
Or the sweet recurrent bloom of May,
And let our Lord's grand silence say,
  'Trust Me too with thy Dead.'

SATISFIED.

AFTER the toil and turmoil,
And the anguish of trust belied ;
After the burthen of weary cares,
Baffled longings, ungranted prayers ;
After the passion, and fever, and fret.
After the aching of vain regret.

After the hurry and heat of strife,
The yearning and tossing that men call 'life';
Faith that mocks, and fair hopes denied,
We shall be satisfied.

When the golden bowl is broken,
At the sunny fountain side;
When the turf lies green and cold above
Wrong, and sorrow, and loss, and love;
When the great dumb walls of silence stand
At the doors of the undiscovered land;
When all we have left in our olden place
Is an empty chair and a pictured face;
When the prayer is prayed, and the sigh is sighed,
We shall be satisfied.

What does it boot to question,
When answer is aye denied?
Better to listen the Psalmist's rede,
And gather the comfort of his creed;
And in peace and patience possess our souls,
While the wheel of fate in its orbit rolls,
Knowing that sadness and gladness pass
Like morning dews from the summer grass,
And, when once we win to the further side,
We shall be satisfied.